Blessings
Eva McCall

Also by Eva McCall

Edge of Heaven

Children of the Mountain

Lucy's Recipes for Mountain Living

Murder on Haint Branch

Eva McCall

Moonshine Press • Franklin, North Carolina

Though the premise of this novel was inspired by an actual event, this is a work of fiction. Names, characters, places, and incidents are either the product of the author's imagination or are used fictitiously. Any resemblance to any actual persons, living or dead, or to any place or event, is coincidental.

Published by:
Moonshine Press
522 Allison-Watts Rd.
Franklin, NC 28734

Copyright © 2013 by Eva McCall
All rights reserved. This book, or any part, may not be reproduced in any form without permission.

International Standard Book Number : 978-0-9889431-0-0

Thanks to Henry Fichner for the cover art — Barbara McRae for editing and typesetting — Tyler Cook, my promotional manager and nephew, whose enthusiasm for this project has given it a life of its own — and my family and extended family, who have never stopped believing in me.

In memory of my friend,
Tonda Woodard

Murder on Haint Branch

1

They said he shot hisself, but you don't shoot yourself through the heart with a shotgun and lay it back down on the bed by your side. At least that's what my granny said the day Sheriff Carlson told her that my Uncle Charlie had been found shot dead and lying on his brother's bed.

Granny said, "He loved life and had ever reason to live. He wouldn't just go and shoot hisself. 'Sides he's my boy and Sanders ain't quitters."

The sheriff said, "Mrs. Sanders, people kill their selves all the time. The way I see it, he didn't wanna go off over yonder across waters and get hisself killed by one of them Germans. Decided he'd just as soon die here at home amongst his family. I heared tales that would curl a dead man's toes about them Germans. Can't say as I much blame him, dead is dead. At least you won't have them soldiers from the White House bringing you a letter that says, 'Sorry to inform you.' If you had your druthers, wouldn't you as soon have me come tell you than some stranger?"

Granny bunched up her apron and covered her face. Sheriff Carlson put his arm around her trembling shoulders in an awkward attempt to console her. I could tell Granny didn't much cotton to his touch by the way her shoulders tightened. The sheriff must-a knowed too cause he drawed it back right quick like and jammed his hands in his pocket.

He told her, "Don't you worry about a-thing. I'll get on into town and send out the undertaker. I've already sent someone to tell your neighbors. It won't take long for them to get over here to lend a helping hand. I'll be in and out if you need me for anything. I'll go ahead and file all the necessary reports. You know November is election month and the sooner this is tidied up the better."

My granny stood right there in the doorway and watched that sheriff walk away knowing full well his only concern was winning next month, not that her son had been murdered. I might only be eleven, soon-to-be twelve, but I knowed there was no doubt in her mind that it was murder. More than likely murder in the first degree, planned by someone right here on the branch.

Granny turned and made her way to the kitchen table, and with trembling hands, reached for a cup. "Olivia, young'un, fix your old granny a cup of catnip tea and add a bit of that white lightning I keep for medicinal purposes. And don't you go telling your Granddaddy where I keep my stash, or he'll be a-wetting his whiskers outta it when his jug runs dry."

I reached up on a shelf behind the table where she kept her empty canning jars and got the one that looked like it was full of branch water. As I mixed the tea, my thoughts stayed on Uncle Charlie's killer. Yes, it was murder and I knowed of at least two people here on the branch that had good reason to want him dead, and Sheriff Carlson might just be one of them.

* * *

By the time Uncle Charlie's body was carried home, neighbors had crowded in, bringing all sorts of food and offering suggestions 'bout what had happened. Not that anyone in the family was interested in their opinions. My granddaddy says "opinions are like butt-holes, everyone has one." Well, right now it was gonna take more than an opinion to explain Uncle Charlie being shot.

My granddaddy has lots of sayings and one of his favorite is, "If you wanna know sump'n, go straight to the horse's mouth." I tried that when I asked Granny where babies come from. She said they were found under cabbage leaves. Think I spent one whole morning looking under ever leaf in the garden. When I didn't find the little sister I wanted, I headed on out to the barn and went to where Granddaddy kept old Bess stabled. All I found was a great big mouth grinning at me. When I told Granddaddy 'bout going in search of the truth, he laughed so hard his false teeth jumped out. When he could finally talk, he said, "Ollie, honey, don't you know that means to ask the person who knows what happened."

Granddaddy has called me Ollie ever since I was a little bitty young'un. Said no young'un should be saddled with a name like Olivia. Sounded like some sort of liver disease to him, but that's what Granny had insisted on calling me. It weren't long till everybody on the branch was calling me Ollie.

Well, back to Uncle Charlie getting shot. Looked to me like the only one who knowed the truth 'bout Uncle Charlie would be the one who found him. I'd get on up to Uncle Ray's house and see what I could find out.

I slipped by Mrs. Roper's house. I knowed she'd ask me ever question in the book. Granddaddy says she wouldn't have anything to do if she didn't have that long nose of hern in everyone's business. Come to think of it, she might know more than anybody 'bout the murder. Maybe I'd drop in for a friendly little visit on my way home. Wouldn't hurt none to hear what she had to say.

Halfway up the trail, I heared voices and took to the underbrush.

No sense in being told to run on home and mind my own business when I was doing just that. Granddaddy says one's business is his own, and I have to agree, 'specially when you're out to find a murderer. As I sneaked closer to Uncle Ray's house, I smelled the awfullest scent. Maybe there was a pole cat nearby. I'd better be careful or Granny'd scrub me down with that hard lye soap of hern. She'd done it many-a time when I'd got into the poison ivy. I wasn't hankering for that sort of bath with Uncle Charlie dead and a killer on the loose. That kind-a bath ain't sump'n to look forward to even in good times. I remember one time in particular when I got into the poison ivy. Granny boiled a kettle of water with some of that soap, and then she poured it into a tin tub, stripped me down to my birthday suit, put me in, and scrubbed with a brush until I was beet red. Don't know which would-a been worse, itching or burning.

I was still thinking 'bout the scent when I saw a bunch of men with handkerchiefs tied over their faces hurrying around like their pants was on fire. 'Bout that time a lawman pushed my Uncle Ray around the corner of the house.

"Hey, Sheriff look who I found hiding up in the hayloft."

My heart jumped in my throat. I couldn't believe my eyes. Granny had said Uncle Ray wouldn't be home for another week. But there he stood. He was supposed to be looking over a new logging job in a town called Waynesville. Had she lied? He'd even been talking 'bout getting out-a the logging business and hiring on with the crew that's building the new road. Granddaddy said it was one of them roads built by the Government, and they were gonna call it the Blue Ridge Parkway. You might as well know right up front that Granddaddy ain't got no use for the government or anything they do. But family is everything to him. He's coming home tonight, probably drunker than a skunk. Maybe too snookered to realize there'd been a-killing of one of his own. It usually took twenty-four hours for him to sober up and by that time Granny had his jug emptied in the outhouse stool. Now with all the neighbors around, she wouldn't get a chance to get rid of it this time. That was alright. Granddaddy'd need it when he found out 'bout Uncle Charlie.

Wouldn't mind having a little nip myself 'bout right now if there was some way of hiding it from Granny, but she was sharp as a tack when it come to my behavior. Said she didn't want me to turn out like my parents. I don't know what she means by that. 'Bout all she ever has said was that my mother was a good girl gone bad. Now to me that sounds like one of Granddaddy's sayings. Maybe she got it from him. Any time I press her for an answer, she says she'll tell me when I'm old enough to understand. Granddaddy always gives her a dirty looking scowl when she tells me that.

I'd watched the lawman haul Uncle Ray away. The only thing left up here is me and the buzzards. Guess they'll be around until that smell's gone. Think I'll mosey on in the house and see if I can find anything the lawman might have over-looked. Seeing I'm closer to the ground, I might see sump'n they didn't.

If the odor was bad outside, it was plain gasified inside. I'd have to hurry or I'd smother. Granny sure didn't need another corpse on her hands. I wasn't even sure how she was gonna handle one. I could see right now me and Granddaddy was gonna have to come up with some way to fix her, and I'm sure his saying won't do the job. If I found sump'n in here that proved Uncle Charlie hadn't killed hisself that might help.

Over in the corner was the bed. Looked like the law had took all the quilts and even the sheets, but the straw-tick mattress was still there, soaked with blood and a-stinking to high heaven. Getting down on my knees, I looked under the bed. There was nothing but some sort of cardboard trunk back against the wall. I grabbed a poker and punched around in the straw, still nothing. With the tail of my dress, I picked up the corner of the mattress. Ah . . . what's this? Why'd somebody hide a little black box under here?

As I reached for it, I heared footsteps nearing the front door. Who was coming? What if the killer had come back for this? Whatever this was. I'd better do sump'n and quick or I might be smelling up the mountain just like Uncle Charlie or worse yet get buried alive way up here and nobody would ever know what happened to me. Granny would be too busy grieving, but Granddaddy would miss me right away, 'specially when he needed me to help him find a new hiding place for his brown jug. Lying down, I scooted under the bed and behind the big, cardboard trunk near the wall.

I didn't have to wait but a few minutes till the front door burst open. I peeked out and saw the biggest, ugliest, man on Haint Branch. It was that mean old Yates.

I shuddered as a chair hit the wall then looked at the box in my hand. Was this what he wanted? Steps neared the bed and beads of sweat dripped from my hand that gripped the box. Was I holding some great secret? Me and Granddaddy already shared one big secret 'bout Mr. Yates? Was there more? I had the urge to sling it across the room. I didn't want to know sump'n that might just get me dead, but instead I squeezed harder and waited as he slung stuff around the room. Yates was mad that was for sure, and I needed to stay quiet or as Granddaddy says, "You'll be dead as a door nail." Now, I know what he means by that saying.

Yates swore and moved away and in a few minutes I heared the door slam. My hand relaxed. I had to know what was inside the box while I had the chance. I opened it. Cards! Just plain old playing cards, what kind-a secret was that? Disgusted, I slipped the box in my pocket and slid from my hiding place.

I'd better get on home. There wouldn't be time for a talk with Mrs. Roper today but soon I'd come back and visit. Who knows what she'd seen?

On my way down the mountain, I thought about the secret me and Granddaddy shared 'bout old man Yates. I just happened to be with Granddaddy one day last spring when he stopped by the Yates' with his jug.

Mrs. Yates come to the door and said, "Grady Sanders, can't believe you'd bring your granddaughter with you on business."

Granddaddy grinned down at me. "She's my buddy. If you can't trust a buddy who you gonna trust."

I felt all growed up; my granddaddy calling me his buddy. There weren't a better compliment for a-eleven year old girl.

She opened the screen door. "Olivia, honey, you come on in here and have some cookies and milk while the men folk take care of business."

I looked up at Granddaddy. He'd told me how filthy the Yates were, and I wasn't sure he'd want me to eat sump'n cooked here, but today he must-a thought they'd cleaned up a-bit for he said, "Run on in. Me and Mr. Yates gotta take care of a bunch of business, horse business that is." Granddaddy tousled my curly blond hair and grinned.

And it must a-been they had lots of horse business because they didn't come back till almost dark. They were both singing, 'Oh, How I Love My Little Brown Jug.'

After we left the Yates, I'd asked Granddaddy what kind-a business Mr. Yates was really in. He'd held up his jug. "Ollie, that man might be the dirtiest man in Macon County, but he brews the best jug of white-lightening in these here parts." He give me that crooked little grin of his and tousled my hair again. "Now that's our secret. Secrets is what makes us buddies, hear?"

I'd heared him real well, and even when Granny had asked of our whereabouts, I didn't tell 'bout our trip to the Yates'.

But this time I came home by myself and scared — carrying more questions than answers. Shadows had crowded in and wrapped our old, wood-framed house in darkness. To me it was the kind-a darkness that threatened to pull all the Sanders family into a waiting grave.

*　*　*

I sat cross-legged in the freshly turned earth of Uncle Charlie's grave and surrounded by the faded grave stones of family that had already passed. A bee buzzed around my head. Not just some ordinary bee, a news bee. Granddaddy says they're the bearer of good news. Well, our family could do with a little good news right 'bout now.

I thought 'bout the ways of educated folk. Seems the more some learn the less they know. Take Sheriff Carlson. Last night he comes waltzing into Granny's yard as pretty as you please. They'd put Uncle Charlie's box out there under the big oak tree cause of the smell.

He walks right up to the coffin and pronounces right out loud for everybody to hear "Well now, don't he look natural?"

Natural? Shot plum dead with a shotgun ain't nobody gonna look natural. Then Sheriff Carlson moseys around the yard shaking hands, slapping backs, and kissing babies. You'd never have guessed this was a 'lection year.

And for all his education, you'd think he'd know better. I heared he was at Cullowhee Teachers College for nigh on to 6 months before his daddy died, and he come back to take care of his mother and all them young'un's. But you can't never tell once folks have gone off and learned the worldly ways what nonsense they'll come home with. A wake ain't no place to be 'lectioneering and a-body ought-a know such things to get on in this world.

Granny didn't much like it either. When she saw him, her mouth got tight in that funny way she has of making a straight line with her lips. I tried that once, but my lips always turned up or down, never straight. But hern did. And her brows come to a point over her nose so as to make her look like she had heavy gray wings pasted on her forehead. But she said not a word — not to Sheriff Carlson — not to nobody till he left. She just sat there by the coffin rocking and frowning.

Granddaddy come in with his friends 'bout the time the Sheriff got around to Sadie Jo Miller. Granddaddy and the boys had been out back, um … warming up their innards. That's what Granny calls it. But seeing Sheriff Carlson sobered Granddaddy right up. He walked straight up to the Sheriff and Sadie Jo. He didn't even 'pologize for interrupting. Just grabbed the Sheriff by the arm and steered him toward the road. He was talking, fast and low like so nobody could hear what he was saying. Sheriff Carlson looked like he was being pushed along by a plow; his feet was a-going but his body was a-trying to stay. He kept looking back like he wanted somebody to help him, but they wasn't watching. Leastwise nobody but me, and I wasn't 'bout to cross Granddaddy with his innards warmed up like that. And all the while Granny was just rocking and frowning.

'Bout that time I seen Aunt Birdie, that's Uncle Ray's wife, peeking around the corner of the house. Now you have to know 'bout my aunt then you'll understand why she'd be peeking. She's a pretty woman. Most folks around here say she's the prettiest they've ever seen on Haint Branch. Granny thinks it ain't natural for her to have brown skin with that blonde hair. I wanted to ask her why since I had brown skin with honey blonde hair, but Granny didn't take kindly to children asking growed-up questions. Fact is, lots of folks say I look more like Aunt Birdie than anyone else in my family, but Granny told me right out flat that can't be since we're no real kin. Anyway, Aunt Birdie always acts funny around Granny. Like she's afraid she's going to be give a-jacking-up for sump'n she did or didn't do. So most of the time when she comes, she'll peek around at Granny. I guess it's to see what kind-a look is on Granny's face. If she's all frowned up, I've seen Aunt Birdie hurry away without even saying howdy.

Last night Aunt Birdie was different. There was worry lines around her blue eyes, and she looked like she was gonna rush over and hug Granny which would've been a first as far as I know. Seems like she'd put on some weight, especially in the stomach. Just 'bout the time I thought she was gonna come over to Granny, Uncle

Ray stepped up beside her. I couldn't believe my eyes. I'd seen the lawman haul him off the mountain. Guess they'd decided he didn't have no reason to shoot Uncle Charlie. I could a-told them that. Uncle Ray wouldn't hurt a fly. Been many a-time I'd seen him stop Uncle Charlie from fighting. Oh, I've seen him warm his innards with the rest of the men, but he'd just crawl off and sleep until he was sober. Be only one reason he'd hurt anyone and that'd be if he caught them fooling round with his Birdie. I can't say as I'd blame him for that.

I crowded in a little closer so I could hear what they was a-talking 'bout. Uncle Ray was clutching Aunt Birdie's arm real hard-like. I wanted to kick him in the shin and run but right then weren't no time to start a ruckus. He was a-talking with a real serious look on his face the way Granddaddy looks at me when I've done sump'n he don't like. I know he does that cause he don't like using the switch on me. Now Granny says it don't hurt a young'un none to get a good switching now and then. Said he didn't care to give it to his own when they were a-growing up. Maybe if he'd a-give Uncle Charlie a few more, he wouldn't be laying there in that coffin.

'Bout that time I heared Uncle Ray say, "I might have chicken house ways, but I ain't gonna be hen-pecked."

That sure was a granddaddy saying. He was always a-telling Granny he wasn't 'bout to be hen-pecked. I didn't have to wonder 'bout that saying none cause I'd seen many a roaster with his feathers picked out. Guess the hens just plain got tired of being chased by that over-zealous male and went to a-fighting back. There were plenty of women on our branch that should do that. I couldn't help but wonder if maybe that wasn't what happened to Uncle Charlie.

I know for a fact that he'd had his eye on Sadie Jo for some time. I even heared Granddaddy and Granny talking 'bout it. Granddaddy said that they sure could make some purty babies. Granny just wrinkled up her nose and told him to go chop some wood. He'd left Granny standing there with that worried frown on her face that she always wore when they were talking 'bout Uncle Charlie. Right then I'd decided that there was sump'n secret between them 'bout Uncle Charlie, a secret that might cause lots of trouble if told. I wondered 'bout trading secrets with her, but she slammed the iron skillet down on the stove with such force I'd changed my mind.

As I listened to Uncle Ray talk to Aunt Birdie, I touched the little black box in my pocket. Did these cards belong to Uncle Ray? After all I'd found them under his mattress. Was that why he was upset with Aunt Birdie? Most women thought it was evil for their men folk to play cards. Granny said cards led to all sorts of trouble. I'd wanted to ask what she meant, but I knowed that was one of them things young'uns wasn't supposed to know. I'd have to find a place to hide the cards before Granny found out that I had them. As Granddaddy says, I'd be in more trouble than you can shake a stick at.

I slipped through the crowd and into the house. Now'd be the time to hide them while ever body was busy watching over the coffin. But what was I going to do? Wasn't no place in this house Granny wouldn't find them so I'd have to find another place, but where? Then it hit me. They needed to go with Uncle Charlie, and I'd see to it the first thing in the morning.

*　*　*

And hiding the cards is how come that I'm up here so early in the morning waiting for them to bring Uncle Charlie to his final resting place and pondering the ways of educated folk. I've got to the sixth grade in my short life time and seems to me like I've learned all anybody needs to get along on Haint Branch. Course Granny said I'd need all the schooling I could get since more than likely I'd not stay here. I can't figure out what she means since a-body has everything they need right here. By that I mean food to eat, a warm bed to sleep in, and plenty of folks to love you. I asked her one time when she was a-telling me what I'd need to get along out there in the big old world if my mama hadn't a-knowed enough to make it.

She'd said, "Child, she didn't know enough to even get there."

I'd asked, "Then she's still here?"

Granny once again said, "Someday, when you're old enough, we'll talk about your mother. In the meantime, you learn all you can so you won't go wrong like she done."

Well, there was one way I wasn't going wrong and that was getting caught with these cards. I wasn't sure they had anything to do with Uncle Charlie's death, but I didn't want to find out, so they're going to get buried right along with him.

'Bout then the news bee decided to settle hisself right on the end of my nose, and I forgot all 'bout the cards. Granddaddy says never to make a bee mad or he'd sting for sure. I sat there real still 'til it decided my nose wasn't that sweet and moved on to a bunch of Golden Rod.

I picked up the hoe I'd brought and then laid flat of my stomach. I scratched out a little hole in the bottom of the grave, pulled the box from my pocket, and studied it. There was no reason not to take a look 'fore I put them in their final resting place. Taking off the lid, I pulled out, not one but, two complete decks. They were beautiful and smelled brand new. There couldn't be anyway they'd be connected with Uncle Charlie's killing. I peeked into the box and right there on the bottom was a folded piece of paper. Unfolding it, I could see there was lots of figures and some kind-a strange drawings. Scrunched up in the lower right corner was a list of names. I slipped it into my pocket, put the cards back, placed them on the hoe, and lowered the box like a small black coffin into the grave and covered it with red clay. There! Uncle Charlie would have company while he waited for what Granny called, 'the final judgment'. And the paper in my pocket, it just might help me in my search for the killer.

As I pushed up from the ground and started to brush the dirt from my dress, I caught a glimpse of sump'n moving in the edge of the woods, probably just a wild animal. Back down in Granny's front yard I seen them getting ready to carry Uncle Charlie's box up the hill. Before I could decide what to do, I'm lifted from behind by the nape of the neck. Now I know from living here in these mountains that no wild animal is gonna pick you up like this. It had to be the killer. Here to choke the life out-a me and drop me in that empty grave. If they didn't hurry getting Uncle Charlie up here, there'd already be a-body taking its spot — mine! I tried to pull loose — my eyes closed tight as I struggled. I felt my body being twisted around and slowly opened my eyes to come eyeball to eyeball with old Mr. Yates. I should a-knowed it all along. Bet him and Uncle Charlie had a fight over moonshining and Mr. Yates won.

"What you doing up here by yourself? Seems to me like you'd be down there with your family waiting to march up here and lay your poor uncle to rest." Yates face wrinkled up in a-ugly grin.

I wasn't gonna let him choke me to death without getting in my two cents. Granddaddy had taught me that I might as well go down fighting, and I wanted him to be proud of me. No sense dying in vain. "Seems to me like you done laid him to rest, left us to clean up the stink. Guess there's more stink in your britches than you want that sheriff to know 'bout."

"Gal, the only stink in my britches is the fart I just let go. I ain't the one that killed your uncle, but got myself a good notion who done it."

"Then you don't think he shot hisself?"

Yates sat me down and loosened his grip as he let out a laugh that might have been heared halfway down the mountain if the wind had been blowing that way, but it was a-blowing to the North. Granddaddy says it was a-taking all the hot air out-a these hills and giving it to them Yankees. You might as well know right now that he don't like Yankees. Said he didn't like what they went and done to his grandpappy. When I had asked what it was, he gave me the same look he gave Granny when I asked 'bout my mama. I knowed right then it was sump'n young'uns wasn't supposed to know 'bout. But now I'd found me somebody who thought the same as me 'bout Uncle Charlie. "Who'd you think done it, Mr. Yates?"

"Ain't saying right now. 'Vengeance is Mine sayeth the Lord.' Guess He'll take care of the murderer. Now tell me what you buried down there, Gal." He glanced down the hill. "And we can both get out-a here before we have company and lots of questions to answer."

"I didn't want Uncle Charlie to be bored while he was a-waiting the great judgment day so I brought him his playing cards."

Another roar escaped Yates. I glanced around half expecting to see the dead that was already a' resting here wake up and wander through the gravestones.

"Gal, that's a story I could almost buy if I didn't think you was smarter than that." He let go of me and reached for the hoe I'd left dangling over the hole. "I'll have myself a quick look. Will sleep better knowing there'd nothing important down there."

Now'd be the time to make a run for it, but there really wasn't no reason. Yates wasn't out to harm me. Looked like me and him were after the same thing. I'd wait around and see what happened when he found out I was telling the truth. Looking back down, I saw the funeral procession on its way. There wouldn't be time for him to hurt me.

"Damn, just plain old cards and new at that. Why didn't you send an old pack along with him?"

"Sent what I found, 'sides Granny'd tan my behind if she knowed I even looked at a card, says playing cards'll send a-body's soul to hell."

"Well, since that's where most folks think I'm headed, I'll take these along with me. Save another poor soul the trip." Yates closed the box and put it in his pants pocket and walked toward the trees. At the edge, he turned back. "You sure there's not something else you're hiding, Gal? Might be able to help find the killer if I found the right evidence."

I stuck my thumb in my mouth and shook my head. Right now wasn't the time to give away anything. As Yates disappeared into the woods, I slipped my hand into my pocket and caressed the paper I'd put there earlier. As soon as Uncle Charlie was buried, I'd decide 'bout who to trust.

~ 2 ~

Life had been sort of drab since Uncle Charlie's funeral. Granddaddy was gone again and Granny spent most of time rocking in that chair of hern. I decided to take a dip in the creek since we was having a nice Indian Summer. I'd just climbed up on a tree trunk that had fell over the creek and I pulled my feed-sack underwear loose from my legs, when I looked up to find Sheriff Carlson watching me. "What's wrong, Mr. Sheriff? Ain't you never seen drawers before?"

He slipped his hand in his pocket, fished out a stick of Teaberry Chewing Gum, and held it out to me.

"Plenty of times. Got six sisters."

I took the gum as I studied him. "Why ain't you riding in that fancy car of yourn? The one with County Sheriff wrote on the side?"

"It's such a nice day, and I need the exercise. Besides, don't want to use up the tax-payer's money burning gas. How's your granny doing?"

"As Granddaddy says, fair to middling seeing what she's been through. You come to tell her you've caught Uncle Charlie's killer? That's the only thing that's gonna fix her."

"Ollie, you're going to have to get rid of such thoughts. Your uncle pulled the trigger that killed him. The way I see it, he'd rather die than go off across them waters. Can't say as I much blame him."

"Uncle Charlie wouldn't do that. He liked living. He loved me and Granny too much. He was shot dead, and you know who done it. Why don't you arrest the killer and put him behind bars! That is unless ... "

"Unless what?"

"I ain't saying no more, and you can't make me. Granny is up at the house if you want-a see her. I'd say you'd better get up there and finish your business, if you have any, before my granddaddy gets home. I seen how he showed you the road the night of Uncle Charlie's wake. Don't think he'll be any nicer now."

Digging in his pocket, he found another stick of gum and give it to me.

"You'd better change your way of thinking, Ollie. And don't be blabbing that nonsense around. Won't do nothing but cause trouble and this world has enough of that."

I watched him turn and leave. He'd know what real trouble was if my granddaddy caught him up at the house.

* * *

At the rise in the road, Sheriff Carlson looked back. Ollie still stood there looking after him. For more than one reason, she gave him the willies. He'd have to watch his step or he'd have more trouble than he needed. Trouble worse than living with a father who drank and chased anything that wore a skirt. Worse yet, beat him morning and night whether he needed it or not. That's why he'd went off to collage when the chance came but that escape had been short lived. His old man had died, and he'd had to come home to help raise his sisters. That hadn't been all bad. He'd earned the respect of the people in Franklin. That was why he'd won the election four years ago.

At the porch, Sheriff Carlston climbed the steps, wiped his face with his red bandanna handkerchief, took a deep breath, and knocked on the Sanders' door. The only sound was a squeaking somewhere deep in the belly of the house. While he waited, he paced the length of the porch and thought about the upcoming election. This race was going to be tough because he was running against someone older and more experienced, but he wasn't a native. This county was true to the 'good old boys'. He'd have to remember where his loyalties were when he moved up the ladder. He paused at the door to listen. When it was apparent that no one was coming, he opened the door and called, "Mrs. Sanders, it's Sheriff Carlson. Can I have a word with you?"

Footsteps replaced the squeaking. Eula Sanders walked right by him and onto the porch. She sat down in the swing and shoved it back and forth. "You'd better say your peace and get out-a here. Grady don't cotton to men being around here when he's gone."

"People do gossip even when there ain't nothing to talk about. That's one reason I'm here. There's all kinds of rumors in town about Charlie's death. I'm trying my hardest to make sure the truth is known, but you know human nature."

Eula squinted at the sheriff, letting her gray eyebrows droop almost over her eyes.

The sheriff shifted from one leg to the other. What was it about this little woman that made him feel like he was coming unglued? He'd heard tell she was from a fine upstanding family out-a Savannah, Georgia. It could be the way she spoke, and she did carry herself with a certain kind-a air, not that of the mountain people. Anyway, he'd state his business and get out of here. Right now even the votes he hoped to get didn't seem that important. "Mrs. Sanders, I need you and Grady to support me in the upcoming election so I can see this shooting thing through. I promise I'll do all in my power to prove that Charlie didn't take his own life."

Eula jumped to her feet. "My Charlie might have taken a little nip from the bottle now and then. And I know he cottoned to the women, but he was a good boy — my boy — Sheriff."

"I know just how you feel. And as soon as this election is over, I promise to spend every waking moment looking for his killer."

"Then you believe he didn't kill hisself?"

The sheriff took a few steps backward. She'd lured him into admitting there could possibly be a killer on the loose. He'd have to get out of here. "I'm saying I'll look into all aspects of this case. In other words, I won't leave any stones unturned to get to the bottom his death. Now that I know I can count on your votes, I'll get going. I might have time to check out a few clues before the day ends." He backed toward the steps, turned, and hurried down into the yard.

"Going somewhere, Sheriff?"

He wheeled toward the corner of the house to come face to face with Grady Sanders. "I was — uh . . ."

"Didn't I tell you the night of Charlie's wake that I didn't want to ever see your weaselly little face around here again? Now, get and don't come back!"

The sheriff squared his shoulders and patted the badge on his shirt. "Mr. Sanders, I understand you being upset that night. This here badge gives me certain rights and obligations. I've made the trip up here on foot to save good tax-payers' money. And I might add, just to assure your wife that after the election, I'll do all I can to clear Charlie's name."

Grady took a step forward. "Why you little scum-ball, campaigning in my dead boy's name. Out-a here before I stomp you into this here red clay!"

The sheriff turned to go then wheeled back around. "Now, Mr. Sanders..."

"Out, and don't come back!"

The sheriff rushed towards the road. As he passed the creek, he hesitated and watched Ollie splash in the water. Was it possible this child had some connection to Charlie's death? Wasn't there some gossip about her birth — something about a young woman leaving her with Eula to raise? He'd go over to the court house and Angel Hospital and see what he could turn up. Maybe The Franklin Press would have reports that could help. Yes, he might find the link he needed to solve this case.

* * *

If the truth be known, Sheriff Carlson could have cared less how Olivia Sanders came to live with the Sanders family, but he had to show some interest in what had happened to Charlie and the child could have something to do with it. He remembered it was close to Thanksgiving about twelve years ago when she'd turned up on their porch in a suitcase.

At the newspaper office, he asked to see copies of the papers for November 1930. The headlines of the second one he picked up read: Baby Girl Found in Suitcase on Grady Sanders' Front Porch. He scanned the article but it didn't tell him much, just an abandoned child story.

From the newspaper office, he went straight to the courthouse where he searched the birth records, but there hadn't been any babies born for the month of November, at least none that had been recorded. He slammed the book closed. There was old Granny Zeta who lived up on Black Mountain. Maybe she'd helped some poor young'un deliver and they'd just dropped the child on Grady's doorstep, but from what he'd heard, talking to her wouldn't help. People were saying she was as loony as a bat. No sense wasting gas to make that trip up the mountain.

He closed the record book and turned to leave when he saw Ray Sanders out in the hall and called to him. "You just saved me a trip out to your house. Your mother is insisting that I try and find out if your brother was killed. If I treat this like a murder case, you and your wife both are prime suspects."

"Leave my wife out-a this."

"Why wasn't she home for the four days Charlie lay, dead, up there on your bed?"

"For your information, Birdie won't stay there alone when hunting starts. She goes to her folks till I get home from my logging job."

"Can her parents vouch that she was there the whole time?"

"Ask them yourself, Sheriff. I ain't doing your dirty work." Ray turned and walked toward the door leading to the street. The sheriff followed him. "Sanders, I have more questions for you."

"I ain't answering no more of your questions. Arrest me if you can prove I killed my brother, and leave my wife alone!" He moved into the street.

The sheriff leaned against the doorjamb. "Don't you get smart-mouthed with me."

"I'll get any way I want with you. And you can take my word, Sheriff, my brother is better off where he's at."

Sheriff Carlson stood there, thinking as Ray sauntered across the street. He hoped Charlie's death wouldn't wreck his plans for the future. Looked like most everyone believed he'd taken his own life,

Maybe it'd stay that way, at least until after the election. Moonshining was growing, and unless handled with the utmost care, it could become a real problem. Right now the kickbacks were helping pay for his campaign. And if his career headed for the big time, he'd need more and more funds. He sure hoped Eula Sanders didn't lose her other son, but if she insisted he keep up this investigation, she'd have to live with the results.

* * *

Killing wasn't something Sheriff Carlson wanted to deal with. As soon as this next term was over, he planned on throwing his hat in for a spell up in Raleigh as a state representative. And who knew after that, he might make a run for governor. Of course, he'd have to keep his nose clean or at least keep it from dripping. He figured locking up a lot of drunks, and trying a whole bunch of chicken thieves would be the extent of his duties as sheriff. Now Eula Sanders wasn't going to let up on him until he looked into the death of her son. He already knew how Ray felt about his brother's death. He might have wanted his brother dead if he found out Birdie and Charlie were fooling around.

Somehow, he felt Ray wasn't guilty. First, he'd go talk with that Yates man who ran the biggest moonshining business in the county. Him and Charlie were sort of business partners. Maybe they'd had a falling out. And Birdie, a lover's quarrel could lead to murder. He'd have to talk to Sadie Jo Miller. Her and Charlie had been involved since she moved to the branch some time back. For sure, he'd have to question that traveling preacher man, Richard Rainey, since he was the main transportation for getting the white lightening out of these mountains. Him and Charlie might have had words. There wasn't no use putting off what had to be done. He'd get on over to Yates and see what he had to say.

* * *

Yates corked the last gallon of moonshine and set it on a bench and sat down by it. The last run had been the best this year. Too bad Charlie wasn't here to have a good drink with him. Wasn't anything better in the world than to have a good buddy to share a drink with, and there wasn't a better friend in the county than Charlie Sanders had been. Could it be possible that somebody here on the Branch wanted him dead? He reached in his pocket and got the cards he'd taken from Ollie. He opened the box and shuffled them. There wasn't any marking or clues anywhere.

Charlie hadn't liked the idea of going off to the war. Maybe he did take his own life. He put the cards back in their box. It'd be milking time soon. He'd better get on home. He couldn't afford to let the calf suck all the milk. His young'uns needed it. He jammed his hands into his overall pocket and headed toward the barn only a short distance from the still.

As he rounded the corner of the barn, there stood Sheriff Carlson. He'd been expecting a visit from him but not so soon. "Can I help you, Carlson?"

"Sure can. You know the election is coming up soon. I could sure use your vote?"

"The way I vote ain't nobody's business but mine."

"I understand. And I ain't trying to buy your vote but there's been, what some folks think, a murder here on Haint Branch. And that's not all, some think it's tied to moonshining; I'm thinking, if it was murder, they're probably right. A vote cast in my direction could persuade me to look the other way."

Yates took his hands from his pockets and made a fist with his left hand. "See this, Sheriff Carlson. Charlie Sanders was my friend. I ain't saying there's not folk in these parts that might-a wanted him dead, but Charlie'd not lay still in his grave if he thought I'd sell out just to protect my own hide. Now, it's your job to find his killer, and I'd suggest you be about that business and leave me to my chores."

The sheriff shifted from one foot to the other and spit on the ground. "I hope you're not sorry, Yates. I should take you in right now on the suspicion of murder."

"And what grounds do you have?"

"The way I see it is that you and Sanders were operating a 'still' together, and he found out that you've been cheating him. It's common knowledge that you don't have very good scruples."

"When it comes to my real friends, I have plenty. Now get yourself out to that road and don't let me catch you back up here unless you have a warrant for my arrest. And I might suggest that if you do come back with one, you'd better have evidence that'll lock me up for good or you're buzzard bait."

The sheriff's face turn beet red, and he backed toward the path leading to the road. He stumbled over a log and sat down in the dirt, then stood and brushed the dust from his uniform before turning and heading back where he came from.

Yates watched until he was out of sight then started his chores. He might be a moonshiner, but he was a true friend even to the dead, and there wasn't any power on this earth that could get him to sell out to the law. Carlson would have to find another way to win his election.

Eva McCall

* * *

Sadie Jo was never one to stand on ceremony so the morning that Sheriff Carlson knocked on her door, she put the top back on her nail polish and yelled, "Come on in."

She was blowing on her freshly polished nails when the sheriff strolled through the kitchen doorway and sat down across the table from her. "Howdy, sheriff, what you doing out this way so early this morning?

"Guess you can say I'm here to please Eula Sanders. She claims someone shot Charlie in cold blood. Said he'd never take his own life. What-a you think, Sadie? From what I hear, you and him were kind-a tight."

She raised her eyebrows at the sheriff. "Guess you could call it that. We were . . . let's say sort-a like joined at the hip if you know what I mean." She blew on her nails one last time as she extended her foot under the table and touched the sheriff's leg.

"Could it be that you caught him with another woman and killed him in a jealous rage?"

"Now, Sheriff, do I look like the kind of woman that would get her revenge that way? Ain't never seen a dead man yet that could do a woman any good. No sir, I'd just show him that two can play that little game, if you know what I mean."

"Don't take an educated man to figure you out, Sadie. I'm sure Charlie shot hisself to keep from going off over yonder to Germany and getting killed. That's what I told his mama, but she don't see it that way so I'm gonna do what any good sheriff would do."

"And what's that?"

"I'm questioning everyone who had a reason to want him dead, and as I see it, you fit into that group."

"Well, you can take me off that list, sheriff. I'd rather have him a-live."

"That ain't too hard for me to believe. Do you know of anyone else who'd want him dead?"

"How about his brother, Ray? He was awfully jealous of Charlie and his wife, Birdie."

"Do you think he had reason to be jealous?"

Sadie tapped her nails on the table. From what she'd seen, Ray had plenty reason to be jealous, but she wasn't gonna tell Sheriff Carlson anything that would make his job easier. Let him earn what the county paid him.

"Why don't you ask him?"

The sheriff stood and pushed back his chair. "I've already talked to him. He's glad his brother is dead but I doubt that he did it. If you remember anything that you think might help, let me know."

"I'll be sure and do that, but right now if I was you, I wouldn't plan on that happening."

"You know it's illegal to conceal evidence, don't you?"

"I ain't concealing nothing, Sheriff."

The sheriff walked to the door then faced Sadie. "For your sake, I hope not."

Sadie didn't bother answering him but just kept tapping the table with her nails until the kitchen door slammed. She was sure that the sheriff wasn't too interested in her well-being or who killed Charlie, either. It was all an act.

* * *

The last person Eula expected to show up at her door again was

Sheriff Carlson. She thought Grady had scared him off for good, but she wasn't gonna be that lucky. There he stood on her front porch all dressed up in that uniform of his, acting like he was here on official business. If he planned on winning the election next week, he'd better do lots of business.

As soon as he knocked, she opened the door all proper like and said, "And have you turned up any leads on who might-a killed my boy?"

"No, I ain't yet but that's the reason I need to talk to you again."

Eula stepped out on the porch. "Any talking we do we can do right here on the front porch where the world can see us."

"That's just fine, Mrs. Sanders. What I've got-a ask you won't take but a minute."

"Well, ask and get out-a here."

The sheriff shifted from one foot to the other. "Did your sons get along?"

Eula squinted her eyes like seeing and hearing at the same time was really hard. "Get along! They fought like cats and dogs when they were boys if that's what you mean?"

"No, as men, was there any friction."

"Any, what?"

"Did Ray have any reason to want Charlie dead?"

Eula clenched her fist. The nerve of this man, here she'd just buried her son, and he dared question her about his brother. Did he really think she'd tell him if there was a reason Ray would want his brother dead?

"Sheriff, my Ray wouldn't hurt a fly. He's a good boy. My good boy. The only boy I got left, and you ain't gonna take him from me."

"But you wanted me to find the killer, remember? That's what I'm trying to do."

"You ain't doing no such thing. You're just trying to look good so you'll win the election. My Ray is a good family man so you can just cross him off your list. Now, get!"

Sheriff Carlson moved toward the steps. "If there's something you know and ain't telling me, you could find yourself in lots of trouble."

"Get, and don't let me see your face around here again, and leave my boy alone!" She wheeled and went back in the house to her rocking chair. Lord, would she ever be able to squish all her worries.

3

Life on the mountain changed after Uncle Charlie's death. Granny totally withdrew for weeks at a time and it was just me and Granddaddy most of the time. Sometimes a neighbor would drop by with fresh-made bread or a pie. Granny'd just take it, nod her thanks, and then go back to rocking.

Sheriff Carlson showed up the other day. He gave me a stick of Teaberry Gum and then went to talk to Granny. Granddaddy come home and run him off. When he left he stood up there at the road staring at me some more. I'm sure he's got sump'n cooking in that little pea brain of his. Whatever it is, he'd better stay away from here or my Granddaddy might use him for buzzard bait. He's always a-telling me what he'll use, but I ain't never seen him catch a buzzard yet so I guess it's just another one of his sayings.

Wondering 'bout Granddaddy's sayings can keep a young'un to thinking purt near all the time. Sometimes at school the teacher will catch me daydreaming. She'll say, "Ollie, young'un, where are you?" Well, the truth is, most of the time I'm studying on sump'n Granddaddy has told me, but ever since Uncle Charlie's death, I've been trying to figure out who might have hated him enough to shoot him dead.

That's where my mind was today when she asked me to name the five great lakes. I was remembering how it had smelled at Uncle Ray's house and seeing him being drug off the mountain. I'd just decided to high-tail it back up to the neighbor woman and see what I could find out when Miss Allen popped the question right out-a the blue. I hadn't even opened my Geography book. I fumbled around trying to find the right page, but she'd caught me red-handed, smack-dab in the middle of my wonderings.

Miss Allen come over to my desk, opened the book, and pointed to the answer. Why don't you read them off for us, Olivia, and for tomorrow you can write the names ten times each. That should help you remember."

Now I'd went and done it, more homework. I'd for sure not have time to do much snooping tonight. Besides it was purt near dark by five. The sun don't linger long here in the mountains. When it's dark it's dark, no time to go prowling around for a killer unless you want-a wind up in one of them there sink holes and get washed away by the underground streams or have to out run a mountain lion or some other wild animal. No, I'd just have to put off my hunting until Saturday when I'd have more daylight. And another thing, I'd have to sneak in this writing job when nobody was looking. No way did I want Granddaddy to know I'd got into trouble. He'd promised me whatever punishment I got at school, I'd get the same at home. Lord only knows I'd wear out the lead in my pencil if I had to write any more. It was already so short I could barely hang on to it, and the eraser had buried itself in the metal top. There I went, thinking 'bout burying. What was happening to me?

I counted the sheets of clean paper left in my note book, only ten pieces and four more days of school this week. I'd have to skimp to make it last. I'd write my lakes on my old homework papers or my brown paper, lunch poke. No use wasting good paper on such things. There was the paper I'd found in the cards with the funny looking map on it . . . but I'd left it in my funeral dress pocket.

The bell rang and I rushed for the door. 'Bout the time I thought I was safe, I heared Miss Allen calling my name. Good Lord, what kind-a trouble was I in now. I wheeled and returned to stand in front of her desk. Keeping my eyes on the floor, I said, "Yes, Miss Allen?"

"Olivia, if you don't start paying attention, I'm going to have to talk with your folks. I know you've just lost your uncle and that's hard for a child your age, but you're always daydreaming. I'm surprised you do as well as you do, but that's not all I'm concerned about. Yesterday I found some bad language wrote on the blackboard. Some of the boys said you did it. I've thought about it and decided if you could look me straight in the eye and say you didn't do it, I'd believe you. Otherwise, I have no choice but to talk to your Granddaddy."

My heart pounded. What was she talking 'bout? I didn't know any bad language accept for the "s" word and Granny had scrubbed my mouth for using it. I'd decided that word belonged in the outhouse. Granddaddy had never used the razor strap on me, but I could see him reaching for it as Miss Allen told him 'bout what she thought I'd done. Slowly, I brought my eyes up, and choking back the hurt that rose in my throat, I looked her right in the eye. "Miss Allen, I don't know no bad words, and even if I did, I wouldn't know how to spell them." I seen the corner of her lips turn up as she tried not to smile.

"Olivia, I think you'll be a great lawyer someday. You've cleared your name in one single statement. Spelling is your weakness. You can go, but don't forget your assignment."

"I won't, Miss Allen."

Halfway to the door, she called to me again. "And please do your daydreaming at home, and if you get tired of dreaming, you might want to ask about your heritage. We're going to do a family tree before the end of the year."

I nodded an answer and ran out the door. Daydreaming or family trees were the last thing on my mind right now. I had to get home and find that funny-looking map.

* * *

The house was quiet when I got home. Not even the usual squeaking from Granny's rocker interrupted the stillness. Little goose bumps popped out on my arms and legs. There hadn't been a day since Uncle Charlie's death that the rocking chair had been still. Was Granny alright? Me and Granddaddy was worried 'bout her sump'n fierce, but he said life was for the living, and the way he seen it, me and him were the only ones living here right now. Said Granny was in a world beyond words. I should-a asked him where that was but I knowed he'd just tell me I wasn't growed-up enough to understand. So I went on back to school, and he'd went on back to logging.

Today I was glad for the quiet; it'd give me a chance to look for the map. First, I'd check around and make sure Granny wasn't in the house, and then I'd search for it. If Granny hadn't showed up by the time I'd finished looking, then I'd get worried.

After a good look around the house, I went straight to my room in the loft. The note should be in my dress pocket. I'd left the dress crumbled up on my dresser.

The minute I reached my room, I knowed there was trouble a-brewing. It was clean as the yard that I had to sweep every Saturday morning cause Granny insisted. She said people judged you by the way your house looked on the outside. When I asked Granddaddy if that was so, he said he guessed, but houses were like people. Dressing up the outside didn't make them clean inside. Remembering that reminded me of the way Sheriff Carlson had looked at me in my drawers. I already figured that little fat man was a lot dirtier on the inside than showed in that nice uniform he wore.

Where was my dress! Had Granny found the map and went looking for whatever was drawed on it? If so, we might all be in hot water. What I had to do now was stay calm and reason this out. The only one who'd bother with my room was Granny, but it wasn't her ways to look in pockets. Why one time she'd washed Uncle Charlie's overalls with his money in them. When he found it still in a wet ball, he'd hung the bills behind the stove to dry out. Well, this time we might all be hung out to dry just like Uncle Charlie's money was.

Let's see. That was my good Sunday-go-to meeting dress, and maybe Granny had put it in the cedar chest in Uncle Charlie's room. I hadn't been in there since he was kilt. I'd heared stories 'bout how the dead hang around before they go on to their final resting place. Some people even drape black cloths over their mirror cause they think the dead can come back through the glass. Guess if Granny was in her right mind, she might have done that. Kind-a glad she ain't cause there's enough drabbiness in this house. Course it could be like that old plantation house down the road, haunted cause the slaves murdered the owner for selling off their young'uns. Can't say Granddaddy wouldn't do the same thing if somebody tried to harm me. I know for a fact ghosts live there cause I heared sump'n like chains being drug up the stairs. Guess that's why I didn't have a hankering to go in Uncle Charlie's room. Who knows? He might be hiding in the chest. That didn't make much difference now. There might be more than a ghost hanging 'bout if I didn't find that map. Pushing open the door as slow as I could, I eased inside and stood there a few minutes eyeing the trunk like it was 'bout to eat me alive.

Finally, I got the courage to raise the lid real slow like. Didn't want no ghost to make me wet my pants. And I'd a-done that even if I'd a knowed he was in there cause it ain't every day a-body meets a ghost or a haint as Granddaddy calls them. The lid creaked, and I scooted back to give the haint room to jump out, but the only thing coming out of that trunk was the smell of moth balls. Granny must a-used a peck-and-half. What kind-a haint would wanna live with that smell? I knowed for sure Uncle Charlie's ghost wouldn't hang around sump'n like that. He was always neat as a pin. There's been many a day I've seen Granny wash, starch, and iron his shirts until they'd almost stand alone. Granddaddy used to say that people as particular as him usually married and fell backwards in a cow pie. When I asked him what he meant by that, he said they'd marry someone as filthy as the Yates. Guess Uncle Charlie would as soon be a haint as to live like the Yates.

With one big shove, I pushed the lid all the way open and right there on top was my dress all neatly folded. I grabbed it and reached in the pocket and pulled out the note that I'd put in the day of Uncle Charlie's burial. Then I refolded the dress and hurried back to my room. For a long time, I sat on the bed and studied the funny looking drawing. It looked like a big copper kettle with pipes of some sort running ever which a way. Down in the left corner was a list of names. Ones I'd never heared. Oh, did that say Carlson? It sure enough did. Could it be Sheriff Carlson? It didn't have to be. There was a whole bunch of them around these parts. In the right lower corner was what looked like a map of some mountain. Wait, right there in real small letters was the word "Black". Black Mountain, that was only a hop and jump from here. First chance I got I'd have to go looking around. The squeaking started again and I knew Granny was back from where ever she'd been. I slipped the map under my mattress and ripped open my greasy lunch poke and began to write. Let's see, Miss Allen said I had to write each lake name ten times. Guess I'd have to tote my dinner in a flour sack tomorrow but that was better than wasting new paper on such a worthless job. Come Saturday I'd get on up to Mrs. Ropers and visit with her a spell. See what she knowed, and then if the weather was nice, I'd see what I could find on Black Mountain.

* * *

Saturday brought plenty of sunshine, but it was cold as a well-diggers butt as Granddaddy says. I never quite figured that one out, and when I asked him he gave me that dirty scowl look of his. I knew right then it was sump'n he didn't think he needed to explain to a young'un. Seems like there's lots a young'un ought not know, but if I'm going to have to know so much to leave Haint Branch I'd better get to learning more than I was getting at that there school of Miss Allen's.

I raised my hand and started to knock on Mrs. Roper's door just as she opened it.

"Why, Ollie, I've been a wondering when you'd get around to coming by. I made a batch of cookies yesterday. Come on out in the kitchen and have some while you tell me how your granny's doing since she lost her boy."

I followed her through the sparsely furnished living room.

Wouldn't Miss Allen be proud of me for thinking "sparsely"? Maybe I was learning sump'n after all.

By the time I sat down at the table, Mrs. Roper had me a glass of milk poured and three of the smelliest peanut butter cookies I'd ever smelled, placed in front of me. She poured a cup of coffee and sat down across the table. Her beady little eyes bored into my face. I lowered my eyes, but I could still feel her glaring at me. Gingerly, I nibbled at a cookie. Lord, there I went again, thinking all proper like.

"Ollie, why are you so quiet? Now, I know you've come up here to ask me what I know about the shooting so why don't you ask. As your Granddaddy'd say, there ain't no use beating around the bush."

"No, Granddaddy would say if you want a-know sump'n go straight to the horse's mouth. And that's what I'm a doing, Mrs. Roper. I want a-know right up front who was on the mountain the day my uncle Charlie died."

"Well, child that'd be hard to say since no one rightly knows what day he died. From the smell, he'd been dead awhile."

"Can you remember any of the coming and going's of that week?"

"Yeah, jest like I told Sheriff Carlson. I think about every man and boy on Haint Branch went traipsing up there at one time or other. Didn't surprise me none since it's squirrel season. I even seen Charlie a couple of times."

"When was the last time you seen him?"

Mrs. Roper broke off a piece of cookie and chewed as she studied. "I'd say about four days before he was found dead."

"And who else did you see the same day?"

"Sheriff Carlson for one. Remember thinking at the time he must have took the day off to go hunting. Then there was Mr. Yates and his boy and even your granddaddy. But the strangest was Sadie Jo Miller. She went by here real early all dressed up in her hunting garb and whistling like a man. Couldn't help but think that was unusual since I'd never seen her hunting before. Course I don't see everything that goes on up here." Her eyebrows wrinkled up in a worried frown. "Ollie, you've got me to thinking, and I'd say that's more than that sheriff has done."

"He's been here asking question?"

"Yeah, he called it routine. Sounded like something he was doing halfhearted."

I stuffed the rest of my cookie in my mouth and washed it down with the milk. Mrs. Roper reached to refill my glass, but I stopped her. "I've had enough and thanks for talking to me. You've helped me more than you'll ever know, Mrs. Roper. And please don't tell Granddaddy I was up here. I'd get my backside warmed for pestering you."

"You don't have to worry none, child. Your visit will be our little secret."

She followed me to the door. "The cookie jar is always full and waiting for a young'un. I fed your aunt Birdie's boys cookies the same day Charlie was found dead."

I hadn't remembered to ask about the coming and goings of that day. "Was it before they hauled him off?"

"I'd say so. The boys showed up before your Aunt Birdie did. That didn't surprise me none since she's in the 'family way.'"

I'd heared Granny talking 'bout being in the 'family way', and I knowed that was one of them growed-up things but that's 'bout all. I shuffled from one foot to the other and glanced out the door.

Mrs. Roper touched my shoulder. "I'm sorry. I forgot you're too young to know about the birds and bees."

I stepped away. "I know Granddaddy fusses 'bout the birds eating his cherries, and the mites getting in his bees."

"Ask your granny to tell you about having babies then you'll understand."

"Granny ain't in no shape to tell me nothing. She won't even tell me where I come from. Why don't you tell me what's wrong with Aunt Birdie?"

"She's going to have another baby. I'd say in about four or five months."

I remembered thinking the night of the wake that she was getting fat in the stomach. Maybe that's why she'd been peeking around the house at Granny. I guess the last thing Granny'd be wanting 'bout right now was another young'un in the family.

4

Sadie Jo Miller had her cap set for Charlie Sanders ever since the first day her folks moved to Haint Branch, but now those hopes were buried here in the Sanders cemetery. Wasn't no use in dreaming about him anymore, but she could remember the good times they'd shared. She squatted and placed a handful of plastic flowers on his grave. The woman at the five-and-ten had promised they would last forever. Would her memories last that long? Could they keep her warm when the wind howled down the valley and snow covered the ground? Wrapping her arms around her shoulders, she closed her eyes and let her mind slip back to the day her family had moved to Haint Branch.

The wagon loaded with what little furniture they owned rattled up Haint Branch road, drawing families from their homes to gawk at the newcomers. The only one to act normal was the young man walking toward a mailbox with the name SANDERS hanging from it. He glanced up as the wagon passed, but that was long enough for her to get a good look at his hazel eyes and his two dimples as he smiled and greeted her pa. As their wagon rounded the curve in the road, she'd turned and watched until the head of wavy, brownish-red hair disappeared.

Her mother had given her a stern lecture. "Sadie, I see that look in your eyes. I'm telling you right now we've come all the way from Highlands to here so we can get a new start, and you'd better mind your P's and Q's. You should know there's nothing more that can put a family in bad standing in a community than a girl with loose morals."

"Oh, Ma. Ain't nothing wrong in looking."

"That's what you said when you went ape over that Martin boy. His ma still thinks you're the reason he hung hisself. I'm telling you right now, we've about run out of places to move."

Sadie Jo kept on staring at the last spot she'd seen her new beau and let her ma babble on for the rest of the way. Wasn't any use in saying that she'd left her heart hanging back there on the Sanders mailbox. If she said anything, her pa would head back down the road and up the mountain to where they'd come from, and that was the last place she wanted to be. People weren't too kind when they found Billy Martin hanging in the barn loft. Most said it was because she'd turned down his marriage proposal, but what was a girl to do? She'd just turned eighteen and being tied down to a man and a bunch of young'uns was something she didn't want. Wasn't nothing wrong with marriage, but a girl had to live some before she hooked up with a man for life. And as for young'uns, well, she'd never been too crazy over them. Maybe she would feel different when they belonged to her.

She turned to her ma and asked, "How long did you know Pa 'fore you got hitched?"

"Not long enough," said Pa.

Ma's blue eyes darkened as she looked toward him. "Your pa's right. But I'd say you never know somebody until you live with them."

"Then you think it's all right to shack up with your man?"

"Sadie Jo Miller! We won't have that sort of talk in this wagon. And I'd better never hear of you living with someone without the benefit of a preacher man."

"Ma, ain't no preacher's words gonna make it right between a man and woman, only love can do that."

Once again her mother eyed her pa with a cold glint.

Sadie Jo couldn't help but wonder what was between them. Wasn't love for sure, or there weren't any signs of it. They'd never argued or at least not when she was around. As far as she could see, they kind of tolerated each other. She aimed on having more than what was between them even if it took her a lifetime to find it. But if the young man at the mailbox was a sign of things to come, maybe she'd found what she was looking for.

Footsteps drew her thoughts back to the cemetery.

"You ain't gonna bring Uncle Charlie back sitting there boo-hooing like that. I'd say you best be helping me look for the killer 'fore one of us gets shot dead."

Sadie wiped at her green eyes with the back of one hand as she pushed a mass of red curls behind her ear with the other. "Ollie, you're the last person I expected to see up here on such a nice Saturday afternoon."

She watched the girl twist on a strand of blond hair as tears gathered in her violet-blue eyes. Something was really bothering her — something more than the death of Charlie. She knew Charlie really loved the little girl and that she loved him, but this was about more than Charlie. She stood and took Ollie's hand. "Would you like to talk, honey?"

"Yes, I'd like to know when was the last time you saw my uncle alive."

The cemetery echoed with the question and the child's need to know. Sadie swallowed and looked away. Why would she ask such

Murder on Haint Branch

a question? Did she know about her and Charlie? "Why do you think I saw him?"

"I went to Mrs. Ropers earlier, and she said she saw you go up the mountain a few days before he was found dead. I'd like to know when you took up hunting and whistling. Granddaddy says 'A whistling woman and a crowing hen always comes to some bad end.' And if you know anything about his sayings, you know they carry a bushel of truth."

"Well, all I know about your granddaddy is what Charlie told me. He said you and your grandpa are nigh on to inseparable. I know how you feel because I felt the same way about mine."

The steady tap of a woodpecker interrupted the stillness and for a minute Sadie thought it was the repeated fire of a gun. She felt the tremble of the child's hand in hers. "I'd say let's not worry about me coming to some bad end. And yes, I went hunting with Charlie that morning. I shot my first squirrel and he got two. I left him at Ray's house about noon and that's the last time I saw him. Now, why don't you tell me where you've been to get so much red clay on your shoes?"

"I've been traipsin' around over Black Mountain looking for sump'n."

"Did you find it?"

"No, but it give me time to do some real hard thinking."

"Thinking about what?"

"That Granny's right. I've got lots to learn if I'm gonna grow up and leave Haint Branch. Didn't use't think I'd want a-leave, but that's a-changing."

"I'll tell you, Ollie, you learn all you can and maybe some of these days we can leave together."

"You'd like to go away, too?"

"Don't see that I have anything to lose." She watched as a smile replaced the worried look on Ollie's face. Could this child hold some sort of secret concerning Charlie's death?

5

Christmas crept up. I knowed it was coming, but who felt like Santa Claus with Uncle Charlie in the cemetery and a war going on? Most days I'd come home from school to find Granny sitting in her rocker with her lower lip sucked in and the top one clamped down over it, rocking like she was gonna rock away all the world's troubles. I tried to talk to her, but she'd stare through me like I was a ghost.

Granddaddy was gone a lot and when he did come home it was with his innards warmed real good. He'd stagger through the house swearing and flop at the kitchen table, banging it for his supper. I'd warm up some for him. After a few bits, he'd shove the plate away and say, "Taste like hog slop. I'm gonna go to bed." He'd stumble back to the front room and study Granny for a few minutes. "That rocking ain't gonna fix nothin', woman. You might as well use that energy to cook a good meal." Then he'd wobble off to bed leaving me and Granny alone.

I'd pull up a chair as close to her as I could and talk, but nothing I said helped. Then three days before Christmas I come home to find her in the kitchen making gingerbread, and I knew right then and there that she'd returned from where ever she'd been.

I can still hear our neighbor woman saying, "Miss Eula you gotta live in the land of the living. You got a girl to raise and a man who needs his woman." I wanted to tell that woman I could take care of myself, but Granny had taught me not to talk back to my elders so I lifted my head a little higher and walked away.

Granny handed me the bowl to lick the way she'd always done

and said, "When you're finished go find your granddaddy, and you and him fetch us a tree." Christmas was a-coming after all.

I'd have to hurry before Granny changed her mind and went back to rocking. I was sure Santa Clause wouldn't take kindly to her rocking while he was leaving my presents under the tree. You have to know right now that I'm too big for this Santa Clause stuff, have been since I was six years old. Me and my cousins was playing in the hayloft a few days before Christmas and when I jumped from a rafter into the hay, (sump'n that granddaddy had forbidden us to do), I landed on sump'n. I dug under the hay and felt a cold leg and foot. We spent the next few days convinced that there was a body in the hayloft. Christmas morning, after we'd opened our gifts, Granddaddy went out and came back hauling a life size mannequin for Granny to use when she made her dresses. Thank the Lord, it hadn't been a body.

I licked the last of the batter from the bowl and rushed out to look for Granddaddy. I didn't have to look far. He was busy keeping his jug company. "Granddaddy, she's back. Granny ain't rocking, and she wants us to get a tree. We'd better get to it. Ain't but a few days til Christmas and 'sides who knows she might go back to rocking."

Granddaddy picked up his ax and stumbled toward the woods. "Come on, I'm with you. That woman's like the weather, one minute hot and the next cold."

Me and Grandpa traipsed all over Black Mountain looking for a tree while I looked for that thing on my map. I wanted to tell him 'bout the drawing but he didn't seem in no mood to talk, and I wanted to get the tree and get home for a piece of that gingerbread. Besides, he'd be as mad as an old wet hen if he knowed I was keeping sump'n important from him.

He chopped down a half-growed tree and tied a rope around a branch. We drug it all the way back to the house. He hammered a cross-bar on the trunk, and we took it inside. The warm gingerbread was on the table, but Granny weren't no where's to be found.

"Wonder where that woman has took off to. Could be she's gone to the cemetery. I'll take a look. You bring down the decorations." Granddaddy stopped at the door and looked back. "Santa Claus is gonna have to work overtime."

I went to get the trimmings, but I wasn't sure there was gonna be any Santa Claus. This made the second time Granny had disappeared since the shooting. Sump'n was bad wrong with her. Sump'n me and Granddaddy couldn't fix.

* * *

"Sheriff!"

Sheriff Carlson hesitated, mid-stride, and then slowly lowered his left boot down beside his right. "Lordy," he mumbled. "Thought I'd seen the last of her." It'd been a while, but not nearly long enough. Just the sound of a rocker creaking brought back the image of Eula Sanders 'sitting and rocking' at her boy's wake. And now here she was.

"Evenin', ma'am," he muttered politely.

"Yes, Sheriff, it is evening, but the sun ain't shone no light on them that shot my boy. And neither have you." Her voice was strong. There was a time after the funeral when folks said she'd never speak again.

"No, ma'am," he replied, certain in his answer now that he knew her mission. "And ain't likely to be no more than you know. He done shot hisself. Plain as the day against night, nothing else to be said about it."

"Bet you'd like that, wouldn't you?"

The old woman was inching closer, eyeing the shotgun he held lazily in one hand resting comfortably against the other arm.

"But sons is sons and ain't nobody'd say that my boy was less than his Pa and me. If they did, it ain't so. I'd know if it was. But it ain't. And you know it ain't."

Sheriff Carlson looked into the old woman's eyes and knew that the truth would come to light. Showing mercy to no man or woman either when it came to that. Truth always did win out, and those that feared the truth were lucky to be dead before it did.

* * *

I had me a purty good idea that Granny wasn't in no cemetery. Seeing it was almost Christmas, she'd be on to Sheriff Carlson like a hen after a June bug. Granddaddy's always saying that to me when he wants me to get my chores done. I chuckled. I could see her pouncing on the sheriff's back and letting him have it with her fist. Can't say as I much blame her. He'd won the 'lection, and we'd not heared hide or hair from him since. Didn't think we would, but if there was one thing a-body could count on here on the Branch was Granny's stubbornness. She was like Granddaddy's old blue-tick hunting dog. When he got a-hold of a 'possum, he wouldn't let go even when it was dead. The only thing Granny considered dead was her boy, and we all knowed that. Guess we were afraid of her holding on and what she might do.

Seeing how normal she'd acted earlier, it could be she'd decided to take matters into her own hands. I'd better get on into town and make sure she hadn't got herself locked up. The thoughts of Granny setting in Sheriff Carlson' jail made the little hairs on the back of my neck stand up. Better for me to go than Granddaddy. Seeing his state, he'd break that sheriff man right in two.

I saddled up old Bess and headed off to town. Wasn't that far and if I hurried, Granddaddy wouldn't even miss me. Bess was in the going mood and took of like a spring chicken. She hadn't been out of the barn much since Uncle Charlie died so I guess she was just happy to have some place to go.

The fog was beginning to settle in as we come into town, but I could see Granny with her hands on her hips, giving Sheriff Carlson what for. He was all sort of slouched down on the courthouse steps taking it like a whipped puppy. I knowed he didn't feel a bit sorry, just wanted Granny to think he was a-trying. But, I reckoned I'd better grab her and get out-a there before he decided he'd heared enough. I sneaked up behind and caught her around the waist. "Come on home, Granny. Granddaddy's got the tree ready for the trimmings."

She looked around like she'd never seen me. A wild sort of gaze filled her eyes, and she shrugged my arms away.

"The girl's right, Mrs. Sanders. It's getting late and I got business to tend to. You run along now, and I promise to come by soon, and we'll have us a good long talk."

Granny stepped closer and leaned toward the sheriff. "I ain't gonna be put off. I got rights, you hear, and sinners pay. Pay by burning in hell."

The sheriff stood straight and shifted the gun to his other arm. "I hear you. Now run along. Don't want-a upset the girl, do you?'

Granny looked toward me. For a minute, I thought she didn't know who I was, but then her eyes cleared and she said, "Ollie, young'un, you ought not to be out this late." She turned and stomped off down the street.

I stood there glaring at the sheriff.

He studied me for a-bit before he spoke. "You'd better get on after her and see that she gets home alright."

He reached in his pocket and took out a stick of Teaberry Gum. My mouth watered. Wasn't nothing more in this world I loved better than Teaberry Chewing Gum and seemed like the sheriff had a good supply.

"Take this and have a Merry Christmas."

I snatched the gum and turned to leave.

"Ollie, you know something about the shooting, don't you?"

Could he know 'bout the map or was he fishing? Trying to make me feel guilty cause he hadn't found out who shot Uncle Charlie. I wheeled to face him. "Why'd you ask such a thing?"

He marched right over and took me by the arm real hard like. "I've knowed young'uns like you, always sneaking around getting their noses into other people's business."

He pulled me real hard against him. I felt something hard like a gun in his pocket.

The wheels in my brain went to turning. Wasn't no use in letting him know 'bout the map. That was my business, at least for now. Mr. Yates never guessed there was more than cards in the box. Granny was too busy rocking to be suspicious of anything. When Granddaddy was home, he was warming his innards. Come to think of it, there wasn't no body worrying much 'bout me these days. Why a haint could carry me off, and I'd never be missed. Didn't know why Uncle Charlie had to go and get hisself shot. He always had time for me. I kicked the sheriff right where it hurt the most then jumped on old Bess and took off for home. That sheriff man gave me the willies.

* * *

After the tree was trimmed, Granny went back to her rocking chair like she'd never left. I caught Granddaddy by the hand and drug him back toward Granny's rocker. "I gotta ask you'uns 'bout where I come from. You see we're having to do this family tree project for school and I don't think Miss Allen will take it too kindly when I tell her that I was found under a cabbage leaf."

Granny sucked in her bottom lip a little further and rocked harder. Granddaddy pushed his hands deeper into his overall pockets and gave me his famous scowl. I should-a knowed right then and there I'd not get no truth from them. "You don't want me to fail the sixth grade cause of some old tree, do you?"

Granddaddy pulled up a cane-bottomed chair and sat down. "Seems to me like we've dodged this subject long enough. You wanna tell her, Eula, or do I have to do it?"

Granny never said a word. She rocked so hard the chair moved toward the front door. If her rocker could-a flew, it might have took off. Good thing the door was closed or she might have just rocked right on out into the night. Then I guess we'd see a flying rocker on Christmas Eve instead of Santa's sleigh.

Granddaddy pulled me up on his knee. "The truth is, Ollie. The buzzards might as well have laid you on a rock and the sun hatched you. We don't know where you come from."

I felt my lower lip trembling and tears filled my eyes. "But Granddaddy, everybody comes from somewhere. I wanna be yourn and Granny's little girl. I wanna have my uncle Charlie back. I don't wanna do no old family tree project for school."

Granddaddy pulled me close. I felt the cold metal of his galluses against my cheek. The coolness felt good against my warm skin. But if the truth be knowed, there was a great big hollow spot down in my chest that nothing could fill, not even being in Granddaddy's arms.

"I'll tell you what to do. You draw a great big front porch and put a suitcase on it for your tree. Ain't nobody can fail a child for telling the truth."

"I don't know what to believe. First I'm told that you find babies under cabbage leaves; and then I'm laid on a rock by a buzzard and hatched by the sun. Now, I'm supposed to believe I come in a suitcase." I glanced up at Granddaddy. His blue eyes had lost that teasing look so I knowed he was telling me some of the truth.

He leaned back in his chair and rubbed his chin. "Let's see. It was just past six in the morning, November the thirteenth, nineteen-thirty. I was on my way out to the barn to milk. When I stepped out on the back porch, there was this big black suitcase setting right there at the top of the steps. I thought maybe Charlie or Ray was off to another logging job so I just took my foot and pushed it over out-a the way. When I done that, I seen the sides wiggling, and I hear this noise like a baby crying. Of course, I run back in the house to get your granny. She opens it and there you was all tucked up in a nice pink blanket with a note pinned to it."

By now my tears had dried, and I'd set up on his knee. If he was lying, he was getting purty good at it cause there wasn't a hint of teasing in his eyes. And you could tell Granny wasn't too happy 'bout what he was a-saying for her pasted-on-looking eyebrows were pulled way up on her forehead and she was a glaring at us real mad-like. I ignored her. This was the closest to the truth I'd been, and I needed to know all I could. "Can I see what I come in?"

"You can see the blanket but the sheriff took the suitcase and the note. He wanted to take you too, but Granny had her arms locked around you and there wasn't nobody gonna snatch you away."

I looked over at Granny. The rocking slowed and her eyebrows settled back into place. Her arms were folded across her chest and a soft humming come from her lips. "What did the note say, Granddaddy?"

"It said, 'Miss Eula, I can't take care of my little girl. Since yours died I know you'll take real good care of mine.' Guess that's the reason your granny wouldn't let the sheriff take you. You've been rocked many a night in that there rocking chair. Why when you had the measles, she sat right there and rocked you for two whole weeks. She wouldn't let another soul touch you. When she's feeling better, She'll show you the blanket."

"I don't need to see some old blanket or suitcase. I'm glad my mama seen fit to give me to you'uns. I'll bet there ain't no young'un got a better granddaddy or granny. Think I'll draw a tree with me, you, and Granny under it, and I'll hang a suitcase from a limb."

"And as good as you can draw, you'll get a prize for the most original one. I know you have the craziest family. Now you'd better get to bed."

I slipped to the floor and ran over and gave Granny a big hug. She just kept on rocking and humming. Didn't matter none cause I knowed she loved me anyhow. I turned back to Granddaddy. "I got the bestest family on Haint Branch and my mama knowed that, too, or she wouldn't have left me here."

In my room, I crawled into bed and tucked the quilt under my chin. I still didn't know who my parents were, but whoever my mama was, she must-a knowed I'd be took good care of by the Sanders.

* * *

Grady Sanders stood and stretched then walked over to Eula's rocker. He looked down at her with the same scowl he'd given Ollie earlier. "Well, woman, I hope you're satisfied. It's beginning to look like your scheming has got us a whole passel of trouble. Trouble I can take, but I don't aim to standby and see that young'un get hurt. Hear me, good. I'll do whatever it takes to keep that from happening. I'm gonna try and get some sleep, and I'd suggest that you do the same. Need our strength if the roof caves in." He left Eula alone with her rocking and memories. Memories that would only hurt if told.

6

Birdie Sanders stood calmly on the front porch and watched the storm approach. Rain was coming. She could feel it in her bones. What's more, she could see it as it came over yonder mountain, crossing the valley and pushing its way up toward the cabin. It was the wrong time of year for rain. It should be snow. Snow would cover up all the filth. One of Ray's daddy's favorite sayings was, 'As pure as the driven snow'. One thing for sure, there wasn't much purity on this mountain. The first slow "tink, tink, tink" of the raindrops on the tin roof made her think. Dread lay heavy as a whole week's worth of meals in her stomach. She whispered to the rain, "Wonder when the real storm's coming?"

The baby kicked, and she realized she wouldn't be the only one affected by Charlie's death. She hated the fact that Ray's work at the lumber camp kept him away from home. She'd spent as much time as she could over at her mama's, but sometimes a-body got to needing their own space.

The day she'd found Charlie dead as a door nail on her bed had been one of them kind of days. Her Mama had got up fussing at her pa — not that she blamed her — she had ever reason in the Good Book to preach him a sermon every day. He was just about the laziest man she knew of.

He'd let you breathe for him if it were possible. For all them tombstones that read, "May you rest in peace," she couldn't decide which of her parents would deserve this epitaph more — her pa for finally being delivered from his laziness, or her mama for finally being free of him.

In a gush of wind, a whole bunch of leaves swirled by. She watched them being carried away and wished she could know that kind of freedom, but she knew escape was not something she could hope for. Her hand slipped across the bulge in her belly. Another baby meant less freedom. Even her trips over to her mama's wouldn't be as easy. Ray was happy about the baby. He wanted as many as the Good Lord gave them, but he wanted them to be his. That was a problem because she didn't rightly think this one was.

She hated herself for what she'd done, but Ray was guilty too for leaving her out here as long as a month at a time without another person to talk too. She had the boys, but there's only so much to talk to young'uns about.

She sat down in the porch swing, leaned back, and closed her eyes. The dampness chilled her to the bone. She drew her thin sweater tighter around her shoulders. Her eyelids drooped, her thoughts drifting back to the first time Charlie had come calling to their cabin.

She'd just pinned the last towel on the clothes line and reached for the empty basket. As she whirled around — she found herself in his arms. When she finally found her voice, She'd said, "I think you'd better let me go."

"Why, Sweetheart, you know this is where you've wanted to be for a long time."

She couldn't deny what Charlie said. What woman in her right mind wouldn't want to be held by arms that rippled with such strong muscles? His head of red-brown curls would make any woman want to run her fingers through it. For every lady he met that twinkle in his hazel eyes said, "You were made just for me." Like her mama always said, "That bedroom look will keep a young'un in your belly and your feet bare." Guess that's why her ma had married her pa and had ten of them. She'd glanced around. The boys were asleep and Ray wouldn't be home for at least two more weeks.

Her insides were quivering like a butterfly that was fixing to bust out of its cocoon and there weren't a darn thing she could do but stand and twirl that clothes basket around in her hands. She didn't even have the willpower to push him away. Fact is, she wanted to pull him closer, but that for sure would make her a wanton woman. Women were supposed to act like kissing and all that stuff didn't matter to them. If the truth be known, most women liked it as much as men, but they weren't allowed to say so.

She couldn't find the words to say no but she did try to push his away. He pulled her real tight up against him and kissed her right smack-dab on the lips. The only other man to do that had been Ray. She'd done the duties of a wife, and it'd got her two young'uns and living on a mountain half the time by herself. Why shouldn't she at least have a little of what she wanted. That kiss had plumb left her weak in the knees and wanting more.

She remembered the basket hitting the ground and thinking she needed to get her feet to running, but that wanting got stronger every minute and nothing else mattered much. Charlie picked her up and headed toward the barn loft. She knew what was coming, but she only snuggled closer.

Hay had never smelt sweeter or felt softer. Her and Ray had tumbled in it a few times, but she'd hated the way all them little sprigs stuck to her. Now, even that didn't matter. That throbbing cocoon was about to bust and set the butterfly free, and who was she to deny nature its course.

Now, she wondered if she'd a known the coming events if she'd not killed that butterfly right there in its cocoon, but it was too late. She'd have to live with her sin forever. It wasn't right to punish Ray and the boys for her foolishness.

The day she'd found Charlie dead on her bed, she'd planned on sending him packing. She'd crossed the porch and for some reason looked in the window before opening the door. There laying right on her and Ray's bed was Charlie. Why the nerve of him. Beds were for decent folk. She'd shamed her marriage bed once but had sworn it wouldn't happen again. Haylofts were the place for her and Charlie. Besides how'd he get in there? She was sure she'd locked the door. It'd be just like him to pick the lock. She'd listened for the boys and decided they were far enough away so she could have her confrontation with him. She turned the doorknob and sure enough it opened like it'd never seen a lock. "You can get up from there and out of my house and Ray's bed. Out!"

By now she was all the way in the room. Charlie didn't move. Lord, that smell, it'd stifle a dead man. Something must have crawled in here and died. A large green fly buzzed overhead. She looked up half-expecting to see something dead hanging from the open rafters. Ray had promised her he'd get around to closing off the part of the ceiling over their bed but that's all she'd got. The fly circled and headed toward the bed. That's about the time she realized where the awful scent was coming from. She'd took a step closer and that's when she saw it. A hole as big as her fist right where Charlie's heart had been. A hole full of flies laying their eggs. Her stomach began to crawl up into her throat. Her legs went weak. Not the same kind of weak they'd been when Charlie kissed her, but the kind of weak that tells you your worst nightmare has come true. From somewhere she'd found the strength to make it to the door. The fresh air cleared her head. She had to get away and fast.

The horrible memory burned so vivid in Birdie mind that she didn't hear the thud of boots or the squeaking of boards as steps moved closer. But she did feel the racing of her heart and the urgency to run. To run, not only from the memory of Charlie, but from the horror she'd done. But where would she go? Her mother's sister had already taken her in one time. Besides, Canton wasn't far enough away, no place was.

The horrid memory seemed just like yesterday, but now she was safe on her porch — Charlie, dead and buried and a child on the way. She closed her eyes again and listened to the rain falling softly around her, then she felt the extra weight as it settled in the swing beside her. Instead of moving, she squeezed her eyes tighter and waited. A familiar hand gently brushed a strand of hair from her forehead. The smell of sweat and sawdust told her Ray was home. He was her loving husband. She'd make the best of what she had. From now on, her dreams would be of the man she had married; not the one she'd made love to at least once a week for the last year; not the one that was buried in the Sanders cemetery.

* * *

The rain continued long into the night. Slowly it had turned from the gentle tapping on the tin roof to a steady roar. A noise that even blocked out thoughts and that's what Ray Sanders needed; not to think; not to remember how he'd been handcuffed and led off his own mountain a few months ago. Why in the world would anyone believe he'd killed his own brother? He rose on one elbow. The glow from the oil lamp cast a soft shadow around his wife's head, giving the effect of a sleeping angel. Poor, Birdie. Why'd she have to be the one to find him? He rested his hand on the bulge beneath the covers. He sure hoped the baby hadn't been marked. Wasn't good for a woman to see something bad while she was with child or at least that's what all the old granny women said. Did his mama know Birdie was the one to find Charlie? As far as he knew, she hadn't stopped rocking long enough to ask any details. Maybe that was a good thing. And Ollie, poor child, her Uncle Charlie had been almost like her father. Now all she had was her granddaddy.

Birdie stirred and opened her eyes. "Ray, it's late. Can't you sleep?"

"Guess the rain's keeping me awake."

Birdie slipped an arm around his neck and pulled him down beside her. "The rain helps me sleep; helps me forget; cleans the world for a little while."

Ray pulled her close. "You have been through so much. I'm sorry. I should have been here. Do you want to talk about it?"

"No, I want to forget, but I'm afraid that won't happen until we know who killed Charlie."

"Birdie, we may never know who killed him. Charlie was mixed up with a bunch of moonshiners. From what I heard they was outsiders from over near Grandfathers mountain. Plus, Charlie's been after ever woman on the branch. Probably shot by a jealous husband. And it wasn't me. I trust my wife even if I didn't trust my brother."

Ray felt the tremor that shot through her body. "Honey, are you in pain?"

Just a tinge in my back, I need to turn over."

She shifted and turned her back to Ray.

"Birdie, I'm concerned about my mother, but I'm more worried about Ollie. That child has no one except my folks. Dad loves her but he's gone so much. Do you think you could spend more time with her? Have her up here to play with the boys."

"Ollie's a good child. She'll be fine. But if it'll make you feel better, I'll try and do what I can."

"That's all I ask. I know you have your hands full. Family is important, and like it or not, we're the only one she has."

"I promise I'll try to help more, even with your mother."

He kissed her neck and cuddled her closer and waited until she was sleeping peacefully then slipped from bed. He stepped onto the porch and sat in the swing. The rain slowed and the steady drip from the roof echoed in the quiet. The call of a hoot-owl came down the ridge. He wondered if it was a real owl or a signal from a bootlegger. Well, that was the sheriff's job not his. Right now he had to try and figure out how to make life easier for Birdie. If she'd try harder with his mother and Ollie, it might help keep her busy and not thinking so much. One thing for sure, it'd keep her away from her parents. That bunch over there on Yates Branch would drain the life from a billy goat.

He'd told Birdie he trusted her, and he'd meant it. He also knew Charlie had had a eye for her since they were little. But she always came to him when things got bad at home except that one time when she was fourteen and ran away. She was gone three or four months. When she came back, she said she'd been with her aunt over in Canton. They'd soon settled into their old routine of him being her defender, even from Charlie at times. Yes, he'd always loved her and always would.

At least now he wouldn't have to worry about Charlie. Not that he was glad he was dead, but he'd been trouble all his life. If his mother stopped her rocking and got back to living, life would almost be normal again.

7

March come in like a lamb and Granddaddy said it would go out like a lion. He had all kinds of saying 'bout the weather. He always checked the sky morning and night to see what color the clouds were. According to him, red at night was a sailor's delight. Red in the morning meant a sailors warning. When the dove cooed, it was going to rain, but the surest sign was when his rheumatism acted up. He'd rub his leg and swear it was gonna come the biggest storm of the season. And we usually did have a good shower or two.

As I crouched in the bushes surrounding the Sanders Cemetery and watched Granddaddy dig like he was mad at the world, I wondered if he was in a hurry cause it looked like it was gonna come a spring shower, or cause he was angry 'bout sump'n? There'd been plenty of times I'd seen him mad. He'd never lifted a hand to me, but wasn't nothing unusual for him to come home on Friday night from a hard week at the lumber camp, and swear at Granny or knock one of his boys up the side of the head with any thing he could get his hand on.

Today he had hisself a-hold of a shovel handle, and he was a making the shovel talk to that dirt. I slipped a little closer so I could hear what he was a-mumbling 'bout. He had a habit of talking while he worked. Any time I wanted to know what was going on in Granddaddy's head, I'd try and get close enough to listen. So this morning when I seen him load a box on the sled and head on up toward the family cemetery, I lit-out up the back trail and found me a good hiding place. I knew what was in the box. It'd be a headstone for Uncle Charlie. Granddaddy always says a man who leaves his mark in the world needs to have his grave marked. As I sneaked closer, I wondered what kind a-mark Uncle Charlie had left. If I didn't find out from listening, I'd have to ask Granddaddy when he finished setting the stone.

"Weren't nothing but trouble from the start." Granddaddy mumbled as he threw a shovel full of dirt in my direction, splashing the bushes in front of me with red clay. Gall-dern, why was he so all fired up? If he kept digging like that, he was gonna dig up Uncle Charlie.

"Should a-got rid of him a long time ago." He grunted, throwing another shovel-full of dirt my way.

My heart skipped a beat. Was my granddaddy capable of killing his own son? Surely not, he was good at cuffing them around, but from what I'd seen, most mountain men were like him.

"Must-a broke his mama's heart a thousand times. 'Bout all he was ever good for was pleasing a woman. Guess they're the only ones round these here parts that'll be missing him."

I scooted forward a bit and glanced over at the box still setting on the sled. Old Bess stomped her foot and switched her tail at a big horse fly that had landed on her rump. Seemed she was getting impatient same as me. Surely Granddaddy hadn't killed his own boy and then had the gumption to haul a stone up here and set it. Guess it was 'bout time I let him know he had company. Maybe he'd calm down some with me talking to him.

I eased through the undergrowth until I was directly behind him then crawled out and stood up. Brushing off dead leaves and twigs, I stepped closer. "What're you doing? How come you're digging a hole in Uncle Charles grave? You gonna dig him up and put him some'eres else?"

Grady Sanders hesitated then turned. "Ollie, I'd say it's your mission in life to sneak up on people, and I'm not digging up anyone. I'm gonna plant this headstone right here at Charlie's head. Don't want to forget which end his head is at." He lifted the box from the wagon and opened it.

I could see the inscription real well. It read: Charles Sanders, Born: August 31, 1911 — Died: Oct 14, 1942. "Why does it matter where his head is? He ain't gonna be fussy now."

"You're right, he's not, but don't want him facing the wrong way on Judgment Day. Want him to see the Lord when he returns."

As far as I knowed, Granddaddy wasn't particularly a religious man. Now, Granny was a different story. She was always dragging me to one of them tent revivals where they were always trying to save your soul from eternal hell. Why I remember one time we went to this meeting, and the preacher had this great big box of rattle snakes. He opened his Bible and read sump'n 'bout if a person had enough faith he could reach right into that box and pick up one of them there snakes and not get bit. I don't want-a say he didn't know what he was talking 'bout, but it don't take much horse sense, as granddaddy says, to know a poison snake can't bite unless it's all coiled up and able to strike. The size of that box and the number of snakes made it impossible for that to happen.

Granddaddy dropped the headstone into place, pushed the shovel into the ground, and sat down on the stone. "Ollie, I've been thinking about your granny. Sump'n is awful wrong with her cause she keeps going to that place beyond words. For sure me or you ain't gonna fix her. I'd take her to see old Doc Rogers, but he wouldn't know how to help her. Don't want-a have to take her off over yonder to Morganton to that Broughton crazy house. Most folks don't ever come home from over there. I don't have the money or time to run all over God's creation to try and get help. The way I see it, she puts a lot of store in that preacher man that comes through here holding them tent meetings. I hear he's gonna be coming back soon. I'm leaving it up to you to get her there."

I sat down by Granddaddy and picked a dandelion. Rubbing the yellow flower against my fingernails, I watched the color as it stained. I sure would be glad when I was old enough to go into Jamison's five-and-ten store and buy some of that nail polish. I could hear that preacher man right now condemning me to hell for using tools of the devil. But I knew Granddaddy was right. If there was anyone in these here hills that could help Granny, it'd be the preacher man. So I'd just put away my feelings and do what I must to help her get better.

I threw down the crushed flower and stood up. "When'll he be here?"

"Next week, far as I know."

"I took a few steps down the hill then turned back toward Granddaddy. "This burying stuff — is that really why you marked Uncle Charlie's grave?"

"Now I ain't never lied to you, have I?"

"No, I guess not, leastwise 'bout sump'n really important. Is everybody buried the same way?"

"Far as I know, It's an old custom based on the part in the Bible that says the dead in Christ will rise up to meet Him when he comes from the east."

"So all people are buried facing the east?"

"In all the cemeteries I've ever seen."

"Granddaddy, how do you feel 'bout this religious stuff?"

Grady studied the ground for a while then stood and took the shovel in hand. "Child, I guess I'm to the age that I should be worrying about where I'm gonna spend eternity. I ain't gonna say anything bad about folks that practice religion. Truth is, the way I see it, it's what stands between you and your maker that's important. About the only thing standing between me and mine is the door from here to there. Don't know what's on the other side of it, but when it opens, I'll be happy to see my master face to face." He filled the shovel with clay and threw it around the stone then began packing it down with his boot.

I watched him work for a few minutes. I knew he'd said all he had to say on the subject, but I needed to ask him who he thought killed Uncle Charlie, then I'd make a decision whether to tell him 'bout the map. I ambled back up the hill and waited until he'd finished packing the dirt.

Granddaddy wiped his brow with his shirt sleeve before looking at me. When he turned he said, "I thought you was gonna get on home and work on getting your granny to go to the tent meeting."

"I'm gonna go in a minute, but first I got-a ask you sump'n."

"Ollie, I've had this feeling ever since the funeral that you've wanted to talk. Do you know something about the killing you ain't telling?"

Now I'd went and done it. Got myself in a fix. Wasn't no telling what Granddaddy would do if I told him 'bout the drawing. I didn't want him going off half-cocked and get hisself killed too. Wouldn't be nobody to take care of Granny but me.

A low rumble echoed across the ridge and a streak of lightening caused Bess to twitch her ears. Storms was one thing that mare didn't like. She'd be heading for the barn any minute.

Granddaddy threw his shovel on the sled. "Come on, let's go before we get soaked. You can ask on the way."

The thunder grew closer. Bess didn't hesitate when Granddaddy picked up the reins. I climbed onto the sled. I'd have to be careful and not say anything I'd regret later. "Granddaddy, I've been wondering who you think shot Uncle Charlie? I heared you say some things back there at his grave that makes me wonder if you had reason to want him dead."

"Guess I should a-knowed little pitchers have big ears. What did you hear?"

"You said sump'n 'bout him being no good and you should-a got rid of him a long time ago."

"Ollie, when you grow up and have your own young'uns you'll understand what I meant. Lot's of parents have regrets sometimes and say things they don't mean. Your Uncle Charlie has caused lots of heartache for our family. I should-a sent him toting first time he got into real trouble."

"What kind-a real trouble did he get into?"

"Not the kind I can tell little girls about. Is there anything else on your mind?"

"Yes, you got any ideas on who shot him?"

"Got lots of suspicions, but that's all they are. Don't guess we'll ever know the truth of the matter."

The rain clouds moved closer. Bess began to trot. A rain dove called somewhere back up the mountain. I moved closer to Granddaddy. There was lots I'd like to say 'bout the matter, but it wasn't the right time. He might decide I was too much trouble and want-a send me packing too.

8

Eula Hodges had married Grady Sanders when she was seventeen and followed him all over the southeast on logging jobs. It had never occurred to her not to be content with her life. She was doing what women were supposed to do — taking care of her man.

Her father had come to these mountains as a young doctor, hoping to save the poor mountain people mostly from themselves. He'd left his wife and young daughter alone for weeks at a time while he traveled, delivering babies and passing out pills for the croup or some other illness. He'd come home worn out and the only thing to show for his hard work was a few chickens, a side of pork, or some other kind of produce. His wife soon tired of her lot in life and went back to Savannah, leaving him to raise their daughter. From then on, Eula accompanied her father, soon learning how to assist when needed. She'd fallen in love with tall, curly, redheaded Grady Sanders while helping care for his ailing mother. By the time they were married, traveling and living in logging camps was not a strange way of life to her.

At twenty-one she was the mother of two boys, Ray and Charlie. She loved watching Grady with his sons, and believed she was blessed, but despite her knowing how lucky she was, in her heart something was missing, and that something was a daughter. Time passed and they bought a farm on Haint Branch in Franklin, North Carolina. She'd stayed there so the boys could go to school. Grady still worked timber and farmed on weekends. Then she was pregnant again. Little Alice was born perfect, but three months later they'd buried her on a hill in the west part of the Sanders farm. From that day on, it became the Sanders family cemetery. Within the same year another little girl was born dead and buried a-long side her sister. When Eula was forty, the miracle she'd prayed for happened: pregnant again, and then the birth of another baby girl. Never a day passed that she didn't thank her Lord for her beautiful little Sarah. This was truly the thing they'd needed to be a complete family.

The completeness lasted until the fever hit the county. Little eight-year-old Sarah was the last one on the branch to come down with it and the second one to die from it. Eula rocked her all day after she'd taken her last breath. Finally, Grady's sister convinced her that the child was gone. Grady had the neighbor men dig a grave next to the other babies that were buried in the Sanders cemetery.

From the time Ollie had appeared on her porch, Eula had vowed to protect her from harm no matter what she had to do. And today as she watched her running from the barn to the house, she knew all she'd done had been from pure love of this child.

"Granny! Granny! Granddaddy says the preacher man is coming next week. You know how you love to go to his meetings. Last time when he was here he cured Mrs. Roper's bad back, Aunt Birdie's mother got religion, and another woman got the Holy Spirit. I bet he can make you want-a stop rocking."

Eula sat down in her chair and began rocking again. There wasn't no use trying to explain to Ollie why nobody would be able to fix her. Life had taken its toll and rocking was the only thing that eased the pain because it brought back all the memories of tending her babies and at the same time helped pack down the stuff she didn't want to remember.

"Granny, please say you'll go. Me and Granddaddy are counting on him helping you."

The room echoed with the child's plea. Eula sucked in her breath and bit down on her lower lip. Lord how she hated hurting Ollie, but how could she face a man of God after all that had happened? The chair creaked louder, but not strong enough to block out Ollie's voice.

"If you don't come, I'll go by myself. I want-a see what he does with the snakes this year. Remember, how he let them crawl all over his arms last time besides there's always good music. We ain't heared none of that since Uncle Charlie died. Ain't no body can play a fiddle like he did."

A shudder edged its way down Eula's spine. Fiddle music was her favorite. Her daddy loved playing it. She guessed Charlie got his talent from him. That's about the only good trait he'd gotten from her family. Was there something she might have done to make him a better man? She'd done her share of praying. Why hadn't it saved him from such a horrible fate? Now there was nothing left except . . . a little girl's pleas, and she'd have to try and not disappoint her.

The chair slowed, and she raised her face to meet Ollie's. She'd never been able to deny Charlie anything. She guessed it was because he was her first born and looked so much like his father. Maybe that was where she went wrong. Should she try and do different now? Ollie was her last chance. Well, Charlie never begged to go to the camp meetings. It was a battle to get him to church even when he was little. Maybe if Grady had gone, it would have been different.

"We'll go if you like, but ain't nothing nobody can do to fix what's ailing me."

"Granny, don't say that. You've always told me that God can fix every thing."

"Might be so, child, but I don't have to go no where for Him to do it. Let me know when the preacher gets here, and we'll go for one night but that's all I'm promising."

"One time'll be all it takes. You'll see. I got-a go feed Bess for Granddaddy. He'll be happy you're gonna go."

As the back door slammed, the rocking resumed. Wasn't no use trying to tell Ollie that her and Grady had stopped talking about God and church a long time ago. She guessed if Grady Sanders had ever had any faith he'd buried it along with his young'uns in the Sanders Cemetery.

* * *

Ominous black clouds roiled from the Southwest, bringing the threat of a spring shower. The dogwood, in full blossom, adorned the mountainside like a new bride. The Reverend Richard Rainey pulled off his coat and rolled up his shirtsleeves. The thick black hair on his arms was matted with sweat, but he wouldn't wash until he had the tent set up. He looked toward the clouds. It was going to rain and soon. He wiped his dark wavy hair from his face and then picked up a hammer and began to pound a tent stake. He loved this spot. Here he didn't have to worry about flooding and there was a good view of the valley below. He'd put his truck over there in the grove of pines, a good place to study and sleep. Never was much cooking. These mountain people fed well and after a few fire and brimstone sermons the offering got real good.

He'd tied the last tent rope and reached for his coat when Ollie arrived. She burst into the campsite like visiting with the preacher was something she did every day. He guessed most children were this full of life. He'd not had much experience in this department except for the mothers who took theirs out during the service and returned with a much-subdued child. He'd preached many a sermon on, 'spare the rod and spoil the child', and he was always glad to see his sermons taken seriously. He straightened, squared his shoulders, and faced his visitor.

"Preacher, my name's Olivia Sanders, and I got-a talk to you 'bout my granny."

"And your granny is who."

"She's Eula Sanders, the one who sets up on the front row, nods her head a lot, and says Amen once in a while. Granddaddy calls her a good God-fearing woman. Guess she fears for both her and Granddaddy cause I ain't never seen him inside a church."

"I'd say it's your granddaddy who we need to be worried about?"

"Oh, I ain't worried none 'bout him. Me and him got our own kind-a religion. But you take Granny; she goes strictly by the Good Book. Says that's the only way to Heaven."

"She's right, young lady, and I think you and your granddaddy are the ones who need to get right with the Lord."

"My being here ain't got nothing to do 'bout getting right with God. It's 'bout fixing Granny. Since you were here last time her boy, Charlie, got hisself shot some how. Granddaddy and me think some body killed him. That sheriff says he shot hisself to keep from going to the war. It's driving Granny crazy. 'Bout all she does is sit and rock. Granddaddy ain't got no money to take her to a fancy doctor, and old Doc Rogers don't know how to fix her. I got her to promise to come to your meeting. You think some of your special praying or laying on of hands might fix her."

The preacher touched her shoulder. "I'll make your granny well, but you have to promise to give your heart to the Lord."

"Can't do that, Preacher. I already give it away."

"Well, when you give yourself to God, you won't want to go back to your old sinful ways. Who did you give your heart to?"

"Granddaddy, of course, who else."

"Sounds like I need to meet this man."

"You won't do it here in this tent. He ain't no church-going man, but he's the best granddaddy in the world. I'd say he's right up there with God. Me and Granny will be here tonight." She backed toward the trail. "And if I was you, I'd start praying real hard that you can fix her or them there snakes might just not scare folks into believing anymore." She turned and fled up the hillside.

Preacher Rainey stood watching her until she'd vanished over the hill. Looked to him like that one spelled trouble. He'd have to watch his step.

* * *

I pulled Granny up the aisle to the very front bench. She needed to be where she'd get the full effects of the preacher's words, and when he let go of that thing he called the Holy Spirit, I wanted it to hit her head-on. The way I seen things, it'd take a whole bunch of spirits to chase away what ever was ailing her. We'd just got ourselves settled when a big burly man come down the center aisle with a huge box. I didn't have to be told what was in it. Ever year it was carried in holding half-a-dozen of them diamond-backed rattlers. I scooted closer to Granny.

You have to know right now that snakes ain't my favorite kind-a creature.

Eva McCall

One time when I was real little me and Granny went to get the cows from the upper pasture. Granddaddy had warned me 'bout how mean a black snake was when he got mad. Don't know what got into me that day less it was one of the preacher's spirits. Anyway, there was a big'n sunning hisself on the edge of the cow-trail. Granny was on up the way a-bit so I got me a stick and starting poking him. I seen right away that he didn't take to kindly to being botheared, kind-a like Granddaddy when he's taking a nap. I give the snake a couple of great big punches. He turned on me and started hissing. "Before I knowed it, he stiffened up and was almost standing on his tail. I remembered how God had made the snake to crawl on his belly after he got Adam and Eve to eat the apple. God never said nothing 'bout the snake walking again, but I allowed the devil could do any thing he wanted, so this one must be full of tainted blood just like some more folks I knowed on the branch, especially the one that had killed my Uncle Charlie.

Maybe some of them folks would come to this here tent meeting and get cured, but right now Granny was my main worry. If we didn't get her fixed soon, she was gonna have a hole rocked in the floor. Granddaddy didn't need another job. It 'bout nigh wore him out trying to keep up the farm work since Uncle Charlie died. I tried to help but there's lots a young'un can't do, like plowing and mowing hay.

I'd got good at milking since me and my cousin, Tilly, learned when we built a play house and decided we needed milk and butter. Tilly tried first but after a few times of getting whooped in the face with the cow's tail and the cow's foot placed squarely in the pail, she gave up. I tried. I'd learned from her what not to do so I made her stand behind the cow and hold the tail. I kept the bucket too high for the cow to get her foot in. That worked find until a stream of pee poured from her and splashed me and Tilly. By then I'd squeezed out enough milk to make us a little pat of butter.

It didn't take Granddaddy long to figure out what was going on, and he declared that if I was gonna drain his cow dry playing house then milking might as well be my job. Every morning before school and right before dark, I'd pull on them teats until they was dry as a bone. It got to be fun cause Granny's cat, Smoky, perched hisself right near my stool, and I'd give him a good shot of milk. Most times I hit his mouth. Granny never scolded me, but I got a few good tongue lashings from Granddaddy.

Tongue lashings must be men's business cause the preacher man was going at it. He was yelling so loud I couldn't make out what he was a-saying. Sweat poured down his face. He took off his coat and threw it toward the man standing by the snake box. It must-a been a signal of some sort cause the man raised the lid and the snake heads begin to appear over the edge. I wiggled closer to Granny. The preacher raised his hands and lowered his voice.

"Before we demonstrate the power of the believers, I want to lay on hands and pray for the healing of the sick. There is one in particular here tonight who needs to be released from the chains of demons. I invite you to come kneel at this altar while I pray and God cleans the evil spirits from your soul."

Granny didn't move, and I whispered, "Don't you think you should do what the preacher says."

"I would but there ain't no evil spirits in my soul or least not now. Can't say there ain't been or will be, but I'm fine tonight."

Eva McCall

I couldn't argue none with her. She seemed like the granny that had raised me. Looked to me like this was gonna be a hard spirit to catch. The altar filled, and I decided most of the folks on the branch must be possessed with some sort of spirit. The preacher looked right at me and Granny. I shrugged my shoulders and glanced over at the snake box. The letters on the side said Kast General Store. And right under them in big black letters was printed Rainey Snakes. I'd seen that handwriting somewhere before. And that name? I'd seen it wrote on something not too long ago. Could it a-been on my map? I'd check the first thing when I got home.

The man had put the lid back on, but I heared the thrashing and hissing inside. Seemed to me like I was gonna have to show people why them snakes didn't bite. About that time the spirit must-a hit Mrs. Rawling right square in the face cause she jumped up from the altar and started shouting. She ran up and down the aisle. Others joined in and 'fore long the whole tent was in a-uproar. Me and Granny moved out-a the tent and into the shadows. The snakes would have to wait till another time cause we needed to get away from here before we were both overcome with some kind-a spirit. Lord knowed one fer house-hold was enough. Besides, I needed to look at the map while the name and the way it was wrote was still fresh in my mind.

* * *

The crowd thinned and Preacher Rainey searched for Olivia and her granny, but they were gone. He'd planned on convincing Mrs. Sanders that she was living with some sort of demon and if she changed her ways, maybe he could have made a convert out of Ollie. Only took a few youngsters to take a stand for the Lord, then they'd all follow.

He hadn't liked the tone of Olllie's voice when she'd come seeking his help. It was for sure that she was her grandfather's girl. As for Mrs. Sanders, she was a good God-fearing woman. Now, from the sound of the old man, he might be part of some kind of plan to make a fool out of his work.

The man in charge of the snakes stepped forward. "You want to use the snakes tonight, Preacher?"

"No, we'll save them for tomorrow night."

"I seen that Sanders young'un watching them. If I was you, I'd keep a close eye on her."

"Don't worry, I'll take care of her." The preacher gathered his coat and Bible and stood straight as a lightening rod as he marched toward his truck.

* * *

Grady paced the floor waiting for Ollie and Granny. He'd heard people say that making a person believe that they were healed was all it took. If anybody could make Granny believe, it would be the traveling preacher man. He had his own theory about him, but it didn't matter who healed his wife as long as she returned to her old self. He heard them crossing the porch and sat down at the table like he wasn't a bit concerned about what took place.

Granny come in and went straight to her chair and started rocking. Ollie followed, looking like she'd got more out of the meeting than Granny had.

"Looks like the preacher man didn't help none."

"I don't understand, Granddaddy. When it was time to go, I drug her out-a that chair and all the way to the tent, even to her seat. Soon as the preacher started his sermon, she was as normal as you or me. When he asked people to come forward for healing, I asked her if she wanted to go. She said there weren't no evil spirits in her. Said there might have been or could be again, but right then, she was alright."

Grady scratched his head. Something was bad wrong and he didn't know what to do. He might just burn that damn rocker then see what happened.

"Granddaddy, you think the spirit that's making her this way is here in the house?"

"No, child, I don't. What ever is ailing your granny is bottled up inside her. We have to find out how to uncork the bottle and get her to face her own demons. Far as I know, she's never done any harm to anyone. Could be the shock of all that's happened over her life is eating her alive."

"You want me to take her back to the tent meeting tomorrow night?"

"No, let's invite the preacher man here for supper and not tell her."

"But who's gonna cook? Me and you is barely making it on our cooking. Don't want-a go killing off no preacher man."

"Don't worry, I'll get your aunt Birdie to cook."

"She's gonna have a baby any day now. You think that's such a good plan."

"Maybe not. Mrs. Roper ain't having a baby, is she?"

"Not that I know of. She's a old woman."

"I'll have her cook and bring it over. How's Wednesday noon?"

"You want me to do the inviting?"

"Guess so. Don't want to have to deal with him anymore than

I have to."

"You know he's gonna try and save your soul from hell while he's here, don't you?"

Grady stood and patted Ollie on the head. "The way I see it, I'm already there, living like this." He looked over at his wife. She had rocked from near the front door to halfway across the room toward the kitchen. Her eyebrows were drooped and her lips set in that familiar hard, straight line. There had to be some way to reach her, and he planned on finding it even if it meant keeping company with that preacher man.

* * *

As soon as I heared Granddaddy and Granny snoring, I pulled the map from under my mattress. Maybe I'd seen the preacher's name on one of them posters they'd put up letting folks know 'bout the tent meeting, but I wanted to make sure it wasn't one of the names on my map. If it was, could it be that he had some connection with what ever was happening here on Black mountain?

I let my finger trace the line down the page. Some of the names sounded familiar and others strange, like they might be from the same place that Mrs. Crome, who lived way up on top of Fox Ridge, was from. I wondered if they were prime and proper, also. I'd already decided that when I growed up I just wanted to be me and not have to act any way.

I come to the very last name and there jumping out at me was 'ainey'. No R, but the same handwriting I'd seen on the box. Ainey was sort of scrounged onto the very bottom. Could be there hadn't been room for the R? Folding the map back into its neat little square, I slipped it back under the straw-tick mattress. Looked to me like

Eva McCall

there was enough reason to keep a eye on that preacher man. There might be more than preaching going on in his life.

9

The day the preacher come a-calling on our family would be remembered by everyone on the branch for years to come. It was not only the day that Sadie Joe Miller met the preacher, causing him to lose his salvation, but it was the day Aunt Birdie's baby come into the world.

If you ain't figured it out by now, Sadie Jo was considered the 'worldly woman' around Franklin and Haint Branch. One of the kind that most decent folk don't want-a get caught dead with. Ms Allen, my teacher, is always a-saying, "Now, class, good behavior is as important as book-learning." Too bad she didn't see it that way whenever she gave me my grade in spelling cause I acted real nice when I spelled a word wrong, which was most of the time. Even when I wasn't spelling, I tried to act nice and prim and proper like Granny had taught me. I guess mountain proper is different from city proper or some folks see it that way.

Anyway, by mid-week of the tent meeting, I'd made arrangements for Preacher Rainey to come to our house for dinner. Granddaddy had got Mrs. Roper to fix a nice meal of fried chicken, mashed taters, gravy, and fresh green beans. She'd even made my favorite, peach cobbler. She'd had to use canned peaches to make it, but that was all right since Granny wasn't cooking none. I planned on eating enough to do me for a few days. Me and Granddaddy wasn't good at cooking too much except taters and 'bout the only way we fixed them was fried. After awhile a person's gut begins to stick together from all that starch. And seeing I'm as skinny as a bean pole, I can't afford to be pinched up much more.

I'd finished setting the table when the preacher arrived. I took his hat and told him he could sit with Granny till Granddaddy come in from the barn. He went right in and pulled a chair up in front of her and begin talking, like talking to a moving chair was as normal as breathing. Granny stared right over his head and didn't say a word. Ever once in awhile, I could see them gray eyebrows of hern twitch and either pull up or down. When she wasn't in her rocking mood, the eyebrows looked as normal as mine. I wondered if the spirit that took her over had sump'n to do with the way they moved.

Finally, Grandddaddy come in from the barn and stood with me in the door watching her and the preacher. Soon the preacher stopped talking and started praying. When he seen the praying wasn't helping, he come back into the kitchen.

Granddaddy stepped forward and said, "Name's Grady Sanders and I assume you're Preacher Rainey."

"You're right, Mr. Sanders."

The preacher stretched out his hand. Granddaddy rubbed his on his overall leg then took the hand, that looked as though it had never used a ax or hoe, into his and squeezed real hard. I seen the preacher flinch just like it might hurt a little bit. It was hard for me not to giggle, but I knowed better or I'd get a good tongue lashing after he was gone. When the preacher got his hand back, he slid it into his pocket but not before I seen how red it was from the squeezing. I knowed Granddaddy had meant to show off his strength for more than one reason. Good thing the preacher man didn't know who he was dealing with.

"Folks, I've never seen anything like this. The demon that's living in that woman is strong as an iron rod. It may take some time to rid her of it."

"Well, right now I'm hungry, and we don't get many good meals around here any more so why don't we eat and then talk about what's ailing my wife. And as for time, Preacher, we don't have lots of that. As I see it, you can either fix her or you can't."

The preacher pulled out a chair and sat down. "That's where you're wrong, Mr. Sanders. God is the only one that can heal your wife. Not me or any doctor."

Granddaddy was already loading up his plate, and I kicked him under the table. When he looked my way, I bowed my head. He grunted and laid down his fork. I glanced at the preacher. "Would you like for me to say grace?" He looked a little surprised but nodded, and I said the shortest blessing I knowed. The way I seen it there weren't no use wasting time telling the Lord what he already knowed. By the time I got the Amen out, Granddaddy was shoveling in his food. The preacher tried to talk but Granddaddy said, "Don't you know your Bible, Preacher. It says there's a time and season for everything under the sun. The way I see it, right now is the time for eating. There'll be time enough for talking later."

I didn't know that Granddaddy knowed anything from the Bible. I didn't speak up to ask where it was in the Good Book. No use showing off how dumb I was 'bout church stuff before a man of God. Now He wouldn't care, but people get hung up on having to act all nicety-nice for the preacher. Me and Granddaddy call that being two-faced. Anyway we sat right there and eat the whole meal without another word. The whole time I'm a-wondering how the preacher was gonna fix Granny and how Granddaddy was gonna keep from getting saved. Well, I should a-knowed the Lord would take care of things like he always does. Most people is so busy trying to fix stuff theirselves they don't watch how God takes care of it.

We'd just finished that good peach cobbler that Mrs. Roper had baked, and the preacher started to open his Bible to lay out the plan of salvation to Granddaddy, when Sadie Jo burst through the door.

It seemed to me like Sadie Jo didn't waste too much time getting over Uncle Charlie's death. I hadn't seen her shed no tears since that day at his grave. Course Granny didn't allow me to spend much time with her since she considered her 'a woman of the world'. When I asked her what that meant, I got the same answer I got when I asked her 'bout my mother. Looked to me like when I growed up, I was gonna find out more than a person could handle. Anyway, I guess Sadie Jo, being a woman of the world and all that stuff was why she was looking at Preacher Rainey with that funny look in her eyes.

Now, seeing how it was her, I couldn't help but wonder if the Lord and the Devil hadn't got their roles mixed up cause the preacher had plain forgot his Bible. He just sat there with it halfway open and his mouth gaping.

"Mr. Sanders, Ray sent me down here to have you go for the doctor. Birdie's in labor. He said to tell his mother to come on up there."

Granddaddy stood and reached for his old straw hat. "Sorry, Preacher, saving my soul will have to wait cause babies don't. Ollie, see if you can get Granny to rocking up the mountain. She'll want to be there. Never misses a birth or a funeral."

I was already pulling her out of her chair. I knowed once I got her out of the house and started up the mountain, she'd more than likely snap out of her rocking mode.

"Come on, Granny. We got-a hurry. Don't want no baby coming into this here world without its granny to welcome it. As I pushed her through the door, I seen Sadie Jo giving the preacher that evil-eye look of hern. I knowed right then and there that there was gonna be some sort of show-down between the Lord and the Devil right there in this kitchen and if I was right 'bout Sadie Jo, the Lord didn't stand a chance.

***

Cleaning up the mess of dirty dishes was the last thing on Sadie's mind as she gazed across the table at Preacher Rainey, but having a little of what waited on the other side might not be so bad. She sidled around the table and reached out a hand with nails painted the color of Raspberries. "I don't think I've had the pleasure. I'm Sadie Jo Miller and you might be . . ."

The preacher let the cover of his Bible drop and stood. His lips moved but no words escaped. Finally, he managed. "I might be . . . still hungry." He reached for the almost empty pie dish.

"Your name, you do have one, don't you?"

"I'm the Reverend Rainey." He took the red-stained-nail hand in his. "I'm holding a tent revival down by the creek. I don't think I've had the pleasure of seeing you there."

"No, and I don't guess you will. Not much of a church going person. I'd rather hold my own little gatherings. You should come some time, Reverend. You might learn a few new tricks that would help you in your preaching."

He dropped her hand. "The Lord is the only help I need in my pulpit."

Sadie Jo touched his cheek and let her hand slide down to cup his chin. "Now, Preach. You should know the Bible tells us that God made the woman as a help mate for man. Why don't you let me help you unwind a little before you go?" She glanced around. "I suspect the Sanders will be gone all afternoon, maybe all night, too. Babies can take a while." She took his hand and pulled him toward the bedroom door. "And so can I."

Charlie was dead, and she was lonely. Men were scarce here on the Branch. Even in town there weren't many. A woman had to do what she had to, to survive. A preacher might not be so bad. Even if she had to sign up for his heaven trip, he might provide her with a way to bigger places here on earth. And she was sure she could take him to places he'd never been.

* * *

Birdie withered in pain and cursed the day she'd ever slept with a man. The shadows moved in and danced about; pulling everything she didn't want to remember into the present. She blinked and pushed at them, but they pulled her into the dark belly of her past.

She'd only been in the fifth grade when Charlie Sanders dipped her pigtail in the inkwell on his desk, but that stain was only a symbol of the one he'd left on her heart years later.

Another searing pain ripped through from her back into her belly. She squeezed her eyes tight. Someone wiped her face with a cold cloth. A woman's voice said, "Try and relax, help's on the way." Relax! How could she do that when she was being torn apart. Why had she let it happen? Why had she let Charlie Sanders ruin her life? She should have ended it after that first time... Lord, why was she hurting so bad. The other babies hadn't been this bad. Was she being punished? Charlie had promised her the world on a platter. Well, what she'd gotten was lots of heartache and plenty of it.

Voices were drowning out her thoughts and that was just as well. If Charlie wasn't already dead, she'd kill him right now. Ray couldn't know this wasn't his baby. Her secret was safe unless . . . no; there was no way anyone could know. But there was the day she and Charlie had made love in the bed. She'd had a creepy feeling that they were being watched. Guilty conscience. Yes, that was it. She was being punished for her sin. The pain eased, but she didn't want to open her eyes, didn't want to see the bunch of probing eyes. She just wanted it over, and then she'd deal. Right now, she had to be careful not to call out Charlie's name. As much as she wanted to curse the ground where he slept, that would also have to wait.

"Push hard," commanded a man's voice.

Thank God, the doctor was here. He'd help her. Another pain swept over her stomach.

"Push and keep pushing until I tell you to stop."

She bore down as she felt her shoulders being lifted. Why didn't he stop the pain? Did he want her to suffer? Did they all know her secrets and think she deserved to hurt? Her face was being wiped again.

"Relax. The baby's not ready to come yet. "I'll give you something to help."

As the cloth with some funny smelling stuff was placed over her nose, the horrifying memories of the first time she'd given birth replaced the pain that racked her body. Dark shadows loomed around her, and she heard her own voice screaming for them to leave her alone. Through the murky midst of the drugs came the faint cry of a baby. Then mercifully darkness, and she slept.

* * *

Preacher Rainey pulled on his pants. He'd let the devil win again, but this time wouldn't be the one that would cause his soul to burn in everlasting hell. No, it'd be the one that had put him in the pulpit on false pretenses. The Bible clearly stated that blasphemy was a sin that would send you to hell. It was too late now. He'd already sold his soul and there was no turning back so he'd enjoy the benefits.

Sadie Jo reached up and tugged at his pant leg. "Preacher man, you want to try and save my soul again?"

"Not unless you want to come to the tent meeting later tonight, Sadie Jo. I've got to go. Besides, the Sanders' might show up any minute."

"They won't be home for a long time, but I don't want to keep you from your calling. That might be the one sin that will send me to hell, and that ain't a place I'm wanting to go. No, sir, I'll take heaven anytime, wouldn't you, Preacher Man?"

He leaned over and kissed her. "Sure will, if what I just had is a taste of what's to come."

"Depends on where this train's a-heading."

"After this week, it's heading on down toward the low country. Got business there."

"More important than business here?"

"I'd say for some folks it is."

Sadie Jo sat up and drew the sheet up under her chin.

"Say, Preacher Man, why don't you take me along? Bet that truck of yours could be mighty cozy."

"Maybe sometime, but this trip is all sold out."

She came all the way up on her knees. Sold out! You mean there's another woman?"

"I didn't say anything about women, although that's about all that comes to my meetings. Women and children, men don't show much interest in things of the Lord."

"Maybe they would if you had someone that would interest them, like a Preacher Lady."

Rainey reached for his hat. "Never seen or heard tell of a Preacher Lady in a tent meeting, but it is an interesting idea. I'll have to think on that one."

"Don't think too long or this one might just find her another pulpit."

At the door, he hesitated then looked back at Sadie Jo, who still sat with the sheet clutched under her chin. A woman preacher, not such a bad idea, but then he'd have to educate her on the main purpose of his mission.

* * *

Aunt Birdie's baby girl was born dead. Now, I don't mean dead like Uncle Charlie, but dead like no light shinning in her eyes. Her poor little body was breathing, but the minute I seen her I knowed her spirit was not there. Of course, I didn't say nothing since everyone was yoo-hooing and awning over how pretty she was. And that she was, little blond ringlets covered her perfectly round head. Her eyes were as blue as a piece of the sky. Maybe the light would come soon then I'd know she'd come to live in her perfect little body.

Aunt Birdie looked faded out also but Uncle Ray said she was just wore out from bringing the baby into the world. Looked to me like birthing and dying was awfully close to each other. Even living hurt. Granddaddy had told that Preacher Man that there was a time for everything under the sun. Looks to me like the Bible knowed what it was talking about since He brought the new baby into the world just when Granddaddy needed to get away from that preacher. Now I ain't saying I don't want Granddaddy to be saved if he needs it. But the way I see things, he looks mighty saved to me since he knows so much 'bout the Good Book, and he's not even a church going man. He knows a lot 'bout everything but I wonder if he knows where this little baby's spirit is. Guess we'll have a talk 'bout it when things calm down.

I touched the pearly white skin on the baby's arm. It felt cold. She made me think of the china doll that Granny kept in her trunk. One time I caught Granny looking at it and asked if I could hold it. She just set her lips in her famous hard straight line and buried the doll under some cloths and closed the trunk lid. I never mentioned it again, but ever once in a while, I'd catch her looking at it. One time I asked Granddaddy 'bout it. All he said was that it belonged to her little girl. It seemed to me like Granny had had her share of hurt and was 'bout to have some more. I looked around to see if she was bothered 'bout the baby, but she was gone.

I tugged on Granddaddy's shirttail. "Where's Granny?"

"She's probably out'n the kitchen fixing some late supper."

He took my hand, and we went into the kitchen, but Granny wasn't there. Granddaddy's brow wrinkled in a frown. "Ollie, you stir up the fire in the stove and bake a fresh cake of corn bread. I'll get on home and see 'bout her."

"I'll go. Ain't no good at building fires."

"I'll start the fire. You're better at making bread than me, and you might even want-a fry up some of them taters over there."

"Granddaddy, what're we gonna do 'bout fixing Granny. Looks to me like that preacher man don't have no cure. And from the looks of things, she ain't getting no better."

Granddaddy hugged me. "It ain't your worry, child. We'll just do the best we can to take care of each other when she's in her rocking mood. Maybe we'll wake up some day, and she'll be back for good."

He stoked the fire and left me alone to think 'bout what he'd said. I knowed Granny wouldn't be back for good, and I was sure Granddaddy knowed it to, but if it helped him to believe it, I sure wasn't gonna say nothing. I'd hurry up and fix supper then get on over to the tent meeting and see what was happening.

10

As Grady stepped onto the porch, he could hear the creaking and groaning of the rocking chair. He knew his wife had retreated to her old ways. He also knew that there wasn't much use in trying to fix what didn't wanna be fixed, and that's just about what he'd decided about Eula May. He'd had Ollie take her to the tent meeting to get healed and that hadn't helped. He'd even had that Preacher Man up to the house for to eat and that didn't help. If it hadn't a-been for Birdie's baby deciding to come into the world just at the right moment, that preacher might a-had him talked into getting stuck under the water down at the swimming hole. He'd never figured out why them Christians thought all that water was gonna fix what-a man had done wrong. Now he knowed for a fact that God could fix stuff. He'd seen Him do it plenty of times. He had enough 'have too's' in his life, and right now one of them was to get Eula in bed and clean up the table. He didn't have to look to see that the dishes were still there. He knowed Sadie Jo wouldn't risk breaking off one of them nails to clean up the table. He smiled at the thought of Sadie Jo and the preacher being left alone. He wondered who'd won that round, the devil or the Lord. If he was a-betting man, he'd put his money on the devil.

He sure had hated leaving Ollie up at Ray's, but she'd have time to get home before it got too dark. That was if she come straight home. Be like her to head to that tent meeting. He didn't know if she went because she enjoyed it or if she was up to some sort of prank. Never could tell with that young'un. Sometimes she was so serious that it worried him, and again, she'd be so full of the old devil he'd swear she'd fell out-a the devil's back pocket.

The rocker stopped as he stepped into the living room. Eula sat there with her lips clamped together and her eyebrows drooping, looking like she didn't have a friend in the world. He squatted and touched her on the hand. "Well, we've got a new grandbaby. Pruty little thing, don't you think so?"

She didn't answer, but he felt a faint quiver in her hand. "Eula, this baby might be what we need to get back to real living. New life can do that for people." He took both of her hands in his. "Honey, remember when we had Charlie. I can still see that glow showing in your pretty eyes. We were so in love and so happy. Who would have thought life could get like this. Please try and be like you used to be. I know Charlie's gone, but we've still got Ollie and Ray and they need us. Ollie needs a home that's full of love and laughter, and we can still give her that. And we can be good grandparents to Ray's young'uns."

Eula's eyebrows shot up and her chin jaunted out. "You think we've had trouble then you ain't seen nothing yet. That old devil is still a-rearing his head even with Charlie in his grave." Her chair began to rock again and this time it almost bounced off the floor.

Grady got up and stood looking down at his wife. Once the rocking started there was no use talking to her. He'd clean up the dishes and try and get some rest. If the devil was on the war-path again, he'd need his strength.

* * *

I heared the racket before I got to the meeting place. Sounded like a bunch of wild cats screaming. Granddaddy's right 'bout one thing. He says there ain't nothing reverent 'bout a crowd of people yelling and screaming out'n the dark even if it is to praise the Lord. He says if you have to glorify Him at night it's more pleasing to the Lord to go 'Coon hunting. At least out there in the dark all by yourself you can see the stars, and the sound of them blue-tick hounds running is pure music to God's and man's ears. And the way he sees things is that if man is pleased, God is pleased. Guess I agree with him since he knows so much 'bout the way the world runs.

I slipped right up close to the pulpit. There sat Preacher Rainey holding one of them big diamond-backed rattlers. The congregation stood with their eyes closed and arms wrapped around each other. They swayed back and forth as they hummed a tune I'd never heared. Granny says they're singing in the spirit. When I asked her what she meant, she said you don't repeat any words you just hum what ever words the Lord puts in your mouth. Well, now I'm here to tell you, it'd be a good thing the words were hummed if they were coming out-a Granddaddy's mouth; otherwise, the ladies might get embarrassed. And I'm sure they wouldn't be words that the Lord had put in his mouth.

One time I wanted to try and use one of Granddaddy's words so I climbed on top of the corncrib where Granny couldn't get me and shouted some of them out. She just looked up at me and never said a word. That night when we sat down at the supper table, she handed me a wash cloth all suds up with homemade soap. She said, "Ain't having no foul-mouthed young'un eating at my table." I looked at Granddaddy for help, but he just lowered his head and studied his food while I cleaned my mouth out as good as I could. Later he told me he was sorry I had to be punished for his sin. I told him not to worry that I'd heared them on the playground at school. I even told him how some of the big boys had took a stick of chalk and laid it flat and wrote the four letter 'F' word in letters the size of the blackboard then told the teacher I had done it. He wanted to go right up to that schoolhouse and give that teacher a piece of his mind, but I told him that was alright that I'd took care of it. I didn't tell him how I'd cried because I was afraid the teacher would tell him or Granny, and they'd believe her, instead of me.

If the preacher caught me doing what I was a-fixing to do, he'd tote me off to Granddaddy and insist that he punish me. Granddaddy would tell him he'd tend to it and as soon as the preacher left, he'd slap me on the back and say, Ollie, young'un, I wish I'd thought of that. That's why I'm doing this so Granddaddy will be proud of me.

I found me a great, big, long stick and slid it across the ground straight for the box marked Kast General Store, with RAINEY SNAKES right under. The box was setting right behind the preacher's chair so he never seen it tip over and them big old copperheads and rattlers slither out toward the crowd. I scooted back into the bushes. Wasn't no way I was gonna miss this show.

Mrs. Roper was the first to open her eyes at the very moment the biggest of the copperheads slid toward her feet.

I saw her mouth open but the words must a-been stuck in her throat. She backed up and knocked one of the Yates young'uns to the ground. By then eyes were opening and someone 'bout the middle of the tent screamed. "The devil has done and turned them snakes loose on us." Preacher Rainey looked around at the box and saw it empty. He dropped his snake into the box and closed the lid. He then turned back to the congregation. "Have faith brothers and sisters. The Lord is testing us."

People were scattering in all direction. The singing group gathered on the stage and begin to sing, "Shall We Gather at the River." Well, the way some of them folks were running they'd never put on their brakes in time to stop at the creek so they'd get a free baptizing out of this deal. Maybe my efforts weren't gonna be a waste cause I was sure there was some that'd never make it to the swimming hole down near the big old Oak tree without a little help.

I sneaked away into the dark. Not only would Granddaddy be proud of me, but the Lord would be pleased that I'd helped Him out'n His work.

* * *

I'd crawled through the split rail fence and headed up the little ridge running off Black Mountain when I heared the voices. Could it be some of the people that had escaped the ruckus back at the tent meeting? Didn't sound too much like leftover religion talk to me. It sounded more like a riled up bunch of men. Squatting down, I worked my way closer. It was too dark to see who they was but some of the voices were familiar. I was sure I could hear Sheriff Carlson telling the men how to take the back roads out. They were loading boxes onto Preacher Rainey's truck. Sure wished I could see what was in them but there was no way to do that. Maybe Preacher Rainey was helping one of the neighbors' move, that'd explain all the boxes. Best thing to do was get on home, then come back when it was daylight and look around.

I'd started to creep backward and head on home when I heard one man say, "Let's take a break and have us a drink of some of this stuff."

Good Lord above, it was a whole load of moonshine. Had to be, weren't no way they was a-hauling spring water off this mountain, although I'd heared that in them fancy eating places down in the low country, fresh spring water was served. Granddaddy always says that after water has run over nine rocks it's pure. Seemed to me like by the time mountain water flowed all the way down to the ocean, it'd be mighty pure. Surely Preacher Rainey wouldn't be helping a bunch of bootleggers. Maybe he didn't know what he was a-hauling. I'd just lay low and not tell a soul what I'd seen or heared, and maybe I could fine out where they was a making it. Then I'd know if the map I'd found in Uncle Charlie's cards had anything to do with moonshining or his death.

* * *

As soon as Eula heard the seesaw of Grady's snoring she stopped her rocking and went to the old trunk in the far corner of the living room. Raising the lid, she dug under a pile of mothball smelling clothes and pulled out a delft doll. The tiny features resembled that of a fashionable young lady, but age had turned the once white dress to a light tan color. The long blond hair lay in perfect curls down her back and the red bow in it now drooped from age. Eula smoothed the dress and cuddled the doll the same way she'd once held her own little girl to her breast.

The soft hum of a lullaby rose from her chest and through her lips, but with it also came the sound of a mother's heart breaking for what she'd lost.

"Granny, what's wrong?"

Eula looked up at Ollie. She hadn't heard her come in, and she didn't want to have to explain how holding this doll helped ease the pain of her loss or the pain of what was yet to come. She studied the child. How she'd like to tell her about how she'd raised her little girl till she was eight years old and then the fever had claimed her. She'd like to tell her — no, wasn't no use robbing a girl of her childhood. She tucked the doll back into its resting place and closed the lid on all the memories she had buried there.

"Ain't nothing wrong that a cup of hot chocolate won't cure and I'm a-fixin' to make you a cup. It's late and something warm will help you sleep." She took Ollie by the hand and led her to the kitchen, warmed two cups of milk, and stirred in some of her Coco mix. Her mama had showed her how to make this when she was lots younger than Ollie. Thoughts of her mama caused her eyes to sting. Why had her mother left and not taken her? Had she been some sort of bad seed her mother didn't want to be saddled with? Animals abandoned their young when there was something wrong. One time their old Collie dog had pups, and she'd refused to feed the runt of the litter. She remembered trying to hand feed it, but it still died. Would Birdie tend her baby?

"Granny, is there sump'n wrong with Aunt Birdie's baby?"

Granny poured the warm milk into the cups. "Ain't nothing wrong that time won't heal. Now, drink your hot chocolate and get to bed. A growing young'un needs her rest." Eula returned to her rocking. Maybe if she rocked long and hard enough, every thing would be alright.

* * *

I didn't wait for the rocking to start. As soon as Granny left the room, I grabbed my cup of hot chocolate and headed to my room. I needed to take another look at the map. Maybe I could place the voices I'd heared with some of the names. It was too late to stop what was happening right now, but once I knowed more, I'd tell Granddaddy. He'd help me find out what was going on, and if it had anything to do with Uncle Charlie's murder.

11

Aunt Birdie and the baby didn't get out much. At first this was expected, but as the weeks wore on and they didn't show up at the church or in town, people started to talk. Said lot's of strange doings were going on up on Haint Branch lately. Some were saying that Birdie must have had sump'n to do with Uncle Charlie's death and that had marked the baby.

I went straight to Granny when I heared a bunch of the neighbor women talking 'bout the baby being marked and asked her what they meant. She wasn't in no talking mood even though she'd took a break from the rocking chair. So I went on out to the barn and found Granddaddy taking a snort from his brown jug. When I asked him how a baby got marked, he laughed and said that was just a old wives tale and took another swig. Seems ever time I ask him some sort of important question, he answered me with sump'n I don't understand anymore than what I've asked. Now I have to wonder 'bout marked and old wives tales, too. Lord will I ever get all this learning done.

Of course, I knew Aunt Birdie well enough to know that she didn't care what people thought. She didn't even care what Granny thought, when she told her to stay in bed nine days after the baby was born. When I asked Granny why she had to do that, she said things had to have time to settle back in place. I don't rightly know what things she was talking 'bout. The only thing I know 'bout settling is that when Granddaddy boils his coffee ever morning he puts a little cold water in it to settle the grounds to the bottom.

Given my little bit of knowing 'bout settling, I guess that Uncle Ray must be pouring cold branch water over Aunt Birdie's head to settle her down. It's a good thing that baby come in warm weather or Aunt Birdie might take a death of cold then who'd look out for that pitiful little baby of hern.

I guess seeing how people were a gossiping and Granny didn't talk much, mostly rocked all the time, that's why I figured it was time I checked up on Aunt Birdie and the baby. Can't say I was looking forward to it but looked to me like somebody had to see 'bout her.

When I got to the house, Uncle Ray was a hoeing corn out'n the corn patch and his boys were a pulling weeds and feeding the hogs. I went on in the house and found Aunt Birdie rocking the baby and nursing her. I set down at the kitchen table and watched her until the baby had finished and went to sleep. "What's her name?"

Aunt Birdie put her in the cradle and covered her with a blanket. "We call her Ruth Ann. Named her for Mama and my grandma."

"She looks more like the Sanders to me."

"She's too young to look like anyone yet, but it don't matter who she looks like as long as she's alright."

"Guess you're right."

Aunt Birdie folded a bunch of diapers and didn't say much more. I watched her for a few minutes then started to leave but the baby cried really hard, and I asked if I could hold her.

"Sit down and I'll let you rock her."

For all the rocking I done, it didn't help to quiet her down. Finally Aunt Birdie took her and tried to rock, but it didn't help. "I'll get on home and see 'bout Granny. If you need me to help, send for me."

Aunt Birdie didn't say nothing, but I seen tears slide down her face. I knowed there wasn't no use talking anymore 'bout Ruth Ann so I headed on home and left Aunt Birdie alone. It was plain to see that young'un wasn't normal. Marked or unmarked it didn't matter. Sump'n was mighty wrong. I seen that Aunt Birdie was as caught up in making her baby be all right, as Granny was caught up in her rocking.

* * *

Birdie looked down into the dead eyes of her baby. She'd love her little girl into being alright. Let people say what they wanted to, she'd not listen. She held her close and hummed a soft lullaby. Singing had always quieted the boys when they were little, but it didn't seem to help Ruth Ann.

Ray came in. "Corn's doing fine. Daddy says it should be knee high by the fourth of July, looks like it's going to make it." He looked down at the baby. "She cries an awful lot. Think we should have the doctor come back and take a look at her? She's not growing like the corn is."

"Seems to me like every body likes to talk without knowing what they're talking about."

Ray took a dipper of water from the water bucket that set on the cook table. "Don't you think you're being a little too much on edge when it comes to the baby?

Birdie's arms tightened around the little girl. "She's mine, and I'll be the one to say what I think she needs, and when she needs it."

"Well, I'd say you need to do something soon. Don't think we've had a good night's sleep since she got here."

Birdie rocked a little harder. "Ain't nothing we can do but wait. She'll outgrow her fussy stage soon. Mama says it's just the colic. I've been giving her a little catnip tea along."

Ray threw the rest of his water out the kitchen door. "Well, if she's not doing better by the time I go into town Saturday, I'm going to speak to Doc Rodgers."

The baby had quieted to a soft whimper. Birdie laid her back in the cradle then turned to Ray. She'd not allow him to go off talking to people about her baby even if it was the doctor. "I'll have you know right now that if I think she needs a doctor, I'll say so. Until then, you just tend to growing corn and leave the young'un raising to me."

Ray moved toward the door. "Too bad my brother didn't live to see his niece. Maybe he'd know what's ailing her."

"As I remember he never showed much interest in our other young'uns."

"No, but he always showed interest in their mother."

"He was your brother, Ray. Family is always interested in family!"

Ray took a step closer. Birdie saw the muscles in his jaw tighten and his fist close and open. She knew she'd have to tread gently and not let him see her true feelings. Wasn't no use crying over spilt milk as Granddaddy says. What had happened between her and Charlie was water under the bridge. She'd have to be the one to live with the guilt.

"I know you and him always had something going and there ain't no use denying it! I'd say there's something wrong with that baby and it's God's way of punishing you." The color drained from his face.

Birdie walked over to the cradle. "God ain't in the trouble-giving business, especially to a little baby who ain't done no harm to a living soul." She patted the baby on the back. "Now your brother is dead and so is our talking about me and him. I'm your wife and the mother to your young'uns and that's all I've got to say." She watched as the color came back to his face. He turned and stumbled out the door. She let him go. Wasn't no use saying another word. Life was the way it was, and talking wouldn't change a thing.

* * *

When I left Uncle Ray's house I seen him coming down the hill from the cornfield. I took off down the hill toward home, but as soon as he got close to the house, I sneaked back and crawled under where the dirt was dug out from under the kitchen floor where I'd left Aunt Birdie sitting. I'd begin to find out that the only way I was going to learn anything was to do lots of listening. From what I'd seen of the baby, there was sump'n wrong and my aunt wasn't gonna say so.

I didn't have to wait long until I heared them talking as plain as if I was right there in the room. Uncle Ray was worried 'bout the baby and from the sound of Aunt Birdie's voice, she was too, but she sure wasn't gonna let Uncle Ray try to fix it. His voice got real mad like and he started talking 'bout Uncle Charlie and Aunt Birdie. She stayed calm and didn't say too much. Then it hit me. Could Uncle Ray have killed Uncle Charlie because he liked his wife? Lord, this was getting crazier all the time. Granddaddy had said he'd wished he'd got rid of Uncle Charlie a long time ago. Now, I know my granddaddy couldn't kill a fly, but what did he mean? It looked like Uncle Ray had more of a reason to want him dead. There was the sheriff and the Yates man and all the moonshining business. Looked like the map I'd found might not have too much to do with his death when there was plenty of people right here on Haint Branch that wanted him dead.

12

Fred Yates fumbled with the pistol in his pocket. Wasn't no use having it out where it could be seen but it made him feel lots safer knowing it was close by. There had to be a new moonshine-still in the area. His business had slacked off too much. Yes, there'd been a tent revival going on, but even if some of his customers had got religion it wouldn't stop them from relaxing a little with a good swig from the jug.

He parted the laurel thicket and stepped into the clearing where the tent revival had been held. He considered himself a good God-fearing man but even Christians had to make a living. Moonshining was about the only way to survive here in the mountains of Western North Carolina, especially since them town people wouldn't let no factories come into town. Said they didn't want the air all populated with smoke from them paper mills, but the real reason was that the big shots wanted to stay in control and run the town. That was alright as long as they let a-feller make a living. Sheriff Carlson knowed which side of his bread was buttered so he turned a deaf ear to the moonshining business. Now of course, that deaf ear got him a vote or two ever four years.

He tightened his grip on the gun as he kicked at a great big rock. He half-expected to see a big rattler or two under it, but when nothing slithered out, his hold relaxed, and he sat down on one of the deserted benches. Too bad he hadn't made one of the meetings. His wife and young'uns had come every night and had reported to him the many faith healings and souls saved. Didn't look to him like God would send people to hell for keeping their families fed but according to Preacher Rainey that's where all bootleggers were headed. Well, let him just keep on a-thinking that, and he'd keep on a-believing, and on the judgment day they'd see who was right.

Fred had been so lost in thought that he didn't hear the footsteps behind him. He didn't realize there was another soul around until Sadie Jo Miller spoke.

"It looks to me like you're a little late with your confessing, Mr. Yates."

"I ain't in the confessing business. Besides, you have to do something wrong to confess, and I ain't done nothing except make a living for my family."

"Some folks consider the way you do that a sin."

"And are you one of them folks, Miss Miller?" Fred watched her saunter around and sit down on the other end of the bench. Here was temptation in real flesh. That was the kind of sin that would for sure send a man to hell. One thing he knowed and that was to keep his distance or he might give in to this temptation, seeing it come in such a cute little package. His grandmother used to say that behind a pretty face laid a whole graveyard of dead bones. Reckon she meant that a pretty face had destroyed many a man. He'd make small talk and get out-a here as soon as he could.

"I'd be the last one to say what's wrong or right and from what I've found out 'bout Preacher Rainey, I'd say he don't have no room to judge."

Fred leaned forward. Maybe he'd misjudged his visitor. It sounded like she knowed some stuff that might shed a new light on lots of things. Could she know why the camp meeting had come to a halt so soon? It'd been his understanding that it was suppose to last the rest of the month. "Did you know the preacher personally?" There was no mistaking the twinkle that came to Sadie's eyes. Fred had seen it many a time in his younger years, the light that came from the eyes of a girl in love.

"I'd say as personally as a girl can get."

"Then why would he up and leave so soon if he was sweet on you?"

"That's what I aim on finding out. Ain't no man gonna do me like Charlie Sanders done me. I loved that man from the day I set eyes on him, and what'd it get me?"

"Why don't you tell me?"

"It got me a broke heart and a hard row to hoe as my mama says."

"What row is that?"

"Having to live with the whispers behind my back about how he'd a-never married me cause he was so in love with his brother's wife."

"That so, and do you think he was in love with Birdie?"

Sadie's eyes narrowed and she slide down the bench a little further. "Call it love or lust, but I know what I seen with my own eyes."

"What was that?"

"Them making out in the barn loft. They didn't think nobody was around, but I'd come up to help Birdie finish a quilt, and she wasn't in the house. Her clothesbasket was laying out there under the clothesline like she'd just dropped it and run. I went out to pick it up and that's when I heard noises in the barn and went to see. It about broke my heart to see him loving another woman, but I vowed not to say a word. I'd win him back if it was the last thing I done. It was a fact I'd as soon seen him dead as having another woman. Don't take that the wrong way. I didn't kill him, but as much as I miss him, I'm glad he's gone. I'd a-never been his first love. I think with this preacher man I was the first, and I'm sure I'll be the last."

"How can you be sure?"

"A girl's got her ways."

"Does she also have ways of finding out other stuff?"

"What kind-a other stuff?"

"Stuff like I just asked."

"Ain't saying nothing, but you just keep your eyes and ears open, and it won't be long that you'll hear tell of Sadie Jo Miller becoming the wife of that Reverent Rainey."

"Hope you're not biting off more than you can chew, young lady."

"I'd say you'd better be more worried about the preacher. Looks like he's got hisself tied with a bunch of men straight from hell. They won't let nobody stop what they're doing. If I'd have to guess, it'd be that bunch that done my Charlie in."

Fred felt the cold hard metal in his pocket. Wasn't like him to want to harm a soul, but a man had to do what he had to so he could protect his way of making a living. "Maybe I could help your preacher friend." He waited for Sadie to answer.

After a few minutes, she rose and edged her way toward the road. "Guess I'd better be going. Ma will be wondering what happened to me, besides I can't talk about what's going on. Wouldn't want my preacher man to get mad at me and lose my only chance to see what's on the other side of these mountains."

Before Fred could say anything, Sadie Jo disappeared as quickly and quietly as she'd come. He pulled the gun from his pocket and rubbed his fingers over the handle. His finger itched to pull the trigger, but he'd not go off half-cocked and kill for the pure pleasure.

Eva McCall

A man needed a good reason to take the life of another, and in his book saving his livelihood was a good reason, and he figured it would be a good reason in God's book also.

* * *

I stayed real quiet in my hiding place until old man Yates and Sadie Jo had finished their little talk. I hadn't started out to eavesdrop like I had up at Uncle Ray's. I'd happened by here on my way home. Thought I'd check out the spot where the truck was being loaded last week and see if I could find out sump'n. Instead I found myself right in the middle of their little talk. Now I ain't saying I'm sorry for listening to what they had to say. Looked to me like the only way I was gonna learn sump'n was to listen real well. And by just listening, I found out there was lots of people who wanted Uncle Charlie dead. Well, maybe not Mr. Yates but from the way he handled that gun he was a-wanting somebody dead. I'd better get on home and think 'bout having me a talk with Granddaddy. Maybe he could shed some light on what was going on.

* * *

I went straight to my room and pulled the map from under the mattress then went in search of Granddaddy. I knowed he'd be better at taking care of moonshiners than he was at fixing Granny. I found him slumped over the plow out'n the garden. At first I thought there was sump'n wrong with him, but then I realized he was just knocking off all the red clay that had stuck to the plow blade. Lord, what would I do if sump'n happened to my granddaddy. He was the only one that really understood me although I'd begin to feel like maybe Aunt Birdie was taking more to me. She'd been talking 'bout going shopping with me before school started if she could get

Granny to keep the young'uns. Granny was so off and on with her rocking I wasn't putting much hope in that. Besides it takes money to buy and there wasn't much of that to be had. Granddaddy hadn't worked on his logging job much this summer, but he'd been busy with the farming so we didn't go without food. I didn't care much 'bout shoes until it got cold weather and there'd be plenty of time to get them. Most of the kids here on the branch started school barefooted.

When Granddaddy seen me coming, he sauntered over to the edge of the garden and flopped down in the grass. "Where have you been most of the day, Ollie? Don't you know them weeds need to be pulled out-a the beans and fed to the hogs?"

"I ain't forgot, but I ain't seen much of the new baby so I went up for a visit. Granddaddy, she ain't like other babies I've seen. What-a you think is wrong with her?"

He patted the grass. "Come sit, child. I knowed we was gonna have to have this talk sooner or later. Was hoping things would change but it don't look like there's much chance of that happening."

"Chance of what happening?"

Granddaddy studied my face for a while then gave a deep sigh. "It looks like your little cousin ain't long for this world."

"Why would that happen? Can't the doctor mend her"

"No one knows why things like that happen. Some folks say the mother marks them by sump'n she done while she was carrying the baby."

"I don't think Aunt Birdie would do anything to hurt her own baby, do you?"

"It ain't sump'n the mother does on purpose. I've heared it said that if a woman hangs out clothes when she's carrying a baby it will be born with the cord wrapped around its neck. Who knows if that's so, but I know your aunt wouldn't hurt a fly on purpose. Nature sometimes makes mistakes, and I suppose that's what happened to Ruth Ann."

"Uncle Ray wants to fetch the doctor back out to see her but Aunt Birdie don't want him to."

"Your aunt don't want to admit there's anything wrong with the baby."

I watched granddaddy as he pulled on a blade of grass and little lines formed between his eyebrows. It was the sort of look he got when he was worried 'bout Granny or me. "Granddaddy, being growed-up brings lots of trouble, don't it?"

"Trouble comes at any age, but when you're young you don't look at things the same way. Besides, a young person thinks they've got lots of time to fix things, but when you get my age, you realize time's a-running out. Guess I need to be preparing for that great judgment day."

"Don't talk like that, Granddaddy. Nothing is gonna happen to you.

Granddaddy gave one of his short quirky little laughs that I'd learned meant he was real nervous like.

"Let's hope not. Don't know who'd take in a-old woman that rocks all the time and a young'un your age, especially one as scrawny as you."

I knowed Grandddaddy didn't mean nothing bad, but it did kind-a hurt my feeling that he hadn't noticed that I'd begin to fill out in places. I dropped on the grass beside him and pulled me a blade of grass and ran it between my teeth. We set there for a while without saying much. I suppose he was a-thinking on what the preacher man had said 'bout going to heaven, and I was a-thinking how me and Granny would manage without him. I wasn't worried a-tall 'bout where he'd go since he was the best man on the branch.

I slipped my hand into my dress pocket and touched the map. I'd come out here with ever intention of showing it to him, but now I wasn't so sure. A voice inside me said, "You know when you let go of that map things are gonna change." Yes, but wasn't it 'bout time sump'n changed. It sure looked like nothing was gonna change with Granny or the baby.

My fingers tightened around the paper. If I didn't do it now, I'd never show him and it might be too late. Could already be I'd waited too long but seeing how they were hauling moonshine off the mountain maybe it wasn't. I jerked the paper out-a my pocket like it was one of Preacher Rainey's snakes and thrust it toward Granddaddy. "Take this and look at it. I found it the day Uncle Charlie was brought home dead, and I've tried the best I knowed to make heads or tails out a it. Thought I might find out who'd killed him, but it's beginning to look like 'bout everybody on the branch had good reason to want him dead."

Granddaddy sat up and took the map and unfolded it real gently like. He studied it for some time then folded it up and put it in his shirt pocket and just as gently he said, "Ollie, why don't you tell me where you found the paper?"

"You know how you always say that if you want the whole truth you've got to go straight to the horse's mouth. Well, that's what I decided to do the day Uncle Charlie was brought home dead. I went up to Uncle Ray's house to see if I could find out who might-a killed him. I found a little black box full of playing cards and this was under them."

"Where are the cards?"

"I was gonna bury them with Uncle Charlie but when I went to put them in the grave Mr. Yates come along and said he'd get rid of them for me. Seeings how I knowed Granny would be plenty upset if she found them in the house, I let him take'm."

"I'd say that was a smart move, young Lady. Your granny would a-had a heart attack if she'd found you with them cards. I seen her rip a deck right out-a Charlie's pocket one time and burn them in front of him. Why don't you tell me what you've been doing with the map?"

"Mostly keeping it under my mattress, but once in a while I take it out and study it then go looking for the moonshine still."

"Ollie, you could've got yourself killed." He patted his pocket. "This here is plans for a big operation and the people involved sure wouldn't let some young'un mess up their plans. But since you've been nosing around, is there any thing else you'd like to tell me."

I threw my blade of grass down and looked Granddaddy right in the eye. "I seen a whole bunch of men loading boxes on Preacher Rainey's truck. Maybe the preacher thought it was spring water, but I don't."

"If I was a betting man, I'd bet you a pair of new shoes that the preacher knows what he's hauling."

"Don't guess it matters much. That was over a week ago. Maybe he won't come back."

"You can bet your bottom dollar he'll be back, and when he does, there just might be a little surprise waiting for him."

My heart skipped a beat. Now I'd went and done it for sure. My granddaddy would get mixed up with them men straight from hell. He might get killed and it'd be my fault. "Granddaddy, why don't we just forget that I showed you the map? Me and Granny need you too much to have you go off and get your self killed too."

Then Granddaddy laughed his deep belly laugh, not his quirky little nervous laugh. When he stopped, he cleared his throat and said, "Ollie, young'un, you don't have to worry. I like living too much to let a bunch of moonshiners do me in. Pull a-arm full of weeds and get them hogs fed and don't worry your purty little head over that map anymore."

As I pulled the weeds, I felt Granddaddy watching me. When I started for the pig-pen, he called, "Ollie, Why didn't you tell me you're growing up. Didn't you know these old eyes can't see that good? I think you're old enough to learn to shoot a gun, don't you?"

I almost dropped the weeds. Ever mountain young'un lived for the day they'd get to shoot a gun. "I believe I'm just the right age, but let's not tell Granny. She might not like it."

Granddaddy nodded, and I headed on to the pen. I was growing up. Even my granddaddy saw it. I was glad I'd shared my secret with him. It made me feel more like his buddy.

* * *

Grady didn't waste any time looking for the moonshiner's still. He had a good idea where it was but he wasn't interested in closing them down. His intentions were a lot more profitable. Let them do the work, and him and Yates would reap the benefits. He knocked on Fred's door and when no one answered, he went around back to where Yates stored his moonshine.

As he walked in, Fred looked up from corking a jug. "Grady, I'm glad to see you. Hope you've come for a refill. I'll tell you business shore is slow. I'm here to tell you that preacher man must-a saved ever drunk on the branch. I ain't selling enough moonshine to wet a goat's whiskers. I have reason to believe there's a new still but nothing to back me up. Sure hope I don't have to tangle with them. I ain't the killing type but I won't see my family starve."

Grady pulled the map from his pocket. "You're right, Fred. There's a new still, and I have a list of names of who's running it, and a map showing where it is."

"I knowed it as well as I knowed I was Fred Yates." He reached for the pistol that hung over the door. "Come on, let's go get them."

Grady laid his hand on Fred's shoulder. "Let's not go putting our horse before the cart. I have been mulling this situation over ever since I got my hands on this map. The way I see it, we've just fell into a good business."

"I don't see what you mean. Seems to me like they're the ones with the market for their liquor while I'm about to starve."

"That's about to change. What-a you say we help ourselves to a little of their hard work. In other words let's let them make it, and we'll sell it and keep all the profits."

"How we gonna do that?"

"We'll just raid their still. Bring it all here and when their customers can't get it from them, they'll be knocking on your door. You'll have a good supply and won't have to lift a hand. We'll make weekly raids and keep them cleaned out."

"Sounds like a plan, but stealing is against the law."

"So is moonshining. They can't report it. Ain't nobody to tell. See, the Carlson name right here. That low-down sheriff is in on this also."

"How we gonna get it?"

"I figure the first time will be easy, but after that, we'll have to see."

"When do we take our first batch?"

"How 'bout as soon as it gets close to dark, you head on over my way? We'll take my horse and wagon."

He gripped the pistol again. "Do you think we'll need this?"

"Won't hurt to bring it along. Don't think we'll need it this time, but a-body never knows. Don't tell a-soul what we're up to."

"Mum is the word."

Grady left Yates whistling. He'd soon have the moonshiners put out-a business. That was just what they needed for killing his boy. There was one more thing he needed to tend to while he had time and that was to teach Ollie to shoot a gun. She'd need to know how to protect her and Eula just in case sump'n happened to him.

* * *

I knowed the minute Granddaddy told me to keep a-eye on Granny because he had to help Mr. Yates do sump'n that trouble was a-brewing for them both. 'Bout the only time Granddaddy went over to the Yates was to get his jug filled and it was only yesterday that I seen him headed that way with it under his arm. And there was one thing for sure, he hadn't been drinking, which surprised me cause when he's home for very long, he'll start taking little nips. I know he don't think me and Granny knows, but he ain't fooling nobody but hisself. Me and Granny done figured out a long time ago that when his eyeballs start to turn red it's with the help of the jug.

Anyhow, it was getting on toward dusk, and you don't go help a neighbor when dark is a-coming on unless what you're gonna help him with is against the law. Granddaddy hadn't said a word 'bout the map I'd give him, but knowing him, that didn't mean he'd put it in his pocket and forgot 'bout it. More than likely, he had a plan, and if he got into trouble it was gonna be my fault for showing him the paper. I should-a burned it, but it was too late now.

As soon as he'd hitched old Bess to the sled and headed off up the road, I struck out to follow him. I kept my distance, and when he'd slow down and look around, I'd duck behind the bushes. Wasn't too long until he met up with Yates and they talked for a few minutes then headed on up Black Mountain. They sure looked like they knowed where they was a-going. Almost to the top of the mountain, they pulled the sled off the wagon trail, and tied Bess to a pine tree.

I seen a wisp of smoke coming from a hollow off to the left. I knowed right where the still was. There was a little water fall over there, a perfect place to set a still. Why hadn't I thought to look there? I kept far enough behind so if I made any kind of noise they wouldn't hear but tried to stay close enough to at least see what was happening and hopefully to hear what was said. I seen Granddaddy motion to Yates and they ducked behind a bunch of laurels. As they ducked, I seen the guard, sitting, leaned up against a post. From where I was, I couldn't tell if he was asleep or passed out, but it was for sure he wasn't feeling no pain. If my guess was right that would change when Granddaddy and Yates were through with him. I still didn't understand what they were up to. If they knowed where the still was, why didn't they report it, and let the sheriff close them down.

Right before my eyes, Yates grabbed the guard from behind

and tied a gag over his mouth. Then they drug him into the thicket. When they come out, Yates begin to haul tin buckets from the still and stack them near the trail. Soon Granddaddy appeared with Bess and the sled, and he loaded them onto the sled and headed off down the mountain. Well, it didn't take a lawyer to figure out what they were going to do. Why make your own, when you had some one else to do it? I'd have to keep an eye on things and see what happened. Not that I didn't have enough to worry 'bout.

* * *

If I'd planned on worrying 'bout Granddaddy and Mr. Yates for long, I had a big surprise coming. The next week I seen Granddaddy hitch old Bess to the sled and head up the mountain. I guessed it was time that I done some more spying. Really, I don't know why I didn't think 'bout spying when Uncle Charlie first got killed. I might have already figured out who murdered him. As Granddaddy says, "It's too late to cry over spilt milk." Guess he means you can't put the milk back in the bucket. 'Bout the only thing I knowed that was being put in buckets right now was moonshine, and it could be that somebody got killed over it. This time I'd be there to see who done the shooting, and when that no-count sheriff come around looking, I'd point my finger at the guilty one. Of course, if it was Granddaddy who done it, I'd make sure I pointed at somebody else. If him or Mr. Yates done it, they'd have good reason. They were good men even if they liked their liquor.

It wasn't long until Granddaddy met Yates. They stood and talked for a few minutes then headed on up to the still. Surely to the Lord, they wouldn't march in there like they did the last time and take the white lightening.

'Bout a half-a-mile from the place, they hid their horse and sled and went on foot till they could see what was happening. I managed to get a little a-head of them and climbed up in a big bushy White Oak tree. From here I'd be able to see exactly how this killing took place. If it was Granddaddy, what would me and Granny do? I had the urge to run and grab him around the legs and beg him to stop, but I knowed he'd just say, "a man has to do what he has to do." That's what makes him a man, so I sat still and waited for the worst to happen. I should a-knowed they'd have a plan and not go off half-cocked and get hurt, cause what happened next showed me just how smart a-man my granddaddy was.

That preacher man was there with his truck, and even though it was getting on toward dark, I could see a bunch of men loading boxes on it. I seen Granddaddy and Mr. Yates hiding in the bushes, watching. When it was all loaded, the men tied a tarp over it, then went back to the still and filled their mugs. When they begin to either drop off to sleep or pass out, Granddaddy slipped from his hiding place and crawled under the tarp and Yates went back to Bess and the sled. Now what was I gonna do. It was either watch Granddaddy or Yates. It looked to me like Granddaddy was in more danger.

It wasn't long till Preacher Rainey got in the truck and headed down the mountain. I'd seen it all now, the preacher a bootlegger! People would have plenty to talk 'bout when this news got out. Maybe they'd give Aunt Birdie and her poor little baby a rest.

My heart didn't want-a stay in place as I watch Granddaddy ride off with that load of moonshine. I climbed down and followed. It wasn't hard to keep up since the road was so bad they couldn't go very fast. They passed where the horse and sled was hid, and I seen Yates watching thru the bushes. 'Bout that time a box fell off the truck. Granddaddy would for sure get caught. Hopefully, the preacher wouldn't hurt him. At least he had a better chance now that it was one-on-one.

Preacher Rainey didn't notice a-thing. 'Bout that time another box hit the ground. A few more feet and another one followed. By the time the truck reached the main road, Granddaddy slid from under the tarp and dropped to the ground. Just as the tail lights vanished, Yates came into sight. Him and Granddaddy loaded the last few boxes and headed toward his place.

Well, I'd seen it all. A whole truck load of moonshine emptied and nary a shot fired. I had to hand it to Granddaddy. He might not be the richest man on Haint Branch but he was for sure the smartest.

* * *

'Bout a week after I'd seen Granddaddy relieve the preacher's truck of its load of moonshine, I decided to go up and visit Sadie Jo and see if she'd heard from Preacher Rainey. I sure would've like to a-been there when he took that tarp off and found the truck empty. I'll bet he was mad enough to swear, if preachers is allowed to do that. Come to think of it, if they can run whiskey, why can't they use a few choice words? Lord, it looked like I'd never understand this growed up business. In November, I'd be thirteen and maybe things would start looking different.

I found Sadie Jo out on her back porch painting her toenails a pretty raspberry color. I asked her where she found that color of polish and she said, "Jamison's five-and-ten" and never looked up or missed a stroke. I seen right then and there, it was no use talking cause she weren't in no talking mood. I sat down on the top step and waited. As she dabbed the last bit of polish on her little toe, I said, "Have you heared from your preacher boyfriend?"

Her hand jerked, and she painted the whole side of her toe. I saw her lips move, but I couldn't hear what she said, but I'd guess it was the same sort-a word the preacher said when he found his wagon empty. "Ollie, look what you've made me do. Hand me that bottle of polish remover."

I looked around but all I seen was paint peeling and flies swarming. "Where's it at?"

"On the railing, hurry, when this stuff dries it's hard to get off."

I handed her the bottle, and as she wiped at the stained toe, I said, "You painting your toes for your preacher boyfriend?"

Her hand shot up and remover dripped from the rag she used. "Ollie Sanders, where'd you get the idea that I had a preacher friend?

I set back down on the steps. Now that I had her interest, I aimed on finding out all I could even if it took all afternoon. "Granddaddy, says that little pitchers have big ears."

"And just what does that mean?"

"I guess it means that I listen too much, don't you?"

She finished cleaning up her toe and repainted the nail. When she'd finished, she come and sat down by me and stretched her feet out so the sun could dry her nails. "Why don't you tell me what you've heard?"

I thought 'bout what she'd told Yates but decided not to let her know I'd over-heared them. Best just to keep it like rumors. "Oh, you know how people gossip. They've 'bout wore out Aunt Birdie and the baby so I guess they thought they'd give her a rest and talk 'bout you for a while."

Sadie wiggled her toes and watched as the color turned darker.

"You afraid them toes will stick together?" Is that why you keep wiggling them?" I asked.

"No, silly. I was admiring the job I've done. Hey, why don't we paint yours while you tell me who 'they' is."

"Granny'd kill me if she seen my toes looking like I'd waded in a berry patch."

"Thought your granny didn't notice much these days."

I looked out over the weed-grown yard and remembered how I'd left Granny rocking, full force, in her chair. Sadie was right; she'd never even look at my feet, and why not. Granddaddy had said I was growing up and looked to me like a girl growing up should have a little fun. "Let's do it."

Sadie went in the house and came back with a pan of water and a bar of soap. "Here, wash and dry your feet real good."

As I washed, she set back down by me and said, "And these 'they' people, who are you talking about."

I scrubbed one last dab of dried mud from between my toes and said, "The ladies that come calling on Granny. I think they're her quilting friends."

Sadie picked up my clean left foot and started painting my big toe. "And what do they say."

"They say that Preacher man is sweet on you, and it's a shame cause you'll break his heart just like you done Uncle Charlie's heart. One of them even said it was the work of the devil to stop the preacher's good work as a minister."

Sadie hesitated before she went on to the next toe. She finished it then picked up another before she spoke. "You don't believe everything you hear, do you, Ollie?"

"No, I don't, but I've seen how that preacher man looks at you. If I was a grown-up and knowed all the things a grown-up is suppose to, I'd say he's plenty sweet on you. Have you heared from him since he went away?"

She finished the toes on my left foot and reached for the right one. I stretched the painted toes out'n the sun just like I'd seen her do. This sure was nice, acting like I was all growed up, but if Granny was in her right mind and could see me, she'd tan my backside and tell me she didn't want me to be a good girl, gone bad. Oh well, as Granddaddy says, make hay while the sunshine lasts. I glanced up and found Sadie studying me. It looked to me like she was a splitting to tell sump'n to somebody. I didn't say a word until she'd finished my toes, and I'd put them all in the sun to dry. "Have you?"

She slid her legs out beside mine and said, "Ollie, can you keep a secret?"

"Granddaddy and me have secrets. He says that's what makes us buddies. You can ask him. I'm the best secret keeper this branch has."

Sadie screwed the lid on the polish real tight-like and reached for the pan of water. Before she could get it, I threw it out across the water-thirsty yard. I had the feeling if she got up; she'd lose the urge to tell me sump'n really important. She set the polish down by the remover and pulled a letter from her pocket. "I got this in the mail this morning. What I'm gonna tell you is sort-a hard even for me to understand, but I believe it cause it happened. Preacher Rainey wasn't a real minister of God's word. He used preaching as a cover up for his moonshining business."

I wanted to giggle in the worstest of ways, but I had to act surprised, and most of all, I had to act real growed-up. I turned slightly toward Sadie, propped my elbow on the porch, and slide down another step until I could rest my face in my hands, then opening my eyes as big as I could, I looked up at her and said, "Really?"

She nodded. "But he is now." She looked down the road like she expected him to show up at any moment.

I was getting more confused by the minute. Finally I said, "He is now, what?"

"A real minister of the word."

"And what brought 'bout his sudden change." Sump'n was happening deep inside me. It was like I knowed how to make her say the things I wanted her to. Was this part of growing up? If it was, I really liked it.

"A miracle from God."

"Like Jesus raising Lazarus from the dead?"

"Sort-a. But God emptied a whole truckload of moonshine. Gone. Not a trace of liquor anywhere."

Now, I really had to work at not laughing. Granddaddy would bust a gut laughing if he knowed he'd been the one to cause the preacher to get religion. "Maybe they were so drunk they forgot to load the truck."

"No, Preacher Raincy don't drink."

I wiggled my red toes some and thought of what to say. I knowed exactly where ever box of that moonshine was, and I supposed God did too. The Yates' young'uns would come to school with new shoes on their feet. Maybe God did have sump'n to do with this. "So, what did he do when he seen it was gone?"

When she'd finished telling me how Preacher Rainey had fell on his knees right there in the street of Atlanta and asked the Lord to clean him and make him worthy of spreading His word, tears were running down her face.

I didn't say anything right away. I knowed she needed time to quiet herself. Good Lord, this growing up seemed to have lots of twists and turns to it. When the tears stopped and she'd wiped her face dry on her sleeve, I said, "And what does this mean for you and him?"

She looked back down the road. "He said he was gonna come and ask my pa for my hand in marriage. Can you believe it? Him showing up and, on bended knee, asking Pa to marry me, just like out-a them romance magazines."

Sadie Jo married and to a preacher, now that would be a miracle. I couldn't quite figure out how the Lord was gonna clean her up. I'd say by now my granddaddy was short on helping. "And are you gonna say yes?"

She glanced back at me then studied me like she'd just realized she'd spilled her guts to a young'un. "Oh, Ollie, I'm sorry. I can't expect you to understand. Someday when you're all grown up, you'll know what I'm talking about."

It looked to me like I understood lots more than she did, but that was alright. "You gonna go away with him?" Now it was me who felt like crying. I was 'bout to lose the only real worldly friend I had.

She put a arm around my shoulder. "Yes, but I'll come back. I could never not see you again. If I'd a married your Uncle Charlie, you would have been my niece? Can we pretend that you are?"

Suddenly, I didn't want-a be all growed-up. I wanted to be

Granddaddy's little girl and Sadie Jo's niece for a long-long time, but that same sump'n that had told me I could get her to talk, told me that change was happening even as we talked.

13

The day the Carnival came to town was the day that Sheriff Carlson's sin got the best of him. It was the week of the Fourth of July. Hot as blue blazes and not even any of them thunderhead clouds reared their ugly heads over the mountains. It looked like it was going to be a long, hot summer. The people in these parts of North Carolina swore that if it rained the first day of dog days it'd rain every day for the next month. If it didn't, people might as well plan on a good drought, but the heat of summer wasn't the only thing burning in Franklin.

The fire that burned in the sheriff's belly wasn't the kind that got kindled on the first day of frost. It was the sort that had smoldered since he was a young boy, or some people might say, men like him were born with the spark already lit. Today it didn't matter where it came from. It only mattered that someone was going to get burned.

He hadn't even planned on going to the carnival, but he needed to check it out. Make sure every thing was safe. He'd even been against it coming to town, but the businesses loved it because it drew people into town from all the hills and hollers. And he knew with them gone from home, it'd give the moonshiners an opportunity to load up a good shipment of white-lightening. He looked up to find Sadie Jo Miller walking his way. "Wait up, Sadie. Care to have a cup of coffee with the sheriff?"

"Why, Sheriff Carlson, aren't you afraid I'll taint your reputation?"

He took her arm and guided her toward a booth that sold refreshments. "I'll risk it for the pleasure of a good looking woman's company." He ordered two coffees. "Let's stroll down toward the river."

They walked in silence for a few minutes. "We haven't talked since I questioned you about Charlie Sanders death, have we?"

"No, don't guess we have? Ain't been no reason as I see it. Did you found out anything about who might have done my man in?"

"If it was a killing, Sadie Jo, there sure aren't many clues. Oh, I can name several people who might have liked him dead, but there's no way of proving any of them done it. For instance like you, I see you as being a one woman man. Could be you shot him in a rage of jealousy because he was seeing another woman. I've known of cases where the people got so mad they don't remember what they did."

"That's not me, Sheriff. I remember everything I've ever done. Can't say there wasn't times I'd-a liked to have killed him, but as I see it, there ain't no man worth frying for." She looked at him and grinned. "At least not that kind of frying. Get what I mean?"

He slipped his arm around her waist and pulled her closer. "I've always got what you meant. You're the kind of woman that will always need a man. Now that you don't have Charlie maybe me and you could fry up something."

Sadie stepped away and looked the sheriff up and down. As the heat grew, Sheriff Carlson stood there in the middle of the path and waited for her response. There wasn't a line of women beating a trail to his door. Most of his friends were married and had families. He wasn't anxious to have a bunch of mouths to feed, but he'd like to have a little loving once in awhile. Maybe it would ease the restlessness that burned inside him.

"No offense meant, Sheriff, but you just ain't my kind of man. If you're worried about me getting lonely, don't. I'm getting awfully sweet on that traveling preacher, and he's crazy over me."

The mist from the river crowded in and for a minute the sheriff felt like he was going to drown in it. Sadie Jo and Preacher Rainey, well, that wouldn't last. The preacher would move on soon and then she'd be lonely. He'd have to wait, but in the meantime, he'd see what he could do to quench his thirst.

***

Ain't never been nothing made as good as cotton candy, or at least that's what I think. Granddaddy says a good chew of home-cured tobacco is lots better. I tried it once and turned green around the gills. At least ways cotton candy won't do you that way but it will make you sick as a dog if you eat too much and most everyone thought that was what happened to me the night of the carnival.

I'd begged Granddaddy into letting me go with Uncle Ray and Aunt Birdie. He didn't think it was such a good idea seeing all that went on at them places, but since Granny stayed in her rocking chair so much and Aunt Birdie's baby wasn't doing right, I guess he felt sort-a sorry for me.

Anyway, after supper we toted Ruth Ann off over to her other granny's and left her, then we went on into town. Ever once in a while, I'd slip my hand into my dress pocket and feel the coins that Granddaddy had give me so I could have a few rides. He'd warned me not to spend it on the fortune teller booth. He didn't have to worry. I had all I could do worrying 'bout what was going on now. I sure didn't want to know what tomorrow held. It wouldn't take a fortune teller to see what was going to happen to Aunt Birdie's baby. Poor little soul, she hadn't growed a-smidgen and still wasn't alert. I felt real bad for Aunt Birdie cause I knowed how bad she wanted to have her own little girl.

When we got to the carnival, the Yates family was there. Me and one of the girls rode the ferris wheel, then I headed straight for the cotton candy machine and got me a whole bunch wrapped around a stick. It was pink and sticky but sweet as sugar and as light as air. I nibbled at it real slow like while I went to hunt Aunt Birdie and her boys. Granny had told me a long time ago that when I was in town I was suppose to stick close to the grown-ups so I figured I'd better still mind her. I took the short cut behind some of the booths cause I knowed they'd be over by the place where they was shooting at ducks for free stuffed animals. Granny says them places is a rip-off. That you can buy what you want cheaper than you can win one shooting, but Granddaddy says you wouldn't have the fun. And sometimes half the fun in getting sump'n is in the way you earn it.

I'm here to tell you my granddaddy must-a had a whole bunch of fun in his time cause he don't do nothing the easy way. Granny gets so disgusted with him. Take the time he decided to raise chickens for a living. Right up and quit his lumbering job and started building chicken coops. It wasn't long until our whole hill-side was filled. Then he ordered all these baby chicks from a catalogue. We kept them in by the stove at night and put them out'n the sun during the day, but we weren't the only ones that like chickens. Them big old hawks picked them off like shelled corn. He finally managed to raise 'bout a dozen, and we got a few eggs before the foxes finished off the brood. He went back to his lumbering job and the coops were used as kindling for the kitchen stove.

I'd just started down the path when from behind me a handkerchief-covered hand slipped over my mouth and the scent coming from it was worse than what I'd smelt on the mountain when Uncle Charlie was shot. Before the scent overwhelmed me, I felt myself being pulled against the rough texture of a man's clothing then darkness slipped through his fingers. The next thing I remembered was someone yelling.

"There's a girl over here behind the elephant tent. Looks like she's been hurt,"

I moved and my legs were still attached. I had to get up. I had to pretend I was all right no matter what. I stood and felt lightheaded so I steadied myself on the tent pole. I felt sump'n wet running down my legs but didn't look. Truth was I didn't want to see. I just wanted to run and never stop. Something bad had happened to me, so bad that it was better not to think 'bout it. I'd act like I'd stumbled over the tent ropes and hurt myself. No one would question that. It would have been a good plan if my stomach had-a stayed still but it crept up just like it did when I'd smelled the scent at Uncle Ray's. First thing I knowed all that cotton candy I'd eat was on the ground and my head was a-spinning again. I hung on to the rope for dear life but the darkness claimed me again. The next time I opened my eyes I was laying on a cot in some sort of make-shift first-aid tent.

A lady dressed in white pressed a cold washcloth to my forehead. "I think you've had too much of that cotton candy and looks like your leg is all scratched up. Do you remember what happened?"

"I was looking for my aunt, and I took the short cut behind the tents. I guess I tripped over a rope and fell." I set up. "I've got to go find her. She'll be worried."

"You stay right where you are. Tell me your Aunt's name, and I'll have one of our men look for her. Don't want you running off in the dark and getting hurt again."

"Her name is Birdie Sanders and my Uncle's name is Ray. Tell them to hurry. I want to go home."

She called to someone down the way, and I sank back on the cot, happy not to have to go look for them on my own. The truth be knowed, I doubt if my legs would have carried me outside this tent. More bile crept up into my mouth and I swallowed, determined not to empty my stomach here. I knowed there'd be plenty of time for that when I was alone. What I didn't know was that being alone would bring more than losing my stomach. It would bring nightmares of a man with a funny-smelling handkerchief.

* * *

Losing my stomach convinced my Aunt Birdie that I was suffering from a dose of the summer flu so she put me right to bed when we got back to their house. I let her think what she wanted. I didn't tell nobody what really happened. Wasn't no use stirring up trouble when there was already enough. With Uncle Charlie dead, Granny rocking, and now a baby that wasn't right, the family sure didn't need a young'un that had got herself into a passel of trouble by not staying with the grown-ups. I'd learned my lesson so I'd just pay the price. Why if Granddaddy knowed that somebody had hurt me, he was liable to go off half-cocked and kill that somebody, and then where would me and Granny be?

Granddaddy had promised to teach me to shoot, and as soon as I felt like it, I'd get him started. From now on, I'd take care of myself. I bunched up my pillow and buried my head in. I sure was glad I was spending the night here. If I'd been home, I'd be getting a good tongue-lashing from Granny on the evils of such places as a carnival. Another wave of cotton candy tried to escape my stomach.

Aunt Birdie seen me struggling to keep from being sick and set a pan on the bed and said, "Sometimes it's best to just get it out-a your system.

What was wrong with me was sump'n that I'd never get out-a my system, not in a million years. I closed my eyes and let sleep wash over me, but as I sunk into dreamland, I felt the roughest of trousers against my legs then that awful smell. I fought to escape and as I did I seen short, stout legs hovering over me. Slowly, I opened my eyes to find Aunt Birdie holding the pan and the last of the cotton candy in it. Gently, she wiped my face with a cool cloth and told me to try and sleep that she'd be right there if I needed her.

As I closed my eyes, I wondered if my mother was anything like Aunt Birdie. Would she wipe my face and sit by my side? Granny had said, when I growed up, she'd answer my questions, but the way it was looking, she wouldn't be answering too many question no matter who asked them.

The next time I woke it was morning, and I felt lots better. Maybe the whole thing had been a nightmare. I raised up on my elbow and seen Aunt Birdie nursing Ruth Ann. I watched and marveled at how gentle she was with the baby. If God had to give a baby with problems to somebody, He sure picked the right woman. Love was stamped all over her face. Right then I swore that when I got growed-up I'd find my mother, and when I did, she'd fix every thing that had went wrong in my life.

* * *

Life felt pretty much normal after awhile but my nind and heart was full of questions and secrets. I sneaked off to my room and laid down on the bed. There was so much I'd like to tell Granddaddy. Wouldn't he get a big laugh out-a knowing he'd helped the preacher find salvation? Maybe I'd just tell him. Seemed we needed a good laugh around here. I was glad I'd give the map to him since I wasn't getting any further along in solving Uncle Charlie's murder than that sheriff was. But on the other hand, I wasn't getting paid either. I hadn't been able to keep my mind on much of anything since what happened to me that night at the carnival. Mostly, I tried to put it out of my mind cause it still hurt sump'n fierce when I peed. If it hadn't a-been for Granny's rocking mood, I'd ask her what was wrong, but seeing how she never sat still long enough, I'd tried to manage, and for the most part, I was lots better, accept for the bad dreams.

14

Grady pulled down his .22 riffle from the rack near the back door. With it purposely aimed toward the ground, he walked toward the barn. If he was gonna teach Ollie how to shoot, he'd have to start by teaching her the right way to handle a gun. His pa had taught him to always carry it pointing toward the ground. Another fact he'd stressed was never to aim a gun unless you planned on pulling the trigger. It was certain that whoever killed Charlie was a good shot. Not everyone could aim and hit their target. He remembered when him and Eula was first married, she couldn't hit the broad-side of a barn. First of all, he had to convince her that it was important for her to learn, and then it took him several months to teach her to aim. But once she got the hang of it, she'd become a good shot. Women needed to know how to handle a gun in order to survive in these mountains.

He'd finished setting a row of pork-and-bean tin cans on the rail fence in front of the barn when Ollie opened the back door and headed toward him. She walked almost drudgingly up the path. He'd noticed lately there'd been a tinge of lines between her brows. She'd been spending lots of time with Birdie and the new baby. He was glad. A young'un her age needed to be around women folk, and with Eula rocking all the time, she wasn't much company. Maybe she was worried about Ruth Ann, or it could be Eula's rocking. "Get yourself up here," he called. "This rifle needs to be loaded."

She raised her head and looked toward him. He saw the lines disappear and a broad grin break across her face. "You mean I can do it?"

He took a shell from the pocket of his vest and reached for the rifle he'd laid on the back of the wagon. "Only if you're ready, remember, never load a gun unless you're gonna use it. And more importantly, don't aim unless you're gonna shoot and always keep the barrel pointing toward the ground when you're carrying it." He placed the gun in her trembling hands. "Steady now." He showed her how to break down the gun and place the shell in the chamber.

She looked up and smiled at him. "Don't you think I'm all growed-up now, Granddaddy?"

"I think you have a good start on the job. Let's see you knock one of them cans off the fence."

Granddaddy watched her raise the gun and take aim the best she could. He didn't offer to help. He would, but not until she'd tried. As her finger squeezed the trigger, the barrel of the gun dropped and a second later the rail of the fence was sent splintering in all directions. "Good first try. Come sit over here on the wagon and let's talk about guns. There's lots more to learning to shoot than just squeezing the trigger."

She laid the gun down on the wagon bed and crawled up beside him.

"Good, you remembered what I said about how to handle it. Guns are to be respected. The most dangerous thing about a gun is the user, not the gun itself. When you have your target, make sure there's nothing on the other side of it. You might be shooting at that can over there but there could be a cow standing on the other side." He picked up the gun. When you're finished, it has to be cleaned and oiled and put back where you found it. Do you understand?"

"Yes, right in the gun rack by the back door."

"And before you take it, you're to ask my permission. Do you get that?"

"I'd never take it without you knowing."

"I'd hope not unless there was some sort of emergency and you had to, then I'd understand."

"Can I shoot again?"

He took a few more shells from his vest. "Yes, but I'm about out of ammunition. I'll get some more when I go into town Saturday. In the meantime, you can practice cleaning the gun."

This time her hands didn't shake as much as she dropped the shell into the chamber and took aim. The sound of metal echoed, and for a moment, the can tittered on the fence then fell to the ground. He could see she was going to be good, but what else had he expected.

"I did it, Granddaddy. I hit the can. I really did."

"Yes, but this is only the beginning. Run on to the house and check on your granny. We'll save the rest of the shells for tomorrow."

Pointing the barrel toward the ground, she handed him the gun. "I'll do better. I promise."

"I know you will. Here, take the gun and put it back. We'll clean it after supper. And remember never take a loaded gun into the house."

"I'll remember, Granddaddy." She hesitated, looked toward the house, and then back at him.

"Is there something wrong, Ollie?"

"Can we talk for a spell?"

"I thought when I seen you heading this way that you had something on your mind. Out with it?"

"You haven't mentioned the map since I give it to you. I was so afraid you'd go off and get yourself hurt or killed and I'd be to blame."

"So that's the reason for them lines between your brows. You had me really worried. There wasn't much to that map. Didn't have nothing to do with Charlie's death. I suspect he might have had some dealings with them, but as far as I know, they had no reason to want him dead."

"So you knowed all 'bout what was going on before the map?"

"I'd heared rumors and even knowed some of the men who were involved. All the map did was show me where the operation was."

"Was?"

"Yeah, it didn't take them long to find that business in these parts ain't too profitable. They moved out a little while back, lock, stock, and barrel. Not a sign of them anywhere." Grady ran gnarled fingers though graying hair as he studied Ollie's face. If he wasn't mistaken he could see laughter hiding behind those big, blue, eyes of hern. And if he was a betting man, he'd bet she knew ever move he'd made since she'd given him the map. That was alright. As soon as she learned to shoot, she'd be safe.

"There's sump'n else I think you'd like to know."

For a moment, he wondered if she was going to confess to snooping. "What's that?"

"I seen Sadie Jo and she says that preacher man is coming back, and he's gonna ask her pa if they can wed. And you know what else she said?"

"Ain't no telling."

"She said. . . ."

Grady saw a shadow cross her face. "What'd she say."

"I just remembered that I told her I wouldn't tell. "It's a secret between us. You understand, don't you?"

"Course I do, young'un. I wouldn't want you to go back on your word."

"Thanks, Granddaddy. Now I'll check on Granny."

He watched as she ejected the used shell and headed toward the house. She was growing up, and sooner than he'd like, he'd have to lose her to another man just like Sadie Jo's pa was gonna do. That man had better be worthy of her or there'd be reason to do lots of target practicing.

* * *

Halfway to the house, I seen Sadie Jo ambling up the road. There was sump'n in the way she walked that told me she had news. I sure hoped it was good. We'd had enough bad around here to last for a while. It looked to me like Aunt Birdie's baby was in trouble of some sort. She wasn't doing nothing but eating and crying. The day I'd over-heared her and Uncle Ray talking it sounded like he wanted to try and fix her, but Aunt Birdie wasn't in no mood to talk 'bout it.

As far as who killed Uncle Charlie, I'd 'bout decided that was the sheriff's worry, not that he was gonna worry too much 'bout it. And Granny, I'd noticed that she rocked more when things upset her, so me and Granddaddy had been real careful lately not to irritate her or say much 'bout what was a-happening. Of course, if the baby died we couldn't keep that from her, but the way she'd acted after it was born, I didn't see her caring too much.

By the time I'd reached the back door, Sadie Jo turned up the path to our house. I set down on the back step and waited. When she was close enough, she held up her left hand and I caught a glimpse of something shiny. A ring! Lord a mercy, that preacher man sure must-a got a good dose of sump'n.

"He really come, Ollie, and look what he give me, an engagement ring. We're getting married September the eighteenth. Will you stand up with me?"

For a minute, I couldn't breathe. I thought this sort-a thing only happened in romance magazines and here a whole true story was unfolding right in front of my eyes. I was even being asked to be part of the story. I wiggled my toes and thought 'bout what they'd looked like when Sadie Jo had polished them. If I was gonna be in her wedding, they'd have to be painted again, and I'd have to have a pair of shoes. The ones from last spring were too little, but if I got my toenails polished, I'd have to have some of them sandals so they'd show. I didn't know how Granny would take to me asking for that kind-a shoe. I could hear her saying, "them ain't sump'n you can wear to school." Maybe Aunt Birdie would get them for me.

I took Sadie Jo's hand and studied the ring. It weren't big, probably from one of them cracker-jack boxes. Way Granddaddy says you can find almost anything you need from one of them. But this one sure looked real, and with engagements, I guess real is what counts.

"Well, Will you?"

"What will I have to do?"

"Just stand there and when Ernie puts the wedding ring on my finger, you'll hold my bridal bouquet."

"Bridal Bouquet? Where you gonna get one of them?'

"Mama said she'd make me one from wild flowers."

"You think she can."

"I know she can. She used to work in a flower shop."

"Really! Your mama had a real job? I didn't know women worked away from home."

Sadie sat down by me, holding her ring so the sun would make it glisten. "Yes, Mama could have owned her own shop if she hadn't a married my pa."

I wanted to ask why she'd choose marriage over having her own business but I didn't. That was one of them growed-up questions. I guess when it comes to love, it always wins out. I didn't rightly know if that was a good thing or not. Maybe my own mother had chosen a job over keeping me. If that was so, then she didn't love me or my pa. I'd never thought much 'bout who my pa was. For some reason that didn't seem as important as knowing who my mama was. Well, someday I'd be all growed-up and somebody would have to tell me sump'n. There might not be no more to tell than Granddaddy had already told me. It could be that I'd have to get use to being called "the suitcase baby."

I wiggled my toes. "Will you paint my toenails again?"

"Yes, and your fingernails too."

I drew my hands behind me. "No, I don't want my nails polished."

Sadie pulled my hands from behind me. "And may I ask why not?"

"They're ugly."

"They're no such thing. There ain't a ugly thing about you, Olivia Sanders. What or who give you such an idea?"

"If I was purty then why didn't my mamma want me?"

"Pretty ain't got nothing to do with wanting, child."

"I guess you're right. Granddaddy is always a saying 'purty is as purty does'. I try and act purty most of the time."

"And I'd say you do a good job at it. You've made us all right proud of you, Ollie. Ain't many young'uns could deal with what you have and still keep such a pretty smile. Now, how about standing up with me?"

"I'd like that."

She reached in her pocket and pulled out a bunch of money all rolled up. "Preacher Rainey give me this to buy my wedding clothes. See if your grandparents will let you go into town with me sometime soon, and we'll have us a fun day getting ready."

I swallowed at the sight of so much money. That preacher man must-a got salvation and his pocket filled at the same time. Well, I wasn't gonna question the ways of the Good Lord. I was gonna just enjoy the harvest, and not say a word 'bout how he become a real preacher man.

15

August ain't good for much of nothing here in the mountains except laying down by the swimming hole, and that's 'bout all me and Aunt Birdie and her young'uns done that summer after the baby was born. She'd spread out a quilt under the old oak tree and put the baby where the sun wouldn't hit her. I'd swim with the boys for a while, then I'd lay by little Ruth Ann and try to get her to look at me.

One day, without thinking, I blurted out sump'n that I'd never even thought 'bout. Aunt Birdie had just settled down with one of her romance magazines. One that Granny said she'd better never catch me with or she'd warm my back side good no matter what Granddaddy said. Well, I ain't told her, but Aunt Birdie lets me look at hern all the time. I've even read some of the stories. They sound 'bout like the people here on Haint Branch. Could be that's why Granny don't want me knowing that the same thing goes on in real life as it does in books.

Anyway, I asked Aunt Birdie if she thought Ruth Ann could see. She laid down her magazine and grabbed up the baby and hugged her tight. "Of course, she can see. Why would you think she can't?"

I got all tongue tied and flustered cause she was so upset. Finally, I managed to say, "Uh . . . it's just that her eyes don't move around like the Yates baby does."

"Them Yates young'uns are the ones that ain't normal. Ain't you ever noticed how dumb they all act?" Aunt Birdie gatheared up her belongings and called to the boys that it was time to go home.

I wanted to beg her to stay a little longer, but I seen the way she was packing stuff up that it wouldn't do no good. When she finished, she said, "Olivia, you'd better run on home and see to your granny." That 'bout broke my heart cause she'd usually take me home with her, and we'd bake cookies while the young'uns took a nap, but I seen right then that there'd be no cookie baking today. As Granddaddy would say, I guess I really ruffled her feathers and I seen there was no use trying to sooth them.

I stood there watching them disappear down the road and fought back tears. Somehow I knowed that Aunt Birdie thought the same thing I did 'bout Ruth Ann. All of a sudden Uncle Charlie being dead didn't seem as bad as it had last fall. I'd like to have him back but not as much as much as I'd like for my little cousin to be able to see.

* * *

I soon found out that seeing ain't all there is to life. I figured if Ruth Ann didn't see maybe God would give her other ways to grow. But Ruth Ann didn't . . . grow, that is. She just didn't seem to care much 'bout being here on this earth. I discovered that the day me and Aunt Birdie was gonna take her to see the granny-woman who lived way up on Rocky Face Mountain. Folks here on the branch believe that the granny-woman has healing power. I don't thing she has anymore than my own granny. If Granny was in her right mind and wanted to, she'd fix little Ruth Ann up good with one of her poultices but for some reason Granny ain't never took to Ruth Ann. When I asked her, she looked away and said "I'm too old to fool with babies. That's why God gave them parents."

I would-a took her to see a preacher man, but Aunt Birdie ain't much on that religious stuff. I don't know anyone who practices faith healing besides Preacher Rainey and he ain't around that often.

When he is, he spends most of his time with Sadie Jo. I guess that's because they're getting married soon.

Anyway, the day we set out to see the granny-woman was a nice Saturday in early September. The early morning fog still clung to the tops of the mountains, but the sun was fast burning it off. I knowed it'd be real hot by the time we reached the old woman's cabin. I had fixed us a jug of fresh spring water and put some side-pork between some biscuits. Figured we could stop and have a picnic under one of them big, shady oaks. That was a nice plan but as Granddaddy always says, "Plans get you into stuff that you've gotta work your way out of." Don't rightly know what he means by working your way out, but I'm always trying to fix things when they don't turn out the way I want them to, so maybe that's what he means.

We'd just finished off the biscuits when Ruth Ann turned as grayish-blue as Granny's old work apron. Aunt Birdie didn't seem to get too upset, just blowed in her face.

I screamed. "She's gonna die."

Aunt Birdie looked at me as calm as if she was telling me to set the supper table. "She ain't gonna die. If she was, it would have already happened. She does this all the time."

"Aunt Birdie, what are you gonna do if the granny-woman can't help?"

She laid her hand on my shoulder and squeezed right gently like. "Ollie, when the time comes, there ain't much I can do except help her be where she ought-a be. Now let's get on up to the cabin."

I gathered our trash and stuck it behind a tree stump. Granddaddy wouldn't like it if I left a mess in the woods. Aunt Birdie was already headed up the trail. Wonder what she meant by helping

Ruth Ann be where she ought-a be? Looked to me like she was right where God wanted a baby to be, and that was with her mother and father. Maybe Aunt Birdie knowed sump'n other folks didn't. I'd ask her later when she had time to talk to me. She'd been awful nice to me since the baby had come, before she'd shy away when I tried to talk to her.

Aunt Birdie was at the old woman's door by the time I caught up with her. I'd heared stories 'bout Granny Zeta but I wasn't expecting what I saw. Her long nose curved under and made a hook at the end. I couldn't help but think it was too bad it didn't curve up then she could have used it for hanging sump'n, maybe like her nightgown so it would hide her not having teeth. Maybe I could get Granddaddy to whittle her some teeth out of Locust wood.

Granny Zeta took one look at Ruth Ann and said, "That young'un needs a good dose of my special tonic. Come on in here and have a cup of tea while I doctor her." She shoved a wad of course gray hair behind her ear with one hand as she pushed Aunt Birdie through the door with the other. She looked down at me. "You can wait out here. Don't want too many seeing me work my magic."

My heart sank as she went inside and left me standing alone on the porch. I wasn't gonna get to watch her make my little cousin better. I heared voices inside then it struck me that the window was open, and if I was really quiet, I could eavesdrop and learn what she done. After all, I was getting good at listening when I wasn't suppose to. I squatted right below the window. I heared her say, "Looks like your young'un has the mark of death. There ain't much I can do to stop that, but I can give you a tonic that will make the passing easier."

I heared Aunt Birdie say, "You want me to poison my own child."

"No, I want you to help her return to her maker."

I raised up a little and saw Aunt Birdie's face. It was all purple and mad looking. For a second, I thought she was gonna hit Granny Zeta but instead she whirled and started toward the door. The old woman followed her, and as Aunt Birdie stepped onto the porch, Granny Zeta slipped sump'n in her pocket, mumbled a few words, and watched as Aunt Birdie fled toward the steps.

Aunt Birdie hollered for me, and I run for the steps. It looked to me like we'd better make tracks off this mountain before we all had a hex put on us.

❧ 16 ☙

The day Sadie Jo come to get me for our shopping trip Granny was in one of her real bad rocking moods. When I asked Granddaddy if I could go, he said yes, but not to be fooling around that pool hall by myself. Said a young girl could get her self in a whole passel of trouble. He didn't have to worry; I'd learned my lesson real good at the carnival.

As soon as we were out of Granddaddy's hearing, I said, "Sadie Jo, why's the pool hall such a bad place to be."

She looked at me like I'd just crawled from behind some big rock. "Ollie, you're growing up fast. I guess your Granny ain't been in no shape to see that. Ain't there been no body that's told you about the 'facts of life'?"

I studied on what she'd said for a few minutes. I could tell her lots of facts but none of them had to do with what was wrong with being around a pool hall. "What-a you mean?"

"Sex. Ain't nobody told you about that?"

"I don't know why they'd have to, seeing it's all around. Why ever time I gather the eggs, I see the chickens doing it. And that old bull of Mr. Yates has just 'bout rode our cow to death lately."

"You know if animals do it, then so do people."

I thought on this little bit of news for a few more minutes. I couldn't see nothing too alarming 'bout it. I'd figured out a long time ago that I wasn't laid on a rock and the sun hatched me like Granddaddy once told me or found under a cabbage leaf either. That was just some of his crazy sayings. "Are they doing it in the pool hall?"

"Not that I know of, but there's lots of dirty old men that hang out in there and a young girl don't need to hear all they talk about. Ain't lady-like."

"I guess you'll have to learn all them ladylike ways now that you're gonna be a preacher's wife, won't you?"

"Guess I will. I've been thinking 'bout that lots lately. I think I'll take some courses on how to act more lady like. Ernie says the Lord can take care of fixing lots of things. Said He'd done it for him, but I can't see that it'd hurt to give Him a hand."

I remembered how Granddaddy had give Him a hand in helping Preacher Rainey find salvation, so I knowed first hand that the Lord used helping hands. "I know the Lord uses all the hands he can get since he don't have none of his own."

"Ollie, if I have any young'uns, I hope they're as smart as you."

"If I'm so smart, why can't I figure out who killed my Uncle Charlie? And smarts sure ain't helped me fix Granny, and then there's Aunt Birdie's poor baby. I went with her up to see Granny Zeta, but that was a wasted trip."

"What did the granny woman do?"

"She didn't do much. Course I had to stay out on the porch, but I peeked through the window. I heared her say Ruth Ann had the mark of death. Guess that's because she turns blue all the time. All I know is that I wish I had a mama that loved me as much as Aunt Birdie loves that baby."

Sadie Jo looked at me. I could see that she was feeling really sad for me. I pulled my shoulders up real straight and blinked away tears that had gatheared. This was Sadie's time and it weren't fair of me to go whining bout my wants. I'd have to save them for another time.

***

By the time we'd reached Pendergrass's dry good store, we'd left the sex subject way back on the road, and I was glad 'bout that. Not that I didn't appreciate Sadie Jo taking a interest in my sex education, but what had happened to me at the carnival still gave me a funny feeling in the pit of my stomach. If that feeling had gone away, I'd have told Sadie Jo 'bout what happened, but like I say, it's her time and I don't want her to go worrying 'bout sump'n she can't do nothing 'bout. And for the most part, I'm all right except for my feelings. As far as I know, feelings ain't never killed no body yet, at leastwise not here on Haint Branch. On second thought that might not be so. Who ever shot Uncle Charlie must-a had some awful bad feelings 'bout him. I know for sure a shotgun killed him and maybe someday the truth will come to light. In the meantime, we're fixing to have us a wedding and some fun.

Granddaddy says when there's gonna be a wedding, it's a mountain custom to kidnap the groom and take him off somewheres and keep him up all night. Guess that's so he won't be in too good a shape on his wedding day. Now to me that sounds like a mean thing to do. Looks to me like he'd 'bout be all used up by then. Maybe that's what they hope would happen. I was a-hoping Sadie Jo wouldn't be left standing at the altar because of some prank that was pulled on Preacher Rainey. I'd have to remember to tell Granddaddy to make sure he got to the church on time and seeing how he was so good at fixing things for Preacher Rainey, I knowed he'd make sure he was all married off proper like. I kind-a half-way giggled to myself. Maybe it was a good thing that all truth ain't knowed.

I looked around in time to see a long-nosed clerk heading my way, and I laid down the pair of white gloves I'd been fingering. She gave me the evil-eye and said, "You know them are the most expensive gloves we carry. I'd hate for your mother to have to buy them because you ruined them."

I dropped the gloves and glanced around, wishing I could crawl under sump'n or plain just disappear. I wasn't 'bout to tell her that I didn't have a mother to pay. Besides, I don't know what she thought I was gonna do to them.

"We'll take that pair of gloves and finish our shopping down the street at Callhands' dry goods."

I turned around just as Sadie Jo pulled that wad of money out of her bosom. I'd love to had one of them new-fangled cameras that I seen at the carnival, so I could-a took a picture of that sales clerk's mouth. It dropped open so far that it almost rested on her bosom, that is if she'd a-had one. It looked to me like nature hadn't a-been too kind to her. Sadie Jo was a different story. She'd been blessed with enough for both her and the sales clerk.

By now the clerk was giving Sadie Jo back her change, but I couldn't hear a word they was a-saying. I could see Sadie Jo looking my way and giving me one of her sly little grins. I'm sure she was telling that woman where she could stick it, and I'd bet it'd be just like Grandaddy says, "where the sun don't shine." And around here in these hollows, that could be 'bout anywhere.

Sadie stuffed the money back in her bosom and walked right over and took me by the hand, and we headed straight for the door. I heared the lady walking after us but we never looked back. When we were on the street, Sadie Jo said, "Ollie, I'm sorry she said what she did. I hope you don't mind, but I told her you were my niece."

"That's alright. I was mighty scared there for a minute. I was afraid she'd call the sheriff man, and he'd lock me up in jail."

"That'll never happen when I'm around. I don't like Sheriff Carlson, and I don't want him bothering none of my kin."

She squeezed my hand, and we headed on toward Callhands' to finish our shopping. I don't recall a time I've ever felt so good 'bout being Olivia Sanders. Maybe not having a mother wasn't all that bad when you had real family to care 'bout you. What would I do when Sadie Jo moved away with that preacher man?

* * *

Weddings was sump'n that didn't happen much here in the mountains. Oh, I don't mean that people didn't get married, but when they decided to get hitched, they'd just go on down to the courthouse and get a license and say their vows before the justice of peace. I asked Granny one time, before she started rocking, how come. She said mountain folk didn't have the time or money for such foolishness. That's my granny. There's never no time for fun things in life. Why that woman could steal the fun out of a holiday by complaining 'bout how much work it was. Don't get me wrong. I love her, but sometimes she needs to "shit-can it," as Grandaddy says, and live a little.

That's what I thought Preacher Rainey had done when we got to the church for the wedding, and he weren't no where in sight. I'd told Granddaddy to watch out and not let him get toted off somewheres the night before. I wanted Sadie Jo's wedding to be perfect. I should-a knowed it'd be Grandaddy who'd see that Preacher Rainey was properly shivered.

Here I was all dressed up in the nicest clothes I'd ever owned.

Why even my toe-and-finger nail color matched, a pretty bright pink. I carried the white gloves tucked in the sash of my dress. I'd like to have worn them, but that meant I couldn't show off my nails. And for sure, I wanted everyone to see the gloves.

Sadie's ma had made me a head piece with little red roses and baby's breath. I'd fastened it in my hair with side combs we'd bought at Jaminson's five-and-ten. My dress was a pale pink, overlaid in white lace. And them sandals were white and even had a tiny heel. Here I was a-fixing to stand up there with the bride, but the groom was no where in sight. He might not be nowhere around but the Haint Mountain Baptist Church was packed. Ever person on the Branch must-a turned out to see Sadie Jo get hitched.

I looked around for Granddaddy and didn't see him nowhere. But to my surprise, Granny was setting on the back row, rocking back and forth. I sure wish that if she was gonna rock she'd a-stayed home, but on the other hand, I don't guess it matters much since everybody in these parts knowed she weren't quite right in the head.

Sadie Jo peeked around from the corner where she stood, and I seen tears spilling down her checks. She'd been so worried 'bout the Preacher Rainey seeing her before the wedding, she'd hid behind the post in the back of the church. She said it was bad luck. If that be so, I wondered what kind-a luck she was having now. Didn't look like good luck to me.

The minister that was gonna pronounce them man and wife was a-waiting at the front of the church. The woman at the pump organ started to play "Here Comes the Bride." I didn't see how there could be a bride if there was no groom. Anyway, we started just like everything was as normal as apple pie, me marching right in front of Sadie Jo and not a soul but the minister waiting for us. What in the world was we gonna do? Maybe God was gonna zap a groom out-a plain air. As we reached the altar and turned to face the crowd, Granddaddy and Preacher Rainey walked through the back door and down the aisle just like it'd been planned that way. I knowed without a doubt, that Granddaddy had sump'n to do with these arrangements or lack of. As soon as Sadie Jo was properly married off, I'd have me a good talk with him 'bout his pranks.

Sadie Jo squeezed my shoulder and I knowed she was on her way to being a married woman. I'd miss her when she left, but when I got all growed up maybe I'd go live with her and her minister husband in the big city.

* * *

Sadie Jo climbed in the truck beside her new husband. She knew that life would never be the same after today. That was all right. It was gonna be different but a good different. She'd learn the ways of a minister's wife and she'd be good at it. The only thing, she hated to leave Ollie behind. Ollie needed a woman to tell her the ways of the world. Her granny sure wasn't in no shape to do it. If Birdie wasn't so caught up with the new baby, she'd see that Ollie was properly brought up. Somehow, she'd had the feeling that Ollie had wanted to tell her something the day they'd went shopping but had changed her mind. Well, she'd write and maybe Ollie could come to visit next summer.

* * *

I watched Preacher Rainey's truck disappear around the last bend in the road and swallowed the lump that was stuck in my throat. Sadie Jo was off to a new life and I was left here to fend the best way I could. Oh, Granny was around but not worth much. Granddaddy loved me. I knowed that, but if I tried to tell him all the feelings that was churning around inside me, he'd pat me on the head and say that I thought too much. Well, right now he had some explaining to do and it'd better be good.

I looked around. Granny was no where in sight but Granddaddy was sidling off toward the road leading toward the Yates place. I knowed he was on his way to fill up his jug. I ran after him and caught up 'bout the time he reached the trail heading toward the Yates place.

"Granddaddy, I thought I asked you not to let them men kidnap the groom and here you keep him away from the church till the wedding started and me and poor Sadie Jo didn't know if he was gonna show up."

Granddaddy stood there looking at me like I'd just dropped out-a the sky. Finally, he said, "Ollie, I see that you've got lots to learn before you grow up. Get on home and see to your granny. I got business, horse business that is, to see to."

I knowed right then it'd do no good to ask any more questions. Maybe some day I'd learn why the preacher was late for his own wedding but in the meantime I'd work on growing up, since that was when I was gonna find out all the answers to life.

17

Granny balled up her fist and pounded the dough one more time. She wished it was the face of God. A just God would not make a mother suffer so. Her heart ached so bad she couldn't tell where it hurt in her body. And it was His fault. After all, what was a mother to do?

Lord how she wished she had never gone up the branch that day. If she could just turn back the clock, turn her feet toward town and never look to see what sin was laying in wait for her. Pendergrass's Dry Goods had had some new cotton material, and she'd wanted to make Ollie a new dress for school. It was 'bout time she had something other than those feed-sack dresses. As she'd passed by the trail going up the branch, she just couldn't resist the urge to see what Birdie was up to, what with Ray off on another timber job. So she'd let her feet turn where her heart didn't really want to go.

That's when her troubles started. No, that wasn't quite right. They'd started the day she'd married that lumberman with that full head of red curls and teasing green eyes that invited her into his bed. Words were not one of Grady Sander's strong points, but then when a man like him had so many other things going, why should he worry about words. Men! Damn them all. Husbands, sons or kin, they weren't nothing but a bunch of trouble.

She gave one more healthy punch and grabbed the rolling pin and began to smooth out the biscuit dough. That was a mistake. The white pastry brought back the memory of the sheet that had practically covered their naked bodies, sprawled out right there on the marriage bed. Not theirs, but Birdie's. How could she do such a thing? Even if she was willing to defy her vows, how could one brother take his brother's wife? And right there in his brother's bed, you'd think they'd have the decency to use the hayloft. That's where white trash should be, and as much as she hated to admit it that was all Birdie or Charlie were. Just plain ordinary dirty trash and that boy was from her womb, fruit of her fruit. How could a good God allow such a thing?

Taking a glass from the shelf above the stove, she slammed it into the dough so hard that it shattered in her hand. She watched in horror as tiny drops of blood dripped onto the white surface. That's what she should have done that day, stopped it. She could have with one swift movement. It would have been finished for both of them and her also, but wouldn't that have been better than being caught up in this living hell?

She reached for a dish towel to wipe away the blood and saw Birdie coming toward the back porch. Cuddled to her breast was her sin child. Lord, this was the last person she needed to see today. Gathering up the dough, she dumped it into the slop bucket and made a bee-line for her rocking chair in the other room, but she was too late. Birdie was already standing in the kitchen doorway. "Say what you come to say then get on home. I ain't in a mood to mollycoddle a sinner today."

"Granny, I know you've never cared for me, and I'm truly sorry for the heartache I've caused this family. Fact is, most of the time I wish I'd never been born. But I was, and because of me, you're the grandmother to my young'uns." Birdie held the baby out like she wanted to place it in Granny's arms. "Won't you try to love little

Ruth Ann like you love the others?"

Granny looked at the baby. "That young'un don't know love and never will, besides why should I get attached to her since she's not gonna live. Just be more heartache for me, and Lord knows I've had my share."

"Yes, I guess you have, but that's no reason not to love."

Granny halfway rose from her chair. "I suppose that's the reasoning you used when you slept with Charlie in your husband's bed. Seems to me like you could have used the hay-loft if you were gonna be unfaithful. That's where trash belongs." There! She'd said what had been boiling inside her for months! "Is that why you killed my boy? Thought he'd tell his brother what a slut he was married to."

Birdie hugged the baby to her bosom. "I didn't kill Charlie. I'm only guilty of loving him and that's never brought me nothing but heartache." She looked out the window toward the cemetery. "Truth is though, I'm glad he's dead. If he'd a-lived, there might a-been big problems cause I couldn't walk away from him." She looked back at Granny. "Trouble was, Charlie didn't know how to just love one woman. Even If I'd married him instead of Ray, he would have never been totally mine."

Granny stood up, straight. "You little tramp! What nerve, coming down here with that sin child. Now take it and get outta here and I don't want to see you around here again." She turned and sat in her rocking chair. Wasn't much she could do about anything but rocking helped squash down all the pain. She rocked until Birdie was well out of sight then went back to her biscuit making.

* * *

I'd just finished my shooting lesson from Granddaddy. We'd

been at the shooting for 'bout two months, and if I do say so, I was getting good. Today I was in a hurry to get back to the house and see if I'd got a letter from Sadie Jo. I sure missed having our girl talks. As I come around the corner of the barn, I seen Aunt Birdie headed that way with little Ruth Ann clutched to her breast. Trouble was a brewing. I could feel it in my bones so I hurried up and found me a good hiding place right under the open kitchen window. If my arm had a-been long enough, I'd have patted myself on the back cause I was getting good at this eavesdropping stuff. Thing is, if I'd a-knowed what I was 'bout to learn, I might have just kept on walking right on back out to the barn and a-stayed until I seen Aunt Birdie leave. But as Granddaddy always says, "hindsight is always better than foresight," so I set myself up to get a-earful.

First thing I learned was that Aunt Birdie felt like she'd always been a bother to my granny. Maybe that was why she looked so worried when she was around her. The second thing was that Granny believed that Ruth Ann was gonna die. That's what the granny woman on the mountain also thought. The third thing was that Aunt Birdie and my uncle Charlie had been lovers and Granny knowed 'bout them. But the worse thing I heared was Aunt Birdie say that she was glad that Uncle Charlie was dead. That nigh on 'bout shocked me to death. She wasn't the kind-a woman that would want nobody to be dead. Sump'n was really wrong here, and I wasn't sure I wanted to know what it was. If being growed-up was so great, why didn't the grown-ups see what was as plain as a lower lip full of snuff.

'Bout the only facts that I can be sure of now is that Uncle Charlie was dead and buried in the Sanders Cemetery and that Aunt Birdie had a baby that ain't as right in the head as she ought-a be and would probably die. Another fact that I'm having to get used to is that there's people right here amongst us that had good reason to want Uncle Charlie dead. And some of them were people that I loved. Before I'd give my map to Granddaddy, I'd 'bout wore it out looking and trying to figure what it meant, but none of it made enough sense to shed any light on his murder. Some days I find myself thinking that the sheriff might just be right 'bout him shooting hisself. Don't make much sense to go off over yonder and get your self blowed all to pieces when you can do it right here at home and have all your loved ones to cry and take on over you. Why if you died over there in another country your kin would plum forget 'bout you time them government people got around to sending you home.

Granddaddy says that when they bring the soldiers home they have a military funeral for them and sometimes they're buried up there near the Capitol in a cemetery just for soldiers.

Now I know one thing for sure and that is that Uncle Charlie wouldn't have wanted to be buried no where away from these here mountains. He loved his mountains almost as much as his home made whiskey and women.

I stood and looked after Aunt Birdie as a great sadness filled my heart. Could it be that Uncle Charlie's death was going to destroy us all?

* * *

Birdie hadn't meant to go to the cemetery, but she'd been so upset when she left Eula rocking, she needed to calm down before she went home, and the cemetery sounded like the best place to go. When she found herself standing at the head of Charlie's grave, she knelt and rubbed her fingers over the letters on the tombstone. The cold, slick marble gave her the same feeling she'd got back at his mother's. Cold and hard — that was the way Charlie's mother was or always had been toward her. How she wished she could break through that shell. She knelt and straightened the few plastic flowers that lay next to the stone. She'd brought them out in early spring just after Grady had set the stone. "Charlie, since I was here last our daughter was born. I named her Ruth Ann. She's beautiful, but she ain't right in the head. The granny woman on the mountain says she has the mark of death. I guess that's because she stops breathing and turns blue lots. I don't know what to do but keep on loving her. Ray don't say much but sometimes I get the feeling he's glad you're gone. It makes me wonder if he was the one who shot you."

She brushed at her eyes. "Lord how I wish you was here to tell me what to do. Ray wants the doctor to come back out to see Ruth Ann. I'll probably let him before winter. I don't see that there's much he can do but tell us what we already know."

She lowered herself to the ground and lay down, placing the baby between her and the mound of earth. She stretched the other arm over the child and the grave as though she were cradling the two people she loved most to her bosom. Tears bathed the baby's head as Birdie's heart broke in two. She'd do what had to be done to make right the wrong she'd done.

* * *

The sadness I felt after Aunt Birdie left wouldn't let go. That's when it hit me. I needed to go up to the cemetery and say my piece right over Uncle Charlie's grave. It wouldn't help none, but it sure as the world would make me feel better. Seems to me like I'm always a-running in to sump'n that ain't none of my business. That's what happened. I went straight up to the cemetery as soon as I'd thought Aunt Birdie would be home. Well, if home was where she was a-aiming to go, she must-a got lost on her way cause there she was standing by Uncle Charlie's grave, talking. I couldn't get close enough to hear what she was a-saying, but she looked awfull upset. I wanted to run to her and tell her not to cry. That Uncle Charlie wouldn't want us to be sad, but I knowed if she seen me there that'd only make her more upset. Maybe she was like me and just needed to say her piece to him. I'd wait right here in the laural thicket until she'd left then I'd say what I had to say. She didn't stand long till she laid down on the ground and hugged the mound of dirt with Ruth Ann in between them.

It was such a pitiful sight seeing her laying there squalling her eyes out. It made me feel like I'd walked in on sump'n that was mighty private. Sort-a like a man and woman being together. Best thing for me to do was to get on back to the house and wait for another time to say my piece to Uncle Charlie.

* * *

Eula finished the biscuits and shoved them into the oven as Grady walked into the kitchen.

"Nice to see you remembered to fix my supper." Grady slammed the table with his fist."

Little beads of sweat formed on her upper lip, and she wiped with her arm. A tight band of concern closed around her chest. Had she gotten so neglectful of her family that they worried they'd starve to death? She studied his face, looking for signs of teasing, but didn't see any. Maybe now that she'd spilled her guts to Birdie, she wouldn't feel the urge to rock as much. "She was here this afternoon. I got a few things off my chest so maybe I'll feel better."

"Eula, pray-tell you didn't go running your mouth to that girl about sump'n that ain't none of our business."

"I'd say it's our business when what she'd done hurts the whole family."

"Ain't you learned, woman, that sometimes it's better to let sleeping dogs lay?"

"And ain't you learned that sleeping dogs don't always stay asleep. In our case, they're liable to wake up any time."

"Well, until they do, I think it's best to let them rest. Where's Ollie?"

"I thought she was out with you, shooting."

"She was, but I sent her to the house over a-hour ago. I told her to bring me the milk buckets as soon as she filled the wood box for you."

Eula's heart quickened as she took the last stick of wood from the box. Something wasn't right here. Ollie might be a little mischievous but she always done what she was told. Could she have overheard her and Birdie. And if she did, what would it do to her? Would she have understood? She was glad she hadn't had that 'bird and bee' talk with her yet. Soon she'd tell her the ways of man and woman, but she wanted to give her a little bit more time to be a young'un.

"Do you think she overheard me and Birdie?"

"Probably not, but if she knowed the truth we wouldn't be worried about her being hurt. Guess she decided to play hooky from her chores. Bet she's playing in the creek. It won't be long to cold weather."

Eula glanced out the kitchen window. Lord, how she hoped

that young'un hadn't heard. She didn't see how she could go on much longer with life caving in around her. "I guess you're right. Best thing to do is sit Ollie down and tell her who her mother is and have it over with. I have to admit that's one sleeping dog that'd I'd just as soon be dead."

"It ain't gonna go away. Do you want-a tell her or do you want me to."

"Tell me what?"

Eula wheeled at the sound of Ollie's words. "Uh . . . where you been? I'm out-a stove wood."

"I'll get some as soon as I know what I'm supposed to know. Or should I get it while you decide who's gonna tell me?"

Eula slipped her hand in her pocket. "Ain't no use in getting all worked up over good news. We knowed you'd been waiting for a letter from Sadie Jo so we was a-fussing over who was gonna tell you?" She held out a white envelope with Olivia Sanders printed on the outside. "The wood can wait till you've read your letter."

Eula was relieved to see the tell-tale signs of worry being chased away and replaced with a big smile and dimples so deep a grain of corn could hide in them. No, the secrets of life wouldn't be revealed to this child for a while. There'd be plenty of time to tell all later.

* * *

I didn't waste no time getting up to my room to read Sadie's letter. She'd said she'd write but it had been over a month and I hadn't heared a word. I guess that's cause she was busy being a preacher's wife. As I gently loosened the seal, I couldn't help but wonder if being a preacher's wife would be any different than any other wife. Looked to me like being a wife was the same, but what do I know since I'm just a young'un? Maybe after I'm all growed up and know all 'bout the ways of the world, I'll see the difference, but for right now all I have is what I'd seen here on Haint Branch. And believe me, some of the stuff that goes on up here ain't fitting for even the most growed-up. Why one day last summer I found Mr. Clawson and his neighbor's wife out'n the cemetery and they sure wasn't digging no grave or putting flowers on one either. I wanted to tell them this cemetery was only for the Sanders' and they'd have to find another place, but I didn't want them to know what I'd seen so I left them there with the dead and hoped some spirit got them for sinning.

I unfolded the one page letter and began to read.

Dear Ollie,

I'm sorry I didn't write you right away but this preacher wifing sure keeps a-body busy. as soon as we arrived, the church ladies give us a wedding shower. I got lots of nice things. Gadgets that I didn't know existed. Can you believe they make a can opener that all you have to do is twist a little handle and it cuts the top of a tin can? At home if we got anything in a can, Ma'd take the butcher knife and hammer and cut it four ways and dump out the contents. And I got a egg beater. You put the eggs in a glass jar and screw on the top then crank a little handle and your egg whites fluff up the best you ever saw. No more beating them with a fork.

I'm excited for you to see all the stuff when you come for a visit. Why we even got one of them new fangled camera's. If I get up for Christmas, I'm gonna bring your granny and my ma one of them egg beaters.

Now for the serious stuff, Ollie, young'un, I wish I'd told you more about the ways of life and all the worldly stuff. When you do visit, we'll talk. Promise me that right now you won't let the boys fool around with you. You're such a pretty young girl I'm sure they'll want-a try stuff, but don't let them. Save yourself for the right man. If I'd a knowed what I do now, I would have. Preacher Rainey says he knows first hand that the Lord forgives, but that don't keep me from remembering all the worldly stuff I done.

That's enough of my preaching. Tell your grandparents I said hello. Hope your granny ain't rocking as much. We'll pray for her. And hope to see you at Christmas. Will write when I have some time, but write me and let me know how you're doing.

Love, your aunt, Sadie Jo Rainey.

I folded my letter and slid it back in the envelope. Sadie Jo Rainey. That name sounded so good, and it looked like she was a-liking married life. I could hardly wait to see her and hear all 'bout the wifing business, and I'd cherish this letter cause it was the first real one I'd ever got.

18

For the most part, I'd managed to forget 'bout the night at the carnival. Sometimes the dreams still come but I was able to manage. The one I hated most was the one where the legs tried to wrap around my neck and strangle me. I'd wake up in a sweat, and it'd take hours to get back to sleep.

It was hard for me to keep my mind on my school work, not because of the dreams, but because I was either thinking 'bout that poor little cousin of mine or missing Sadie Jo. I was in my missing Sadie Jo mood when the teacher said. "Olivia, tell the class about your special person."

I squirmed around in my seat for a few minutes. How was I gonna chose between Granddaddy and Sadie Jo? I stood and said, "I have two. You all know my Granddaddy, Grady Sanders. He lives here and has helped raise me. But my favorite person that's not real family is Sadie Jo Miller. I was in her wedding this fall. She married Preacher Rainey and moved to the big city to be a preacher's wife."

"And what makes her such a good friend?"

"Cause she listens and thinks of me as family."

"You may sit down, Olivia. You see, class, family can be more than the people who live in your house."

Now I wished I'd been listening to the lesson instead of having my mind on sump'n else, but it looked like I'd give the right answer. I looked down at my book and seen we was studying 'bout families in our health class. As I thumbed through the pages, I seen we were gonna learn all 'bout the human body. I remembered the little talk me and Sadie had earlier. Maybe I could write and ask her some questions so I wouldn't be so dumb when we got to that section. It sure looked like Granny was never gonna be in a-asking mood any time soon.

She wasn't even in a listening mood the next night when my belly started to cramp really bad. I laid in bed and pulled my legs up to my chest trying to make it stop but that didn't help much. Finally, I dozed off to sleep and woke some time in the middle of the night and my sheet felt all wet and sticky. Now, I done it, wet the bed. I hadn't had that sort of accident since I was four years old. I lit the lamp and started to pull my night gown over my head when I seen there was blood ever where. It was even streaming down my legs. Not like the little bit at the carnival, but real blood ever where. Was I bleeding to death? I pulled off the pillow case and folded it and placed it between my legs, then crawled back into bed on the dry side. Sleep didn't come because all sorts of fears kept me awake. Could it be I had some sort of bad disease? Maybe God was punishing me for eavesdropping so much, or I'd hurt myself somehow.

Then I remembered the health book. I turned back the covers and holding my pad in place; I got the book and settled in bed.

Right there toward the back, I found the answer. It told all 'bout how a girl's body changed from being a young'un to a woman. I can't say I liked what it had to say, but I'd been waiting for this growed-up thing and it looked to me like it was finally happening. Lord, how I wish Sadie Jo was here to talk too.

The next morning when I got up I told Granny what had happened. She stopped her rocking long enough to go out'n her bedroom and come back with a stack of rags.

"Here. Use these. There's two big safety pins right on top. Pin them to your underpants and when they're soiled change and wash them out and hang them up to dry." She went straight back to her chair and begin to rock. I wanted to ask all sorts of question. Like how come it hurt so bad. The book called it menstrual cramps but it didn't say nothing 'bout so much pain. And how was I gonna go to school with this bunch of rags between my legs? I was sure glad it was Saturday and I didn't have school. What if it got on my clothes and the other young'uns saw it? Why in the world did I ever want-a grow up. I went back to my room and pulled out my tablet of writing paper.

    Dear Sadie Jo,
    Granny gave me your letter. I was so happy to hear from you. I'm glad you like married life. I can't wait to see all your new stuff. I got sump'n new but it ain't no fun. I got these awful cramps in my belly and woke up with blood all over. Granny gave me some rags to ware pinned to my drawers. I read what this is all 'bout but I wish you were here to talk to. Granny ain't one to talk 'bout such stuff. In fact, even before she started rocking she was always telling me not to ask so many growed-up questions. Now that I'm 'bout growed-up I wonder what she'll say. There's lots of stuff that she could tell me if she'd just stop that darn rocking and be the old granny that took care of me when I was a little young'un. I've always been able to talk to Granddaddy 'bout anything, but this just seems too private. You know, woman stuff. I'd go up and talk to Aunt Birdie but she is so sad these days. I found her in the cemetery the other day crying over Uncle Charlie's grave.
    You don't have to worry 'bout me and no boys. I've seen and heared enough to know they spell trouble. I'm gonna grow up and move away from here, find my own way in the world.
    I'll be looking forward to your visit at Christmas, and

maybe when school is out, I can come down to Atlanta for a spell.

Your loving niece, Oliva Sanders

I folded the letter and put it in a envelope then slipped out to the front room and took one of Granddaddy's stamps. I'd put it in the mail box on my way to school Monday, that is if my belly quit hurting so bad.

* * *

Eula knew that Ollie didn't know she'd heard her come into the front room, and she even knew without looking what she was after. That was all right. Let her write to that Miller woman; the woman that had helped put her son in the cemetery. They'd all have a day of reckoning and hopefully she'd live to see it.

She wished she'd talked more to Ollie about becoming a woman, but somehow the desire to be the woman Ollie needed in her life had died along with every thing else. Maybe someday before Ollie married there'd be a time when they'd have a good heart-to-heart talk about being the right kind of woman. She hoped so because she'd hate for her to be the sort of woman her mother was.

She set her lips in a straight line and pushed the floor hard with her feet. There! The sound of the chair drowned out the beat of her heart and squished down all the pain. Hopefully tomorrow would be a better day.

* * *

Tomorrow wasn't a better day. It was a day filled with regrets. It all started when Eula decided to go up to the cemetery. She'd fixed breakfast for Grady and Ollie and left it on the stove before she headed out. She wished there were some flowers to take but it had already frosted and killed every thing. She took along a rake to clean off the fallen leaves.

When she arrived, there Birdie was, bent over Charlie's grave like she was his widow or something, and she had that sin child of hern clutched to her chest. This weren't right, and she was gonna put a stop to it right now. She walked right up to where she was and grabbed her by the shoulder.

"What are you doing out here? Don't you have a husband who needs you? Take that sin child of yourn and get off my property."

"I ain't hurting nobody, am I? Ray won't talk to me when he's home. Mad cause I don't want the doctor to come back out and take a look at Ruth Ann. I told him it's a waste of money. There's nothing he can do to fix her. Charlie always listened to me. I thought if I come up here and unburdened my soul maybe I'd be able to find some answers. You can't deny me that, can you?"

"You've made your bed now sleep in it. That's all I've got to say, now get!"

She stood there and watched Birdie trudge back down the hill. How she hated her for what she'd done to the Sanders family. Why couldn't it be Birdie who was laying here under the cold sod instead of Charlie? As Birdie faded from sight, she turned and tended the graves of her loved ones as though she were serving them a meal in her kitchen. That was all she could do to make right the wrong that had happened.

* * *

I knowed there was sump'n wrong the minute I woke up and didn't hear Granny's rocker. Thank God my belly wasn't hurting as bad so I crawled out-a bed and went hunting her. The kitchen was empty but breakfast was setting on the warming shelf of the stove. I called but she didn't answer. Where would she take off to this early? It was Sunday but it was too soon for church and besides she didn't go much anymore. When I was a little young'un, she'd scrub me good and clean in the tin wash-tub behind the cook stove so we could go to church on Sunday morning. She sure didn't leave any dirt for the preacher to clean up. A while before Uncle Charlie's death she'd quit. "Cold turkey," as Granddaddy would say. Never give the first reason. That suited me fine. I'd learned more 'bout God from Granddaddy than I'd ever learned in church.

I went to the back door and looked out. Through the heavy mist I seen her heading up the mountain with a rake over her shoulder. Right away I knowed she was heading for the cemetery. Guess I'd tag along and see what she was up to. Maybe if she got busy working up there, I could talk to her 'bout this woman thing that had happened to me.

Well, was I ever wrong cause when I got in sight of the graveyard there she was giving Aunt Birdie what-for. I wanted to rush over and protect Aunt Birdie and the baby, but I knowed it'd only make things worse so I just stood there and watched Granny send her toting back down the hill then go to work on the graves like she was digging up the dead. Let her dig all she wanted, I'd go with Aunt Birdie and maybe she'd feel like talking.

I followed her to the fork in the trail. Instead of taking the one heading toward her house she headed on down the path that passed the pond where we went swimming. The only time anybody ever went down there was when they wanted a good swim, surely she wasn't gonna go in that cold water this time of year. I had to run to keep her in sight. I thought 'bout yelling out, but I didn't want her to tell me to go home until I seen what she was up to.

As I come around the bend in the trail, I seen her all bent over the hand rail on the foot log that crossed over the stream that fed the pond. What was she doing? Then it hit me that she might be thinking of dropping Ruth Ann in the water. I froze in my tracks at the thought of such a thing. No, my aunt wasn't capable of such a act. Maybe she was looking at sump'n like a big fish. Granddaddy said there was big cat fish living in it, but he'd rather fish in the creek for the brown trout. I yelled and she straightened up.

"Ollie, what are you doing up here so early?"

I managed to get my legs going again and walked toward her. "I seen Granny take off toward the cemetery this morning and since she don't get out-a her rocking chair much, I was worried."

Birdie moved toward the other end of the foot-log. "I don't think you gotta worry about that old woman. She's got more zip in her old bones than all of us put together."

"Aunt Birdie, Why don't you and Granny like each other?"

As I joined her on the other side, she took my hand. "Honey, it's not a matter of liking or disliking. We just see life different, I guess."

I thought 'bout what she'd said for a few minutes. I sort of understood. Granny was all business. You could tell that by the way she went 'bout doing her work, like she was out to kill a snake. I don't think she's ever enjoyed life like Granddaddy has. Could be she needed a little nip from his jug once in a while.

"I understand. Like Friday night I woke up in the middle of the night with a awful belly ache. There was blood all over. I was really worried until I found the answer in my health book. Saturday morning when I told her all she done was give me a bunch of rags to pin to my drawers. There was so much I wanted to ask her but she just went back to her rocking."

Aunt Birdie squatted right down beside me and pulled me close with her free arm. "You poor child, course you need someone to talk to. Come on home with me, and we'll bake cookies and have us some girl talk."

She stood and took my hand again. "Aunt Birdie, what was you looking at in the water?"

There was a long silence, and I'd begin to think she hadn't heared me. Finally she said, "The future."

"You mean like next summer when we'll be swimming again?"

"Something like that. Now let's hurry and get them cookies to baking."

As we headed toward her house, I didn't need water to see the future. My nose could already smell the peanut butter cookies that would be baking in Aunt Birdie's oven. And that girl talk, the questions were fighting in my head as to which one would be asked first.

* * *

Now you have to understand, cookie baking to Aunt Birdie is a real science, not like Granny's. Granny just throws a bunch of stuff in a bowl and mixes it up. First, Aunt Birdie sets all the ingredients on the table and then she gets her mixing bowl and measuring spoons out. She follows the recipe to a tee and as soon as she's put in sump'n she puts the container away. One time I asked her why she did it that way and she said that was so if she lost her place in the recipe she'd know she'd already used it. I guess with young'uns running around it'd be easy to lose your train of thought. Why sometimes

Granddaddy will come in the house and stand and look a-bout like he's lost his head or sump'n. When you ask him what's wrong he'll say, "I come after a coal of fire and forgot where we keep it." I laugh and point to the cook-stove cause Granny always has a fire in it, even in the dead-heat of summer.

That's why today had throwed me into a tether. Nothing a-bout the whole day was even close to normal. Granny wasn't rocking like she did most of the time. Granddaddy hadn't come home from the logging camp like he usually does. Aunt Birdie was acting like Granddaddy did when he'd lost his head. She put the baby in the crib and stood looking like she was confused 'bout what to do next. When I asked her if we were gonna start the cookies, she looked at me like she'd forgot I'd come home with her. Finally, she said, "Cookies, of course. You get out the stuff."

That shocked me cause she always did it all. She said I was her tester. That ever cookie baker had to have someone to tell if the dough was right. Well, it looked like that was gonna change also. Why'd things have to keep changing? Looked to me like they should stay the same long enough for a-body to get use to them.

I'd just greased the cookie sheet when Aunt Birdie come in carrying a blue box in one hand and what looked like a long piece of elastic in the other. She handed me the box.

"You'll find some store-bought sanitary napkins in there. Use them when you go to school but wear the rags at home. The napkins are expensive so I only use them when I'm going somewhere." Then she held up the elastic. "This is a belt to hold them in place."

After she showed me how the belt worked, we started the cookies and talked. First, we talked a-bout what I'd learned in my health book then 'bout my feelings. Feelings ain't sump'n that's easy to talk 'bout. I asked her what love between a man and woman meant. She gave me the same look that I'd got all my life and started to say sump'n 'bout when I growed up, but then stopped and looked me square in the face.

"Love is a drawing-together between a man and woman, a special feeling that God gives them so they're attracted to each other. I guess that's so He can keep the earth full of people."

I studied on what she'd said for a few minutes. It seemed to make good sense to me. I guess God had already give Will Ramey at school that special feeling toward me cause he was always pestering me. But so far God hadn't give me the same kind-a feeling, and I hoped He'd forgot because I sure wasn't ready to be that growed-up yet.

"I sort-a know what you mean, but how 'bout love in general. Like what I have for my family?"

Aunt Birdie laid down her spoon and smiled at me. "Ollie, young'un, you're sure full of questions. The way I see love it's like our swimming hole. When the pond gets too low for it to drain, the water gets all stale and mucky looking. When we don't love that's what happens to us. If we stay like that spring out there, where we get our water, flowing and always a giving, our love will grow stronger and the farther it reaches out the stronger and clearer it becomes."

Aunt Birdie opened the oven door and put the cookies in to bake then picked up a stick of wood to feed the stove fire.

"Do you think that my mother loved me and that's why she give me away?" I listened as she shook down the ashes from the fire box and it sounded like she was real mad at the stove.

"Ollie, I think your mama done what she had to. Sometimes

love ain't got nothing to do with some choices."

"I don't know much bout choices yet, but I guess with all this growing up business, I'll have to learn."

Aunt Birdie turned toward me and tears were streaming down her face. I hadn't meant to make her cry. It looked to me like she had enough to make her sad without having to worry with me. I'd get on home and see if I could find out some more of this growed-up stuff from Granny or maybe Granddaddy.

19

By Christmas Birdie knew if Ruth Ann didn't die before spring, she'd have to make some kind-a decision. She couldn't go on this way much longer. She'd take out the envelope the granny woman had given her and look at it but she didn't have the nerve to look inside. Looking would give her the knowledge to take her own child's life, and she wasn't ready for that sort of learning yet. She'd look at the sleeping child and think about how easy it would be to hold a pillow over her face until she'd stopped breathing. No. That would be too hard. Oh, the neighbors would think it was a natural death, but she knew she wouldn't be able to finish what she started. She could not help her breathe when she turned all blue, but that seemed so heartless. When the time come, it would have to be something that she could carry through with.

"Looks to me like you're gonna be feeding that young'un as long as you live." Ray moved toward the chair where Birdie was nursing Ruth Ann. "Sometimes I wonder just how God does punish people. Don't seem fair that He'd do it through an infant. Look at her, perfect to the eye but all messed up on the inside."

Birdie ran her hand gently over the baby's head. "The way I see it, God ain't in the trouble giving business. People make their own troubles."

"So you're saying we made our baby the way she is?"

Birdie began to rock. "I guess I'm responsible, she growed inside my body. Ma told me I'd mark her cause of finding Charlie dead and seeing all that blood. And that awful smell, it still makes me sick at my stomach"

"Guess it depends on how much stock a person puts in old wives tales. I'd say there's nothing to them. I'll bring the doctor out to have a look at her or we can take her into him."

"I've already told you there ain't no doctor that's gonna fix Ruth Ann, but you might want-a see if you can find some help for your ma. Ollie worries about her. I told her not to. I wanted to tell her that Eula was too ornery to have much wrong with her."

"I don't think there's anything wrong with my ma. All that rocking is just her way of coping with all the bad things that have happened."

"You could be right, but Ollie is growing up and she needs a woman to talk to and Eula ain't doing it. She was here the other day, and we had a good long talk."

"What did you talk about?"

"Women stuff, you know how a young girl's body changes, boys, and such. Mostly she wanted to talk about feelings."

"Feelings! Why in the world would a young'un like Ollie want-a talk about such a thing?"

"Yes, feelings. I don't find that strange at all. I remember having all these strange emotions when I was growing up and having no one to talk to."

"You had a ma. Didn't she talk to you?"

"No, she just told me she had her problems, and I'd have to work things out for myself."

"Your folks was always a strange lot."

"They ain't no stranger than your family, and talking about family, did you realize that Christmas is only a few days away. I'd like a tree for the boys."

Ray shoved his hands into the pockets of his overalls. "I'll fetch a tree but I can't bring the spirit of Christmas with it." And he was gone leaving behind a feeling of defeat.

Birdie rose and watched him trudge off up the mountain. He was so right. This would be a Christmas without any spirit.

* * *

If we'd a knowed this would be the last Christmas we'd all be together maybe it would've been different. Granny wasn't in no mood to do baking and what's Christmas with out her gingerbread. Granddaddy moaned and groaned when I asked him to fetch a tree but he did it anyway. Said he was only doing it because of me.

I remembered how last Christmas I'd had to go looking for Granny and found her threatening the sheriff cause he hadn't found Uncle Charlie's murderer. I knowed right then and there he wasn't too interested in finding who killed Uncle Charlie. Since I'd give Granddaddy my map I'd not bothered trying to find out anymore — or, I could say since I'd found out that the murderer could be someone right in my own family, I'd stopped trying. I wouldn't want to have to watch that sheriff lock up my kin folk. He'd get the last laugh and I wouldn't like that no more than my granny would. So as Granddaddy says, it's best to let sleeping dogs lie.

Anyway, the biggest job at hand right now was getting the tree up, and Granny in some sort of Christmas spirit if that was possible.

Halfway up the ladder to fetch down the Christmas tree decorations from the attic, I remembered that I hadn't seen Granny all morning, hadn't even heared that darn rocking chair and that seemed good. What could she be up to? Surely she wouldn't go back into town and attack that sheriff again. Maybe I'd best go see if I could find her. No sense putting up a tree with a missing granny.

I found Granddaddy out'n the barn and as I opened the door he slid something under old Bess's saddle and stepped in front of it. Acted like nothing was going on, but I knowed different so I didn't say nothing. Let him play Santa Claus for as long as he wanted. I asked, "You seen Granny around this morning?"

He shuffled his feet and pointed out the barn door. "I seen her headed up the mountain bright and early. Had a bunch of pine limbs in her arms. Guess she's gonna try and make the dead feel like Christmas."

"Knowing Granny, she can do it. Never seen nothing like it. If she set her mind to it, she probably could make the dead get up and walk."

"You're right, Ollie. If she'd just leave that darn rocking chair alone, she'd be in good shape."

"Hey, what if we hid it while she's gone?"

Granddaddy scratched his head. "Don't think I've not thought about burning the darn thing, but knowing her, she'd make me build her another one, and I don't have time for that."

"You're right, she would, so I guess we'd best let her keep the one she's got. The rockers are wore a good bit on it and maybe when they're all wore out she'll have to quit. I'll get on up to the cemetery and check on her."

"You're a good young'un, Ollie, even if you were found under a cabbage leaf."

"Oh, Granddaddy, you're gonna have to find a better tale to tell me cause I've out-grown that one."

"Guess you have young'un. Now, get on and see 'bout your granny."

I trudged up the cemetery hill thinking 'bout the kind-a life I'd been dealt. What kind-a mother would leave their baby in a suitcase on a stranger's front porch? Or was it a stranger's porch? That thought jolted me almost plumb out-a my tracks. Why hadn't I thought this through before? Of course, my mother would leave me with folks she knowed. And if that was so, she would have to be somebody from around here? Suddenly, my heart felt lighter and my feet moved faster.

When I reached the cemetery, there was Granny all bent over her babies' graves, covering them with pine boughs like she was trying to keep them warm. Almost made me want-a cry, but I swallowed the lump that was crowding up in my throat and slipped closer. I hunkered down right close to where she was working and watched. I was so close that I could see her shoulders shaking, and when she wheeled around to get more branches, I seen tears running down her cheeks. When she turned to go to Uncle Charlie's grave, she seen me all crunched down in the bushes right near his grave. She just stood there a few minutes and stared at me. Finally, she said, "Young'un, what-a you think you're doing up here so early in the morning? Don't you have your Saturday chores to do?"

I straightened up and went closer. "I come to see if you was all right. Remember last Christmas when I had to go to town and rescue you from that sheriff man. Lord knows what would-a happened if I hadn't a showed up. Don't see too much up here that you could get into but a-body never knows. And you don't have to worry 'bout my chores, I'll get them done. I've got all day."

Granny wiped her face with the back of her hand. "If you're trying to tell me you don't have enough to do, I'm sure me or your granddaddy can find some more."

I picked up one of the branches and laid it on Uncle Charlie's grave. "I don't need no more work. It'll take me most of the day to get that tree Granddaddy brought home decorated. You gonna help me?"

"Don't know. Will have to wait and see how I feel when I finish here?"

I cleaned up some of the trash close to the babies graves and dumped it in the bushes and when I come back Granny was kneeling between them. "Granny, would you like to talk 'bout your dead young'uns?"

She wiped at her eyes again and smiled at me. "Honey, I could talk all day about them but it won't bring them back to my arms so I don't see no use in wasting words."

I understood what she meant. It was kind-a like Aunt Birdie's baby. Wasn't no words gonna fix her either and from the looks of things we'd all be better off if she was resting up here in the cemetery. I watched Granny work for a little while then decided I'd ask her 'bout my mama again.

"Granny, would you have left your babies on just anyone's door step."

"Course I wouldn't have ever left them anywhere. What made you ask such a question?"

"Well, on the way up here I got to thinking 'bout being left on your and Granddaddy's porch. The way I see it, my mama wouldn't just have left me anywhere. No, I think my mama would-a only left me with people she knowed."

Granny whirled toward Uncle Charlie's grave but not before I seen how her face got all stony looking. Wasn't she pleased that I'd come up with some sort of clue as to where my mother might have lived? "Don't you think I'm right, Granny?"

"I think you think too much. A young'un your age don't need to be worrying about such things. Now, help me finish here and let's get on to the house."

We worked in silence. From the look on Granny's face, I knowed there was no use saying anymore 'bout my mother. That was all right. The next time I went up to Aunt Birdie's I'd talk to her 'bout my hunch.

*　*　*

Christmas morning brought little joy to our house. Granddaddy woke up with a bad belly ache. That wasn't like him. I don't remember a time that he was ever sick. Granny had started her rocking at the break of dawn and it looked like it was gonna go on all day. I hurried up and started breakfast. Maybe if Granddaddy had sump'n to eat he'd feel better then I'd give them the presents I'd made.

I carried a plate of soft scrambled eggs and bacon to Granddaddy cause he said he didn't feel like getting up. He tried eating but I could see he wasn't hungry at all. When I tried to get Granny to eat, she just scolded at me so I ate and washed up the dishes. I'd go on up to Uncle Ray's and see what kind-a Christmas they was having. Maybe I could bring back a little Christmas cheer.

Well, if I thought the Christmas spirit was dead at our house, it was buried at theirs. Breakfast still sat on the table and it looked like it hadn't been touched. The boys were nowhere in sight, and I could hear Aunt Birdie rocking in the front room. I'd heared enough of that at home. She looked up when I come in, and I could see she'd been crying and Ruth Ann was asleep in her arms.

"Where's Uncle Ray and the boys?"

"He took the boys over to my parents. I wanted to go but Ruth Ann feels a little warm. Sure hope she's not getting a cold."

I touched the baby's head. She did feel warmer than usual. "Could be sump'n going around. Granddaddy is in bed with a bellyache and he ain't never sick."

"How's your granny?"

"Rocking as always so I thought I come on up here and see if I could find the Christmas spirit. And I brought you'ns some homemade gifts. I'll leave them right over here under the tree and you can open them later."

"Thanks, Ollie, and there's a package there with your name, take it."

I picked up the brown paper poke with my name on it. "You didn't have to, Aunt Birdie."

"I know I didn't, but Christmas ain't about having to it's about wanting to."

"Thanks, Aunt Birdie. There's sump'n I want-a ask you. Sump'n I just though 'bout the other day, but when I asked Granny she clammed up like she always does."

"Child, you know you can always talk to me."

"Well, Granddaddy told me how he found me in a suitcase on their front porch and how Granny took to me right away and wouldn't let the law take me away. I've been wondering ever since and it hit me the other day that my mama must-a been from these here parts cause I don't think a mother would leave her baby with just anyone. What do you think?"

For a moment, I felt like all the air was being sucked from the room. Was I gonna get the same sort-a treatment as I got from Granny? Slowly, Aunt Birdie got up from her chair and placed Ruth Ann in her bed then come over and touched me on the cheek. "Oh, Olivia, you're so smart, but there's some things that's best left alone, and I think this is one of them things."

She was acting like all the other grown-ups now. And I thought me and her was friends. Seemed like there was this line between young'uns and grown-ups and it was looking like I'd never be able to step over it.

"I thought I was getting growed-up enough to not be treated like a little young'un."

"You are growing up, Ollie, and that's why it's so important that you think about living your life so you won't have to make the same kind-a choices that your mother had to make."

"But maybe if I knowed who she was, she could help me not make the wrong choices."

Aunt Birdie's face clouded as though she was thinking sump'n she'd rather not think 'bout. Lord knowed she had enough to worry her to death. I shouldn't a-brought up my problems it being Christmas and all. I'd just get on home and see if I couldn't stir up a bit of cheer on my own. I turned toward the door with my package tucked under my arm.

"Ollie."

I stopped and turned. Aunt Birdie's face had went all soft and sweet looking.

"Yes."

"I can't imagine your mother not loving you. Remember she

loved you enough to make sure you was took good care of and that's the best gift a mother can give her baby."

I didn't answer. Wasn't nothing else to say, but some day I was gonna find my mother.

* * *

By the time I got back home, Granddaddy's bellyache was lots better and Granny had parked her rocker and decided to fix us a Christmas meal. There still weren't no gifts under the tree and that was hard to understand. Ever since I was a little young'un there'd been presents under the tree. Maybe not anything store bought but something that was made especially for me and that made it all the more special. Could be they'd thought I'd got too growed-up for Christmas. I'd never figure this growning-up business out. Looked to me like you were too little or too old depending on the situation. If it was sump'n your elders didn't want-a talk 'bout you were to young, but if it was sump'n they wanted you to do or to tell them then you were all growed-up. Talk 'bout double standards.

While I was busy feeling sorry for myself, Granddaddy sneaked in the kitchen door looking like the cat that had swallowed the last mouse on Haint Branch. He didn't say a word, just sat down at his usual place. I scooted in on the bench behind the table but never took my eyes off him cause he was acting awful strange.

Granny put a pot of pinto beans and a cake of cornbread on the table then went back to the stove and brought us a heaping pot of fresh turnip greens. Wasn't nothing in the world I loved better than fresh greens. Thank the Lord it hadn't been cold enough to freeze them.

I filled my plate. As I was getting ready to dig in, Granddaddy slipped his hand toward my plate and then lifted it, revealing a small package wrapped in newspaper.

A present! I wasn't forgotten after all. I picked it up and said, "Can I open it now?"

Granddaddy smiled. "Guess you can. After all, it is Christmas."

When I ripped away the wrapping and opened the box, there before my eyes was the smallest gun I'd ever seen, its pearl handles glistening in the fading sunlight. "For me?"

Granddaddy lowered his eyebrows like he does when he's getting real serious or mad. "It's for you to learn how to use. And someday when you're grown, it will be yours."

There went that growed-up business again. I just didn't know how much more of this non-sense I could take. Surely one of these days I'd step over that line into the growed-up world. If wearing the rag didn't take you there, what in the world did it take? There must still be some sort of secret that I didn't know 'bout but I could tell from the look on Granddaddy's face that right now wasn't the time for questions.

Granddaddy reached for the greens. "When we've finished dinner, we'll go out to the barn and do some practicing. There's lots of difference in shooting this than my rifle or shot gun. That there is used to protect yourself with, and the others are hunting guns."

"It must-a cost lots of money."

"Cost ain't got nothing to do with keeping my little girl safe. You'll find there's lots of people out there in this big old world that ain't one bit interested in your well-being."

Right then I knowed there weren't nothing in this here world that Granddaddy wouldn't do to keep me safe, and that sure did make me feel special. What better Christmas gift could I get than that sort-a feeling?

20

Birdie stood at the edge of the swimming hole and studied the pool of dark water. She was so lost in her own world that she didn't notice Ollie standing at the edge of the trail. Maybe if she had she wouldn't have had the time to make her plans.

All she could think about was just slipping under the surface and never coming up. Then it struck her. That was the answer! Why hadn't she thought of it before? She knew she'd never be able to take her child's life alone, but her own would be so easy. Ray was a good father, and he'd see that the other children were raised. She slipped her hand into her pocket and pulled out the tiny package the granny woman had put there last fall. There'd been many a night this past year that she'd been tempted to use whatever was in there to help Ruth Ann from this world, but she'd always put it away. She couldn't bring herself to do what she knew Granny Zeta wanted her to. It wasn't that she didn't want to help her little girl be free from her bondage, but she didn't want to do something that might cause her pain. She opened the envelope and dropped the contents into the water and watched them sink beneath the still surface. As the little ripples spread across the pond, she knew what she had to do. This place would become her and Ruth Ann's final resting place. She'd bring her out here and jump. They'd sink to the bottom and it would all be over. She'd die with her love child in her arms.

* * *

It was a long winter. Granddaddy was puny most of the time and Granny's rocking seemed to get worse. Uncle Ray was gone most of the time. Aunt Birdie looked like she was lost in some sort of fog. I really got worried the day I found her out at the pond staring into that dark pool of water. She was just standing there looking into it. I wanted to go up and talk to her, but she didn't look in no talking mood, so I went on home.

I tried to talk to Granny 'bout her but she only lowered her eyebrows and rocked harder. When I asked Granddaddy if there was sump'n we could do to help Aunt Birdie, he said she'd be all right that it was just the winter blues that had her down. Well, I'm here to tell you if that's the winter blues, I don't ever want them. Who'd a guessed that kind-a blues would bring on the troubles that was 'bout to happen to her. For that matter, troubles weren't only waiting for her but the rest of us also.

Granddaddy's chickens had been disappearing. At first he thought a fox or a chicken weasel was taking them but there wasn't any feathers left behind. He said if it was a wild animal there would be more evidence. He suspected it was a two legged animal. In Granddaddy's book a chicken thief was the worse kind. Said a man that would take another man's chickens would steal 'bout anything so he vowed to take care of the thief. That worried me. Not that he was gonna catch the thief but the look on his face when he said it. To my way of thinking if Granddaddy would kill a chicken thief, it stood to reason that he might have killed Uncle Charlie. And the two people I didn't want to be guilty was Granddaddy and Aunt Birdie.

Anyway, the next night Granddaddy loaded his rifle and waited for the thief to strike. He didn't have to wait long. We were getting ready for bed when the chickens begin to squawk. I never heared such a racket in all my days. Granddaddy grabbed his gun.

I moved between him and the door. "I don't want you to go out there. Please let them have the chickens. We can buy some more."

He pushed me to the side. "Ain't the chickens, young'un, It's the principle."

He left me alone with Granny and that darn squeaking rocker. Granny suddenly stopped her rocking and started toward the door.

"No, Granny, you can't go out there. It's too dangerous."

She stopped and looked at me. "Don't tell me what I can or cannot do. Remember, I'm the granny. Now, I'm going out there and save that old man from hisself. You go on to bed."

* * *

At this moment, I realized that Granny had more sense than me and Granddaddy give her credit for. She knowed human lives were more important than a bunch of old chickens, and I wasn't 'bout to go off to bed and leave them out there. I grabbed my coat and slipped out the back door in time to see Granddaddy pin a man in overalls against the barn wall with the shot gun shoved under his chin. Granny rushed up and yelled, "Old man, what-a you think you're doing? Let him go. Did you ever stop to think he might be stealing cause he's hungry."

Granddaddy was so shocked at the sight of Granny that he dropped the gun but kept the man against the wall. "Eula, you're supposed to be in there rocking. Where's Ollie?"

"I told her to get on to bed."

"You know that young'un ain't gonna go to bed with us out here. Get yourself back in the house. I'll take care of this thief. When I finish with him, he won't be stealing no more."

"And you won't be working no more. There's laws against murder, and we don't want that sheriff to get the last laugh."

"You hold him there, Granddaddy. I'll be right back with sump'n that'll make him pee his pants."

I heared Granny giving the thief a piece of her mind as I went in the house. When I come back out, I rushed right up to where granddaddy had the man pinned against the henhouse. I took the lid off the can of black pepper and handed it to Granddaddy. Make him take a big snort of this and he'll be happy to leave your chickens alone."

Granddaddy jammed the jar under the man's nose, and he sneezed so loud it blowed the pepper out-a Granddaddy's hand. Granddaddy let go of the chicken thief, and he stumbled off into the night. I ran for the house before I got a blessing-out from Granddaddy.

I'd learned two things tonight, Grandaddy was capable of murder if his stuff was messed with. That little bit of information didn't make me feel too good. But the second one did. Somehow, I felt better knowing that Granny wasn't as crazy as we'd thought.

* * *

As the weeks slipped by, Birdie mulled over the decision she'd made at the pond. The way she saw it, drowning Ruth Ann and herself was her only hope. It was strange to think of hope being in death. If Charlie did take his own life, did he feel the same way as she was feeling right now? There was a lot she wanted to do while she still had time. First she'd write the boys a letter, something they could have when they grew up and of course she'd have to leave one for Ray. The only other person she needed to think about was Ollie. That young'un would need something or someone to help her understand and it sure wasn't Eula Sanders.

"Aunt Birdie, could we talk?"

"Ollie, how long have you been standing there in the door?"

"I've been here long enough to see that you have plenty on your mind, and I have a few things on mine so I reckoned we could have one of our long heart to heart talks."

Birdie dried her hands on her apron and set down at the kitchen table. "I was thinking there are a few things I want to say to you while there's still . . ." A pot on the stove boiled over and Birdie jumped up and slid it off the heat then sat back down. "Now what was I saying?"

"Sump'n 'bout while there's still . . . but you didn't finish."

"Lord only knows what I meant. Don't know half the time anymore if I'm coming or going. Why don't you talk first while I gather my thoughts? I'll fix you a cup of hot chocolate while you talk, how's that?"

"Hot chocolate in the middle of the week? Granny only let's me have it on special occasions."

"Well, our time is special so we'll have some."

Ollie pulled out a chair and sat down. "I want to talk 'bout you. A little while back, remember, I seen you at the pond then we come up here and made cookies and had us a woman talk. Then the other day, I saw you there again. First I thought you was gonna go swimming, but it was mighty cold, and you didn't have on no bathing suit. When I got home, I asked Granny if sump'n was wrong with you, and she only scowled at me and kept on rocking. When I asked Granddaddy, he said you probably had the winter blues. You're gonna be all right, aint you? I don't know what I'd do without you."

Birdie's heart quickened and she looked out the window. This was going to be harder that she ever imagined. "Everything changes, Ollie. Look out there, Spring is already creeping up the mountain. It won't be long till that mountain is in full bloom. Come September, Fall will start sliding down the mountain over there. The leaves will turn, then the winds will come and blow them down, and it will be winter again. See, life is like that, a cycle and it'll never change."

"I'm beginning to understand that growed-up stuff, but sometimes I'd like for time to stand still a little while so I could get caught up with my thinking."

"We'd all like that, Ollie. Feelings like that don't have nothing to do with being grown up. Remember nothing stays the same for long, but you'll always take things with you from one season to the next, and that's what I want to talk to you about."

"Sounds awful growed-up to me, but I promise to try and understand or take what you say with me until I do."

"That's all I'm asking of you. I want you to remember how special you are to me. I hope all our talks and fun times together will help you over the rough spots in your life. I wish I could have done more for you, but sometimes things are just so that there's only so much a person can do."

"Aunt Birdie, don't talk sad like. Our good times ain't over." Ollie sipped her chocolate and tried to look as much like a little young'un as she could. Maybe if she didn't grow up things would stay the same. "Why, we're gonna get us some good swimming in this summer."

The mention of swimming brought thoughts of the pond and what Birdie had planned. She fought back the tears that suddenly gathered in her eyes. Could she follow through with her plans? It didn't seem as easy as it had standing alone there on the foot-log. She patted Ollie's hand and pushed back the rush of emotion that crowded up in her chest. When she trusted herself to speak she said, "Course we will, now finish your chocolate and get on home before your granny gets worried about you."

"Granny don't worry 'bout nothing much as far as I can see. Now, Granddaddy is another story. I think he worries 'bout me growing up. He bought a handgun at Christmas and he's teaching me to shoot it. He said he wanted me to be able to protect myself when I got out'n the big old world."

"That ain't such a bad idea. Most mountain girls know how to shoot. My pa taught me when I was about your age. You be careful though."

"I will. Granddaddy is a good teacher, and I've learned all 'bout gun safety. But I'm worried 'bout him. He's been puny ever since Christmas."

"I'll have Ray get him to the doctor. Now, get going." Birdie watched Ollie start toward home and wished she could wrap her in some sort of cocoon and keep her safe until . . . what? There'd always be some sort of pitfall. That was why this was called life. She picked up a tablet and sat down at the table. She'd write her letters. Then she'd be ready to finish what she had planned.

* * *

Eula knew where Ollie had gone this afternoon. She sure wished she could keep that young'un away from Ray's wife. That woman spelled trouble, always had and always would. If Ollie didn't show up soon, she'd send Grady up to bring her home. And Grady was another trouble, he hadn't went to work in over a month, said he didn't feel good. It probably was too much of that white lightening. She'd preached at him till she was wore out about drinking and it hadn't changed a thing. It looked like her whole life was one big problem.

The back door slammed and Grady come in. "Where's Ollie? It's milking time, and I can't find her nowhere."

"I seen her head toward Ray's earlier. I wish you'd say something to her about spending so much time up there. You know how I feel about that woman. She has always spelled trouble."

"I know how you feel, Eula. You don't have to tell me. But the way I see it, Ollie could be in worse company. Let it go, woman. We're mighty blessed."

"Don't know what you'd know about blessings since you ain't a church going man."

"Church ain't got nothing to do with belief."

"I ain't as crazy as you think I am, old man. Looks to me like if you think we're so blessed, you'd show it more."

Grady pulled up a chair in front of Eula's rocker. "I know I ain't been the best of husbands, but I've really tried. We're getting old and I'd like for our last days to be like the first ones."

Eula studied him for a few minutes. "I guess you do but how about the stuff in between. That's the filling in life and from where I sit our filling ain't been too good. There's that Lakey woman and then all the white lightening you've consumed. It's probably eaten up your insides. Guess I can forgive the drinking, but not the women."

"Woman, Eula, just one."

"How do I know that?"

"Belief, woman, belief in your husband."

The rocker began to creak. Eula's eyebrows shot up and her lips drew in their hard straight line. She'd not listen to any more of this crazy old man's foolishness. Wasn't no way to flavor up the filling in her life. Even if there was, it'd take a whole gallon to even make it the least bit sweet so she'd not even waste the time trying.

21

Words on paper, even though they were from the heart, were just words and Birdie knew that. There wasn't anything that could say what a hug or quick kiss conveyed. She'd made sure the last few days had been filled with lots of kisses and hugs for her family. Even little Ruth Ann needed to know she was doing the best for her. It was with all this in mind, that she'd set about laying the ground work for her departure.

Every night after the young'uns were tucked in, she sat at the kitchen table and labored over the letters she was writing. To Ray she expressed her love for him and for being the kind of husband who provided well for his family. To the boys she reminded them of all the joy they'd brought into her life and charged them to be good boys for their father so they'd grow into young men that would have made her proud. When she started Ollie's letter, more tears than words filled the page. Finally she wrote, "I love you and someday I hope you'll understand just how much."

She folded the letters and put them away. Tomorrow she'd take Ruth Ann in her arms and they'd go to meet Charlie. She crawled in bed and tucked the blanket under her chin. She wanted to slip her arms around Ray one last time but she was afraid she'd change her mind about tomorrow if she did.

The next morning Birdie went about her chores as usual. As soon as the boys were off to school and Ray had left for the logging camp, she laid the letters on the table and took Ruth Ann and set out for the pond. She tried not to think about what she was a-fixing to do.

She'd already thought it through and all that was left was the doing it.

At the foot-log she hesitated and looked about to make sure she was alone, and then ran onto the log, and without hesitating, jumped. As she felt the water close over her, she prayed for forgiveness.

Instantly, the Lord gave her a vision of the little boys who wouldn't have a mother to tuck them in tonight, a husband who'd come home to no dinner. Then a vision of her aging parents, heartbroken, that their only daughter could take her own life. Her foot touched the bottom and she knew she couldn't take anyone's life, not even her own.

She pushed hard and with her free arm worked her way to the surface. The moment she saw sunlight she grabbed a low hanging limb. She knew she'd be all right but Ruth Ann was blue and there was no way she could make her breathe again.

"Birdie, hang on, I'm coming."

She closed her eyes and thanked God, that He'd not only saved her from taking her life, but had sent Grady to help.

Grady reached the pond as Birdie felt her grasp on the limb slipping. He jumped in, and taking the baby from her, swam to the shore and laid her down, then going back, he tucked Birdie under his arm and swam toward shallow water.

He sat her down. "Are you alright?"

She nodded and pointed toward the baby.

"I'll fetch her, but I think it's too late."

Birdie closed her eyes but this time no prayers came. She already knew it was too late for her baby. It had been too late from the time of her birth, but at least now she'd be at peace. She also knew that any peace for her was gone.

Eva McCall

* * *

The swimming hole weren't good for nothing before or after August. That water never got warm even then, so when the word came that Ruth Ann was dead, drowned in the swimming' hole, guess we all knowed what nobody was willing to say.

I remembered how Aunt Birdie had stood looking down into the dark murky water last winter when I found her out there. I figured it was just because she was depressed over having a young'un that was already dead, but now I know she was thinking about how she'd send little Ruth Ann on to be with Uncle Charlie I can't say that anybody on the branch blamed her for what they knowed she'd done so their way of dealing was not talking 'bout it, but Aunt Birdie's way was to cry lots. I'd even found her out'n the cemetery one day last fall and she was talking to the mound of dirt. I wonder now if she was telling Uncle Charlie how she planned on helping Ruth Ann from this life.

I didn't waste no time getting up to Aunt Birdie's. Figured she'd want me there to help out. I dreaded going cause I knowed we'd all miss little Ruth Ann, but right now there weren't no time for thinking 'bout feelings. There was a funeral to see to and somebody would have to deal with that sheriff man. That's when it hit me hard that he might put Aunt Birdie in jail. I couldn't imagine my aunt sitting down there all locked up like some sort of criminal. Then I remembered how Granddaddy had treated the sheriff at Uncle Charlie's wake. That give me a good feeling knowing that Granddaddy would send him packing.

When I got to the house, I found Uncle Ray sitting in the swing out under the big oak tree in their front yard. He was swinging away like he didn't have a care in the world. Surely, he wasn't gonna be like Granny and start that moving all the time when things weren't right. I spoke but he didn't answer so I went on in the house and found Aunt Birdie all crunched up on the bed, bawling her eyes out. When she seen me, she just cried harder so I went on out in the kitchen and stoked up the fire in the stove and started making us some hot chocolate. That's when I seen the letters laying there on the table and one of them had my name on it so I opened it. The paper was all wrinkled up from what looked like somebody crying on it. It was from Aunt Birdie and all she said was that she loved me and hoped that someday I'd understand. Understand what? I'd seen how hard it was being a Mama to little Ruth Ann, and as hard as it was, she was in a better place.

I finished the hot chocolate and took it in to Aunt Birdie. When I offered it to her she just shook her head and kept sobbing, "I couldn't do it. Oh, God, why?"

I sank down on the bed beside her and held her in my arms. "But you did do it. Ruth Ann is in Heaven."

"I know but . . . I . . . was suppose. . . ."

Then it hit me what she was trying to say. She'd meant to kill herself also. That was why there was letters on the table. She'd wanted her family to know she loved them. Why hadn't I seen this coming? If I was getting so growed-up, I should have knowed. And Uncle Ray, he lived with her all the time. Surely he'd seen how bad off she was. I wanted to go right out there and give him a piece of my mind but that'd have to wait. Right now I had to tend to Aunt Birdie. First of all, I'd let her cry all the sad out, then we'd plan to put Ruth Ann away.

Eva McCall

* * *

Putting Ruth Ann away wasn't all that easy. Granddaddy said under the circumstance there was certain stuff that had to be tended to so it'd take a day or two. When they did bring her home, it was in one of them little white store-bought coffins. She looked like a china doll, laying there all dressed up in a little pink dress.

The doctor came and gave Aunt Birdie a shot in the arm to keep her from squalling her eyes out. After that she was as quiet and gentle as a lamb. I wanted to talk to her 'bout what had happened, but she wouldn't talk.

Neighbors came and brought all kinds of food, and the night before we took Ruth Ann to the Sanders Cemetery, they sat up with the body. Looked to me like nobody blamed Aunt Birdie too much for whatever had happened.

The next morning we marched up to the Sanders cemetery, and as we gathered around the open grave, the preacher from the little Haint Mountain Baptist church committed her body to the ground and her soul to God. We didn't even sing. I guess that's because nobody felt a song in their heart. We marched back down the mountain as if to say, 'it's done' and we're all glad.

* * *

I was with Aunt Birdie when Sheriff Carlson come out the next day to do his investigating. He said, "Mrs. Sanders tell me just how your baby wound up in the old swimming hole. We all know she couldn't get there by herself."

That's 'bout the silliest thing I've ever heared. Ruth Ann wasn't a year old and even if she'd been a normal baby, she couldn't have got there by herself.

Aunt Birdie forced back a sob and said, "I just couldn't live with what was wrong with her any longer. I wanted to die. I couldn't leave her behind because there was no body to take care of her." She let out the sob and looked around the room.

I stepped up to her and grasp her hand. "It's alright, Aunt Birdie. I know how Ruth Ann always stopped breathing and turned blue. We all know you didn't hurt her on purpose."

"But I did hurt her. I hurt her by bringing her into the world. The best thing I could do was help her not hurt anymore, so I went out to the pond and ran out on that foot-log that crosses the creek and jumped in with her clutched in my arms. I remember sinking and touching the bottom and then it hit me that I'd never see Ray or the boys again. I pushed real hard and forced myself toward the surface. I never was a good swimmer. I couldn't do much and hold on to Ruth Ann, but I managed somehow to grab onto some of them limbs hanging over the edge of the pond. I seen that Ruth Ann was all blue and not breathing. She done that all the time. Ollie has seen it happen lots."

"She's right, Sheriff. We even took her to see Granny Zeta. She said Ruth Ann had the mark of death."

Aunt Birdie wiped her eyes with the handkerchief that I give her. "When I surfaced, I couldn't help her anymore than keeping her out-a the water."

"Sheriff can't you see my Auth Birdie has suffered enough. Why don't you just go and leave her alone."

He give me one of them looks he'd always gives me. One that was like he was a-wanting sump'n I had. "I can't do that, girl. There's a law against what she done, and I'm here to carry it out."

"You ain't done much 'bout finding Uncle Charlie's killer. Why don't you use your sheriffing to find who killed him and leave Aunt Birdie to raise her boys?"

"I'm here to tell your aunt there'll be an inquest into the baby's death tomorrow at the courthouse. That'll determine if she'll have to go to trial."

He turned and left. Me and Aunt Birdie just set there staring off into space. I think we both knowed that probably tomorrow night she'd be sitting in that sheriff's jail.

* * *

It was just a stroke of luck that Grady had decided to go out and check the pond before his grand-younguns done much swimming. He hadn't planned on saving his daughter-in-law from drowning, but now that he had, he wasn't about to see her rot in Sheriff Carlson's jail, even if he had to resort to blackmailing the sheriff. He had plenty of proof that he'd been involved in the bootlegging up on Black Mountain, but hopefully it wouldn't come to that. If the steps he'd taken worked, she'd be home in time to fix supper for her family. He opened the door to the judge's chambers and slid into a seat next to the wall. A long table with chairs around it sat in the middle of the room. The sheriff led Birdie in, and she sat down by Ray. The rest of the table was filled with stern looking men.

No one spoke but Birdie's soft sobs echoed in the quiet. Grady wished he'd had the doctor to give her something, but maybe crying wasn't so bad. A display of emotion from the plaintiff was a good thing.

A sober-faced coroner took the chair at the head of the table and a woman with a pen and paper sat by him. He spoke. "We're here to decide if the plaintiff, Birdie Lee Sanders, is culpable in the death of her own baby, Ruth Ann Sanders. Mrs. Sanders, I want you to recall the events leading up to Ruth Ann's death as honestly and truthfully as you can. Take a deep breath and relax. We're here just to get the bottom of this, not to harm you."

Birdie grasped Ray's hand and began. "I knowed . . . we all knowed from the day Ruth Ann was born that something was bad wrong with her but none of us wanted to own up to it." She looked Ray in the eye. "My husband was the first to admit it. He wanted to bring Doctor Rodgers back out to check her, but I knowed there was no use."

Birdie's voice grew week and Grady was afraid she wasn't gonna be able to say much more.

The coroner turned toward the woman who was taking notes. "Would you get Mrs. Sanders a glass of water?" Then he turned back to Birdie. "Why didn't you want to seek help for your daughter?"

"I did try and get help for her. There's a old woman, Granny Zeta, who lives up on Black Mountain, People say she can cure about anything so I took Ruth Ann up there. She said my baby had the mark of death."

"Did she give you any medicine for the child?"

The woman returned with a glass of water and Birdie took a long sip. When she'd finished, she set down the glass and in a low voice said, "She give me something to help her from her bondage, but I couldn't use it."

"But you could drown her in the pond out on Haint Branch?"

"Drowning her wasn't my plan, Sir."

The group of men stirred uneasily. Birdie continued. "Drowning us was my plan, but I couldn't go through with it. The minute I went under that water I knowed I couldn't kill nothing."

"But your baby is dead and buried, Mrs. Sanders."

"She died every day, sir. Any one can tell you how she'd turn blue and stop breathing. It was me who kept her alive, day after day."

"If you wanted her dead, why didn't you just not help her? No one would have ever known."

"Could you just let your baby die, Sir?"

The room was so quiet that Grady thought all the air had been sucked out, and they were never going to breath again.

Finally, a low moan came from the coroner, and he muttered, "No, I guess I couldn't."

Grady knew now was the time to step forward. He stood and went to the table. "Sir, I'd like to present a witness. Is that all right?"

"Sure, anyone that might help us to understand what took place."

The door opened and Doc Rodgers stepped in and sat down next to Birdie.

Grady faced the group. "As you all know, this is Doctor Rodgers. When I pulled Birdie and the baby from the pond, I knew there'd be questions asked about how Ruth Ann died so I had the doc find out just what happened."

The doctor looked at Birdie. "Your baby didn't die from drowning. I'd say she was dead before you hit the water."

"And how do you know that?" asked the coroner.

"If she'd died from drowning, there would have been water in her lungs. There wasn't a drop in them."

Grady's eyes met the astonished look on the group's face. "Dry as a popcorn's fart, wouldn't you say, Doc?"

"Yes, Grady. Your granddaughter died from lack of blood flow to the brain, and that was caused by a bad heart."

"There, gentlemen, is your answer to why Ruth Ann Sanders died. Now can my daughter-in-law get on home and take care of her family?"

The coroner hit the table with his big gavel and said, "Hearing dismissed."

While every one was talking at the same time, Grady gently guided Birdie and Ray toward the door. He'd done all he could to help Ray and his family. He knew this crisis was over, but with a family like his, another crisis was surely on its way.

~ 22 ~

After the inquest, Birdie went back to the house she shared with Ray and the boys. Anymore she wasn't sure there was such a place as home. Wasn't a home supposed to be a place of feeling loved and accepted? The house where she lived had no feelings of any kind. It didn't have anything. It was just a place to stay.

She went through her routine, but the memory of what had happened to Ruth Ann haunted her day and night. During the day, she'd rush to the crib to change her and find it empty. She'd wake in the middle of the night to the sound of crying. She wasn't sure if it was her dead baby's or her own. Was she going crazy?

Ray didn't come home more than he had too. She knew it wasn't that he liked his work so much but preferred the company of the men at the lumber camp to hers. She guessed that was because she'd turned away from him ever since the baby died.

It was Friday, and she wasn't looking forward to another long weekend with just the boys for company. She could go to her parents, but that was more commotion than she could handle. That's why she'd sent the boys over to Grady's to see if they'd let Ollie come and spend the weekend.

She laid her romance magazine down and gave a heavy sigh, then she heard steps on the porch. The young'uns hadn't been gone long enough to be back. Before she could move, Ray came through the door.

He laid his jacket on a chair. "You look surprised to see me. Were you expecting someone else?"

"Just the boys, I sent them to see if Ollie could spend the weekend with us because I didn't expect you home."

"Didn't expect or didn't want me here?"

"I don't want you here if you're gonna be ugly and show that Sanders temper all weekend. You're not the only one who's hurting. Ruth Ann was my baby too."

"Was she mine, Birdie?"

Birdie was so shocked for a minute she found it hard to breath. This was something she'd never thought he'd ask and something she'd tried not to think about.

"Well are you gonna answer me or just sit there."

Slowly she raised her eyes to meet his. "Are you looking for a way to block out your pain, Ray? If I said she wasn't, would loosing her hurt any less?"

"Don't you think I've tried to reason it all away? Trouble is it won't go away. The way I see things is that if we're gonna have any kind of life together, we're gonna have to start with the truth."

Birdie had never heard the clock tick as loud or the fire in the cook stove crackle as much. Lord, how was she gonna answer his question. If she said what she believed in her heart, would he get so mad he'd hurt her? That was a risk she'd have to take because she couldn't live with herself anymore.

"Ray, I've only really loved you and Charlie. It's not like I've been out to be with every man on Haint Branch. If you can believe that, then maybe, I can make you understand how I felt about Charlie."

"I don't need to know about how it was with Charlie. I need to know if it's me that you've always loved."

"That ain't something I even have to think about. Yes, it's always been you. You were always there to protect and love me, and that's why I love you so much. Now, can I ask you something and you'll tell me the truth?"

"I'll do my best."

"Did you kill Charlie?"

Ray went to the kitchen and poured a cup of coffee then returned and pulled up a chair to face her. "If I said I did, would you love me any less?"

Again Birdie was lost for words. She wasn't sure she knew this man anymore. "I wouldn't love you anymore or any less because love ain't about what we've done or not done. Did you kill him?"

"In my heart, I killed him a thousand times. I wanted him dead because I knew that as long as he was alive you'd never be completely mine. But no, I wasn't the one who pulled the trigger. Sometimes I think the desire is worse than the act."

"I know what you mean. Desire is all I felt for Charlie. Desire is what led to the act."

"I came home to get some answers and see if we can start anew. We have two little boys who need both parents. Do you think we can make our marriage work?"

"That's one question that I can say yes to without any hesitation. And I promise, you'll never have to ask any more questions because I'll never give you reason to have to." Her arms reached out and wrapped around his neck. Feelings of being loved and wanted rushed through her, and finally she knew she was home for good.

* * *

After Aunt Birdie's hearing, my life settled down into a steady routine. That was alright with me since the last year had been so full of ups and downs. School was 'bout out and I wanted to ask if I could go visit with Sadie Jo, but I knowed there weren't no use in asking since Granny didn't cook half the time and Granddaddy was still puny. Looked like the only fun I'd have this summer was going to the swimming hole with Aunt Birdie. And that wasn't a sure thing. I was worried she'd not be able to go back where Ruth Ann had died. Besides I hadn't seen her since the inquest. Could be she wouldn't even want-a see me.

After all my doubts 'bout Aunt Birdie, I was a little more than surprised when the boys showed up on a Friday night and asked Granddaddy if I could spend the weekend with them. He'd studied a few minutes then told me to get my nightclothes and get on up there. I'd asked what Granny would say, and he told me to leave Granny to him. She'd been in a real bad mood since the hearing, and I was glad to leave her be.

When I got up to Uncle Ray's I saw him sitting right there in front of Aunt Birdie and they were talking. I stopped on the front porch so as not to bother them and that's when I heared what I wished I'd never heared. Aunt Birdie asked him if he'd killed Uncle Charlie, and after he got hisself a cup of coffee, he asked her if he said yes would she love him any less. I couldn't believe what I was hearing. I stood there with my feet froze to the porch floor. Uncle Ray killing his own brother. Being home with a rocking granny wouldn't be any worse than spending the night with Uncle Charlie's killer. I pulled one foot free and the other one followed. As I turned, I heared him say, "No, I didn't pull the trigger but in my heart I wanted him dead." I fled down the mountain to the safety of home. Could my quiet-mannered uncle really want someone dead?

Eva McCall

* * *

I knowed better than to say anything 'bout what I'd heared at Uncle Ray's to anybody. Who'd want their neighbors and friends to think one brother could want the other dead. Cain might-a killed Abel but at least it wasn't over a woman. Somehow a woman made the sin sound worse. It looked to me like here on the branch women was at the root of everything that went wrong or at least according to the men.

It's too bad all the men weren't like my Granddaddy. He never said nothing bad 'bout Granny's rocking, just endured all them meals me and him fixed. And he'd done all he could to protect and help Aunt Birdie. Why who'd ever thought to find out what really killed little Ruth Ann but my granddaddy? Guess he knowed that sheriff well enough to know he'd try and say she killed her on purpose. Knowing all that, it didn't surprise me none when a few weeks after me hearing Uncle Ray almost confess to the killing Uncle Charlie, Granddaddy got up on Saturday and said, "Ollie, me and you are gonna build a new swimming hole. The old one's been there so long it's full of all kinds of trash. Let's go down to the lower end of that bottom land and right there where the creek makes that sharp turn, let's pond it up then we'll tear down the old dam."

For the next few weeks we worked every spare minute we had on the hole and by August it was ready. I went up to Aunt Birdie's to fetch her for the surprise. At first she didn't want to come along but with some begging and pleading from the boys, she come. Now I know she wasn't too happy 'bout ever getting in the water again, but when she seen what me and Granddaddy had done, she broke down and cried all over us. I knowed Grandaddy weren't too happy with bawling women, but he made the best of it. Said he wanted to make sure his grand young'uns was good swimmers, but I knowed he really wanted Aunt Birdie to be able to enjoy her season the way she always had. So for the rest of the summer me and the boys splashed in the cool creek water while Aunt Birdie laid on a quilt and read her romance magazines. Oh, sometimes she'd lay the magazine down and join us in a water fight or play a game of hide and seek with us, but for the most part she either read or watched us play. That was alright with me cause ever day she become more like the Aunt Birdie I'd knowed before all the bad stuff happened. Wonder why I didn't know there'd be more bad stuff waiting right around the corner.

* * *

Granny rocked herself right into fall without even knowing what she'd done. After Ruth Ann's funeral, she'd took to her chair again and hardly ever stopped. Once in a while she'd ask some sort-a question that didn't make much sense. Granddaddy would tell her that every thing was fine. Her eyebrows would twitch, and she'd rock harder. That's why it surprised me and Granddaddy when she answered the door on Halloween Night.

Seeing what happened, it was a good thing she did cause Granddaddy was out guarding the outhouse. He'd vowed to shoot any body who tried to push it over. Said he was tired of building a new one or resurrecting the old one ever year.

I called it his studying room. Everytime he got real quiet, I knowed he was a-fixing to say he was gonna have to go out to the out-house and study a while. One time when he was out there studying on whatever he studied on, it come a real hard storm and blowed the out-house over with him setting on the stool. From that day on, any time it come a hard storm, you'd find Granddaddy setting on the front porch doing his studying.

I heared the door open and someone holler, 'trick or treat' and then Granny screamed. "Trick or treat? Hellfire, the house is on fire."

I rushed down the stairs. Granny had grabbed a bucket of water from the table and throwed it on the wall behind the stove. Smoke crawled through the cracks like distorted rays of sunlight I'd seen shining through the dirty kitchen window earlier. Behind the smoke, I saw flames licking at the already weather-worn boards. I grabbed the dishpan and shoved it into the hands of one of the Yates young'uns, who stood looking like they'd been the ones tricked instead of treated. "Bring water and hurry!"

I shoved another one toward the out house. "Get my granddaddy. Tell him the house is on fire."

Granny was beating at the flames with her apron. I grabbed the sack of salt and started throwing it. More flames broke through. Looked to me like the house was gonna burn down in spite of all we could do.

"Stand back."

Granddaddy heaved a dishpan of water onto the wall and shoved it back to a young'un's waiting hands, then grabbed the bucket from another and dashed it onto the wall. By then another young'un appeared with more water, and Granddaddy dumped it too. The flames disappeared but the black smoke poured into the kitchen, making it hard to breath. Granny stumbled toward the living room, coughing. I knowed she was headed back to her rocker. Guess she thought she'd rock the fire out. Too bad we couldn't a-dumped some water on her and a-fixed what was ailing her, but her fire had been a-smoldering too long for much of anything to help.

Finally, the smoke stopped and Granddaddy dropped onto a kitchen chair and buried his head in his hands. The Yates young'uns stumbled off into the dark. I figured their trick or treat trip would more than last them through the year.

"Granddaddy, do you think the outhouse is safe?"

"Ollie, young'un, I'm beginning to wonder if anything on this branch is safe anymore. Trouble just seems to keep a-pouring in. Could a-built two outhouses in the time it'll take me to fix this wall. It makes a body wonder if somebody is out to get us."

"This is our home, Granddaddy. Why would anyone want to burn it down?

Granddaddy's smut covered hand brushed the tears from my cheek. "Don't know, child, but we're gonna fight them demons just like our forefathers done."

"Tell me 'bout your forefathers."

"You run on to bed, I'll tell you some other night. I'm too tired now, and I've got to clean up this mess."

I touched the spot over my heart where I hurt the most. What would Granddaddy say if he knowed how my heart ached to know who killed my Uncle Charlie? And most of all to know who my mother was. I'd better just not complain. It looked to me like Granddaddy had his hands full right now.

23

Granddaddy died the day after I had my hair cut for the first time. It had growed down to my waist and all them curls made me look like a little young'un. And looking that way was something I wasn't a hankering to do, especially with Jake Williams making eyes at me. He'd began right after I'd started getting little bumps on my chest. I'd asked Granny why the knots hurt so much. She'd quit her rocking long enough to tell me hurting was a woman's role in life.

I wanted to look all growed-up like Sadie Jo and go to the five-and-dime and get some of that red polish for my fingernails and toenails. Can you believe having red toenails? It seems to me like the chickens would peck them off. I asked Sadie Joe and she said the secret was to stay out of the chicken house. That would be nigh on to impossible at my house since I was the one who had to gather the eggs.

Anyway, that's why I talked Uncle Ray and Aunt Birdie into taking me to town with them on Saturday. Sunday was going to be my fourteenth birthday and I wanted to look all growed-up. Now I wish I could shrink back into a little young'un, 'specially if it'd give me back my granddaddy.

When we got into town, Birdie went with me to the barbershop. She told Mr. Lawson to give me a bob. I said I didn't want Bob I wanted a haircut. They both had a good laugh and the barber explained that was a hairstyle. While he was cutting, Sheriff Carlson come in and sat down over in the corner — never said a word the whole time, just watched me out of them beady little eyes. By now

I'd learned not to trust him. I wasn't gonna tell the grown-ups 'bout his ways. I guessed somebody should know, but I'd learned a long time ago there was some things that just weren't talked about. He hadn't done much of nothing to find out who killed Uncle Charlie but no body seemed to notice. By now I was sure he was mixed up in the moonshining business somehow. I hadn't put it all together yet. Granddaddy says you gotta row with the oars you got. When I asked him what he meant he said, "Ollie, young'un, it simple means use the sense God gave you." Looked like the sheriff would know better than to sheriff and moonshine at the same time, but what do I know.

After the barber finished, my hair barely touched my shoulders and curled up real nice. Then we went to Jamison's five and dime and bought some side-combs and bobby pins. I studied the polish while Aunt Birdie paid, and I vowed that as soon as I got some money I'd come back and get the reddest one they had. I'd have to get a jar of that remover stuff so I could take it off before I got home cause Granny didn't believe in wearing such stuff.

As soon as we finished in the dime store, we went over to Angel's drugstore and set at the counter and ordered store-bought ice cream. I'd only had it one time before and it was in a cone. That was when I was seven and Granddaddy had took me to town to buy me school shoes. We'd bought it at the same drugstore. When we got outside, I looked that cone over real good and decided right there on the spot that I wanted to know what it tasted like. I held it up in the air and bit the bottom off. Of course, ice cream started dripping 'bout the time we got into Mr. Roane's nineteen-thirty-five Ford. Granddaddy made me throw it out the window cause he said he didn't want me to mess up someone's car that was nice enough to give us a ride home. That 'bout broke my heart right there in front of the drug store.

Today I didn't have to worry 'bout not getting to eat it cause Aunt Birdie asked for it in a dish, and we set at the soda fountain and eat it real slow like.

When we couldn't make the ice cream last any longer, we walked down the street and looked in all the shop windows. Aunt Birdie called it window-shopping. To me it was just another way of saying we didn't have enough money to go inside and buy sump'n. I watched all the women come out with their high heel shoes clicking on the pavement and their arms loaded with packages and right then and there I promised myself that someday I'd have enough money to buy shoes that clicked on the sidewalk. I didn't say anything to Aunt Birdie cause I didn't want to make her feel bad cause we had to look in the windows, but I saw the desire in her eyes as she gazed at a real nice dress.

Finally, she said to me, "Ollie, just one time in my life I'd like to have a store-bought dress."

I slipped my hand in hern and squeezed it real hard like. "Aunt Birdie, when I get a job and make some money, the first thing I will buy, is you a new dress."

She brushed my forehead with a kiss. "You'll be needing your money to buy your own clothes. Maybe I can save enough egg money to get me one."

We walked on down the street, and I wondered 'bout the ways of grown-ups. Seemed to me like nothing they done made good sense. Uncle Ray worked hard at his lumbering job and farmed on the side but they never had enough money. I swore right then that my life wouldn't be like the people on Haint Branch, just getting by from one payday to the next.

* * *

Halfway home we met Granddaddy on his new horse, Daisy. Uncle Ray stopped the wagon. "Where're you going, Dad?"

Granddaddy didn't answer. He was too busy starring at me. Finally I said, "It's me, Granddaddy, Ollie. Don't you like my new haircut?" He still didn't say anything, but he did slide off his horse, and as he did, he broke off half a dogwood limb. Then he pulled me down from that wagon and began to beat me. He whipped so hard he wore off the leaves. When he'd finished, all that was left was a short little stick. He threw it in the gully and swore under his breath, climbed on his horse, and rode on down the road. Little drops of blood begin to ooze down my legs. If it hurt, I didn't feel it because the hurt in my heart was a whole lot worse. Granddaddy hardly ever raised his voice to me. I'd heared Uncle Charlie and Uncle Ray talk 'bout the beatings he'd give them. Now I understood what they meant. I no longer knew the man I'd loved and called granddaddy all my life. Since this morning, he'd turned into some sort of monster. One I didn't care to ever see again.

Aunt Birdie climbed down and wrapped her arms around me. "Ollie, I'm sorry you had to find out what kind-a man your grandfather can be."

I dabbed at my eyes as I tried not to cry. "Why did he beat me? I ain't done nothing. He said I could go to town with you. He even said I could get my hair trimmed."

"Guess there's a big difference in a trim and what you got. I'm

Eva McCall

sorry. I thought it'd be all right when he seen how growed-up you looked."

Uncle Ray reached down to help us back on the wagon. "I think that's the problem. He don't want her to be all growed-up. He wants her to stay his little girl."

He was right. I understood cause one part of me wanted to stay a little young'un but there was sump'n else going on that I didn't understand. A bigger part of me wanted to know what the grown-up world was like. I knowed that soon that part of me was gonna win out and lots of things would change.

Well, they changed sooner than I'd expected for I never seen Granddaddy again. Monday, Sheriff Carlson was back at our door. I knowed the minute I seen him standing there all frowned up that something had happened to Granddaddy.

"Where's your granny?"

"Where do you think, Sheriff? She's in there rocking just like she's done every day since Uncle Charlie's death and it's all your fault."

"Why'd you think that?"

"If you'd half-tried to find who killed him, she'd be better. Me and Granddaddy has tried every thing we know. I even took her to the tent meeting hoping that preacher man could help her but that didn't work either. Ain't gonna be nothing that'll fix her until the killer is caught."

"I think we all need to forget about some-might-have-been murder and tend to the business of living. If you'll just step aside and let me in, I have some news for her."

I planted my feet firmly in the middle of the doorway. "You'll get to Granny over my dead body."

The sheriff slipped his hand around to the back of my neck and pulled my face up real close to his. I smelled the foul order of his breath and felt it against my cheek. My body went rigid as my arms come up and grasp him by the shoulders. I pushed hard and he reeled backwards, catching hisself on the doorjamb.

"Have it your way, Missy. You can tell her they found Grady dead this morning at the lumber camp."

It was my turn to hang on to something. Granddaddy dead. It couldn't be. It'd only been Saturday that he'd beat the daylights out-a me. I'd wished I'd never see him again, but I hadn't really meant it. The welts on my legs had 'bout all gone away. As for my hair, I'd pulled it out as straight as I could so it would be a little longer. I didn't even care 'bout being growed-up for Jake Williams. I wanted things to be the way they use to. Now, they never would be.

I heared the shuffling of feet behind me and turned to find Granny staring at the sheriff. "It seems to me like you take pleasure in coming to my door and telling me my loved ones is dead. I already knew Grady was gone. He came to tell me bye about daybreak this morning." She turned to me. "Ollie, he said to tell you he was sorry for whooping you. Said he never should have done it, but he'd been upset over losing his little girl."

Me and the sheriff were both starring at her. Had she lost what little sense she had left? "What do you mean, Granny? They found him dead at the lumber camp this morning. He couldn't have been here."

Granny moved back toward her rocking chair. "I know what I seen. He stood right over there in the kitchen door and told me goodbye."

The creaking and moaning of the chair started again as Granny's lips come together in the same hard line she wore when she was upset. I knew right then that I'd have to take charge and be the grown-up even if I didn't want to. There was things to take care of and I'd have to see to them.

* * *

Granddaddy's funeral was simple. That's the way he'd a-wanted it. I had his brown jug placed in his right arm, cradled like a baby. Preacher Rainey and Sadie Jo come all the way from down in Atlanta to do his funeral. Guess that was only fitting since Granddaddy was responsible for Rainey's salvation.

The coffin was placed in our front room and Granny pulled her chair right up near it and rocked. Uncle Ray took some of the neighbor men up to the Sanders cemetery and dug a grave right by Uncle Charlie's and Granddaddy's other two dead babies. This was the first grave that had been dug since Ruth Ann was laid to rest.

When it was time to bury him, we all marched up the hill in single line, singing, "When the Roll is Called Up Yonder." I knowed there was neighbors that wondered if he'd be present, but me and Preacher Rainey both knew that if he wasn't there the rest of us wouldn't have a chance. Sadie Jo appointed herself as me and Granny's keeper. It made me feel real good to have the minister's wife by my side. When we got to the gravesite, Preacher Rainey asked if there was anyone who wanted to say a few last words 'bout Granddaddy.

Yates pulled on his galluses and stepped forward. "Grady Sanders was the best friend I ever had. He'd quit anything he was doing to give a neighbor a helping hand, even to stealing moonshine." The crowd laughed then Yates continued. "I'm gonna miss him but not like his woman and Ollie will. I want them to know I'll be there for them." He stepped back in line.

Uncle Ray removed his hat before he spoke. "There ain't a better father and husband in this country. My pa made sure we were raised with food in our stomachs and shoes on our feet." He hesitated, "That is most of the time. Ain't none of us perfect. He was always there. Even when we laid little Ruth Ann to rest, he wouldn't let us give up."

I couldn't keep quiet. Granddaddy wasn't just a ordinary man, he was a saint and I aimed on making sure they knowed the truth. I scooted up to the front and then realized if I told everything that he'd done to change the way life here on the mountains had happened that I'd be destroying part of the magic. Why Preacher Rainey might lose his salvation if he knew that Granddaddy give the Lord a helping hand. Mr. Yates would be embarrassed if it was known that he was the one who bought moonshine when he really didn't need it just so the young'uns would eat.

I looked at the coffin being ready to be lowered and remembered the day I'd watched him set Uncle Charlie's headstone and heared him talking to hisself. I had wondered if he had killed his own son. Now I know if we were burying Uncle Charlie's killer there was good reason for him doing it. Granddaddy only done what was best for his family. No, there wasn't no use telling the truth. His good deeds would have to stay between me and him and the Good Lord. That's the way Granddaddy would want it. "I loved him and I know he loved me and Granny." I stepped up to the coffin and kissed the hard cold wood.

As the preacher committed his body to the earth, my heart

turned cold as ice in the middle of the winter. It wasn't fair that the bestest man on the branch was being buried up here on this hill when right over there near the edge of the woods stood Sheriff Carlson. Sump'n told me he'd win the award for being the meanest man in Franklin. Too bad I couldn't prove just how mean he was, or could I?

* * *

After the funeral everyone gathered back at the house to help eat up all the food that had been toted in. I knowed it wouldn't take long to have ever dish in the house licked clean. That was alright. The sooner the crowd cleared out the more time I'd have to talk to Sadie Jo. If I was gonna try and prove how mean the sheriff was, I'd need her help. I weren't sure how preacher Rainey would feel 'bout her helping, and I sure didn't want-a cause trouble between them, but there weren't another soul on Haint Branch brave enough to help me. Come to think of it, there weren't a-body on the Branch that would believe he was evil, but I was 'bout to change that.

"Looks to me like you've got lots going on in that pretty head of yours."

I set down my plate of fried chicken. "Yes, Sadie, and I was just a-fixing to come looking for you. I have to talk to you 'bout sump'n. Let's walk out toward the barn."

When we was by ourselves, I said, "Sadie, I need your help, bad."

"You ain't done and got yourself in trouble with some boy, have you?"

The thoughts of being with a boy hadn't crossed my mind. Good Lord a mercy, I just turned fourteen, but come to think of it, I guess that's old for a mountain girl. I know several that was married when they was twelve. "Of course, I ain't. You don't have to worry 'bout me. I ain't gonna get myself knocked up and have to raise some boy's young'un by myself."

Sadie give me a big hug. "That's my girl. There will be some young man come along and steal your heart, but give yourself time. The way I see it that's about all the mountain people have is time."

"Well, what I want you to help me with will take a little time and planning."

"From the twinkle in your eye, you've got a little devilment up your sleeve."

Sadie looked back toward where Preacher Rainey stood talking to the preacher that had married them. I sure didn't want to get her in a heap of trouble with her new husband. Maybe I should just forget my plan.

"Well...."

"I don't know, Sadie. At first I thought it was a good idea, but now I don't know."

"Tell me and let me decide for myself."

I glanced toward where the sheriff was standing on the front porch. He looked so smug. Lord knowed he had a good setting-back coming and it looked to me like I was the one to give it to him.

"You see Sheriff Carlson standing up there looking so pious. I've been a-thinking it's 'bout time he had his comeuppance, wouldn't you say so?"

"Strange you should say that. I was thinking about the same thing up at the cemetery. What you got in mind?"

"My plan ain't fully cooked yet. Maybe you can give me some help. Ever since I was a little young'un that man has had a-eye on me. You know, like he's waiting for sump'n to happen. There been times he's touched me and it give me the creeps."

"He ain't never, you know, tried to force you into having sex with him, has he?"

"Not that I know of."

"What do you mean? You'd know if he had. And I hope you would have told someone. Always tell, Ollie. Don't let them old men get away with their shenanigans. Remember, there'll be another young girl that'll have to face the same sort of trouble."

"Remember that summer when the carnival was in town?"

"Yes, and your Uncle Ray and Aunt Birdie took you."

"Well, sump'n bad happened to me. Aunt Birdie just thought that I got tangled up in the tent ropes and fell cause there was blood running down my legs. When I started throwing up all that cotton candy she thought I'd eat too much or had the stomach flu and that was why I was so sick."

"And you're telling me that something else happened?"

"Yes, but I don't know what. Someone held a handkerchief over my nose with sump'n on it, and I passed out. I remember feeling the rough legs of trousers against me so I'm sure it was a man. Next thing I remember was someone screaming that I'd been hurt."

"What happened then?"

"Some people took me to the first-aid tent and then found Uncle Ray and Aunt Birdie. They all thought I'd fell over the ropes, and I just let them think what they wanted. Guess I didn't want them to think I was stupid or sump'n. Besides, Aunt Birdie had all the trouble she could handle and it would have only upset Granny more. And you know my granddaddy. He'd a-been out to kill somebody.

Besides I'd been told a hundred times to stay with the grown-ups."

"You poor child, if only you'd a said something."

"No, it was best that I kept my mouth shut. The worst was the bad dreams. They're almost gone now, but ever once in a while I dream of a man's legs wrapping around my neck, and I'll wake up in a cold sweat."

"Do the legs have a-owner?"

I looked back toward the sheriff. "He's a standing up there on the porch."

"So you think it was Sheriff Carlson?"

"That's right, but I can't prove it. Besides, who'd believe me? The way I see it, I'm gonna have to catch him red-handed."

"And how do you plan on doing that?"

"I hear there's a circus coming to town day after tomorrow. I want you to help me get all dolled up in some grown-up clothes and I want to go. I believe, if he tried sump'n once, he'll try again, especially now that I'm more growed-up."

"I don't know, Ollie. This could be dangerous. And there won't be any law to call since we're dealing with the only law in town."

"Remember all them gadgets you got when you was married. You said you got a camera. Did you bring it with you?"

"I did. Took some pictures this afternoon."

"I want you to take it with you to the circus and don't let me out of your sight and the minute that sheriff comes on to me, you take a picture. We'll have him good. He can't weasel out-a it with that sort of evidence."

Sadie stood there for a long time studying me like I'd lost all the sense God give me. Finally, she said, "I guess I owe you that much since I done moved away and left you to grow up here all alone. Now with your granddaddy gone there won't be no body to protect you."

I reached in my pocket and pulled out Granddaddy's little thirty-eight. "Granddaddy might be gone but he left me able to take care of myself." I watched Sadie's eyes get as big as silver dollars.

"Ollie, what are you doing with a gun?"

"Granddaddy give it to me, and he made sure I knowed how to shoot it. Will you help me?"

"Yes, we'll spend all day tomorrow catching up on all the happening here on Haint Branch and getting you ready to rid it of one of its worst citizens. I have to go now but I'll see you tomorrow." She joined Preacher Rainey on the porch where he was unloading the film from the camera.

Sheriff Carlson wandered off toward the road. He'd better enjoy tomorrow, for if my instincts was right, it'd be his last day of sheriffing.

24

Franklin don't get much in the way of entertainment but when it does the whole town turns out. The night of the circus wasn't any different. What a send-off the sheriff was gonna get. Me and Sadie Jo had it all planned down to the last words we was gonna say to him and them words were, 'good bye forever'. There was a few choice things I wanted to say to him but I knowed if Granny heared 'bout it I'd be in for a good mouth-washing with her lye soap so I'd just let it be.

When we got to the circus tent, we parted ways. I looked around until I spotted where the sheriff was then I found me a seat close to him. Now I didn't just set there, I made a few trips out to where they was a-selling pop-corn and drinks. And of course, I had to stop and talk to a few of my school friends. All the time I could feel the sheriff watching me. If I do say so myself, I looked mighty spiffy. Sadie Jo had pinned up my hair almost on the top of my head. She'd painted my nails and even smeared on a little lipstick. Just a light color, said I didn't need to look like a pool-hall girl. When I asked her what was so different 'bout them, she said they were there to serve the men playing pool. I didn't get around to asking her what they were serving cause Granny come in and made me wipe the lipstick off. That didn't stop me none cause as soon as we were out-a sight of the house I made Sadie Jo put it back on. I had on the dress that I had wore to Sadie's wedding. I'd even talked Sadie into hemming it a little shorter, and I wore the sandals I'd wore in her wedding. When I was all dressed up, Sadie had took a small bottle from her purse and dabbed the sweetest smelling perfume I'd ever smelled right behind each of my ears. She said that'd make a good man turn bad. Well, I weren't too interested in turning a good man bad. I just wanted the bad man to notice me or at least smell me.

The last time I sat down, right before the show started, I seen him edging his way toward the end of my row of seats. The bait was working. I could feel it in my bones.

Me and Sadie had planned for me to leave as soon as the lion act come on. I was to head for the outhouse. It'd be sort-a dark out that way. She'd wait inside, and if he followed me, I was to knock on the door. That way she'd be ready with her camera.

I couldn't get too interested in the show. My heart pounded so hard I was afraid the sheriff would hear it and arrest me for disturbing the peace. Maybe Sadie was right. What if I got hurt or even killed? Who'd take care of Granny?

Then there was Aunt Birdie. We'd got awful close since her baby died. I'd hate to cause her anymore grief. Well, it was too late now. Sadie would be waiting with her camera. There was nothing to do but follow through. Maybe he wouldn't follow me. Could be I'd had it wrong all this time. This would prove the town's sheriff good or bad. And right now I almost hoped it'd be good.

The lions were up and so was I. Inching my way down the outside aisle, I made it to the back of the tent. There was no sign of the sheriff. Good. I'd hurry out to the outhouse and get Sadie, and we'd watch the rest of the show and go home. I'd forget how I felt 'bout Sheriff Carlson.

I almost ran down the path to the toilet, but before I reached the door, a hand grabbed me and pulled me into the bushes. This wasn't the way it was suppose to happen. I hadn't even knocked on the door. All was lost.

I was gonna die or worse yet, be scared for life and there'd be no evidence. I was hauled through the bushes to a clear spot then whirled around to face my attacker. I was right. There in front of were the legs that had wrapped around me in my dreams.

* * *

He was pushing into the ground, smothering me right there on the spot. I wanted to open my eyes but I was too afraid of what I might see. Somehow I got my hand into my pocket and a-hold of the gun Granddaddy had give me. Now, if I could just aim it up and find the trigger, I'd fire. At least the noise would bring help even if I didn't free myself. I almost had it. I edged my fingers down beneath the pearl handle and wrapped it around the trigger. Just as I pulled, I opened my eyes enough to see lights flash but I never heared the gun go off. Someone yelled, "She's over here." I felt the weight being lifted from me. I opened my eyes to see Preacher Rainey holding Sheriff Carlson by the throat.

I let go of the gun and tried to sit up, but I was too weak cause I was half-scared out-a my wits. Thank the Lord, the gun hadn't fired. I couldn't think of much worse than having that sheriff dead and bleeding all over me. Talk 'bout having another man's blood on your hands, that would be bad enough, but taking a bath in it was another story.

Sadie Jo dropped down on the ground beside me. "Honey, are you alright? He didn't hurt you any, did he?"

"Just smashed me flat as a pancake. I tried to shoot but the gun didn't go off."

She took the gun from my trembling hands. "That's cause the safety is still on."

"Where'd the light come from?"

"The camera, I got his picture trying to hurt you. We'll fix him good."

I let the tears flow. I didn't care much right now 'bout fixing nobody. All I wanted was to go home and hear Granny's rocking.

* * *

Granny's rocking didn't fix the way I felt. Wasn't nothing we could do 'bout Sheriff Carlson till we got the pictures. In the mean time, that little weasel of a sheriff was free to do anything he wanted. I'd just have to stick close to the house and not let him catch me out alone.

Granny said I didn't have to go back to school right away, said the teacher would understand since my granddaddy had just died so I spent the most part of the week helping her around the house. Ever once in a while she'd look at me and ask if I was sick or sump'n. I wasn't sick like with a cold or anything, but my spirit was in real bad shape. I hadn't quite figured out how I was gonna live without my granddaddy. I had Sadie, but she'd be going home soon and then what would happen?

Granny's rocker wasn't in motion when I come in from milking and doing chores on Tuesday evening, instead she was cooking. I was a little shocked since she'd been bent on rocking most of the time. I acted like what she was doing was the most normal thing in the world. "Are we having company for supper, Granny?"

"Preacher Rainey and Sadie are coming."

"I thought you didn't like them."

"It ain't for me to like or dislike. I went up to the cemetery, and they were up there paying their respects to your granddaddy, and they asked to come over. Said they had something to talk to you about. I'm telling you right now if they have it in their heads for you to go back to that big city with them, you can just forget it. You've got to get your schooling."

For the first time in a long time, I felt loved by my granny. She wanted me. "You don't have to worry 'bout me going no where, Granny. Not for a little while anyway. I like school and my friends, besides I couldn't go away and leave you since we just buried Granddaddy. I'll have to see 'bout getting some sort of work to keep us from starving."

Granny mixed us cups of hot chocolate and set them on the table. She sure was changing, hot chocolate on a week day?

"You don't have to worry about us starving, young'un. I've got a little money put away. There should be enough to do for a few years, but I want-a save back enough to bury me with."

"Granny, you've gotta be dead to be buried, and you're a long way from being dead. I'd say you'll be around till I'm more than growed-up."

Granny took her hot chocolate and walked to the window and stared out into the gathering dusk. "Yes, I know. But your growing up is gonna change things."

"What things?"

"Nothing special, just being grown up makes a difference."

"Don't worry 'bout that. It looks to me like growing up ain't gonna ever happen for me." Then the idea hit me like a bolt of lightening from the sky. "Granny, why don't me and you go back to Atlanta with Sadie and her husband? We could get us a place of our own, and I might even be able to get a job and go to school."

She turned so quick I thought she was gonna hit the hot stove.

"Me in Atlanta? That'd be like putting a bull in a china shop."

I wanted to laugh at the picture of Granny in a big city. It was a crazy idea but who knowed, she might like it.

"Did I hear laughing?" Preacher Rainey stepped up on the back porch. "Ollie, Sadie wants to see you outside."

I looked at Granny half-expecting her to say I was needed in here, but she started dishing up supper and said, "Don't be long. Food ain't no good cold."

"Thanks, Granny. We'll be right in."

I found Sadie standing out by the barn, looking mighty worried. When I asked her what was wrong, she held out the camera and said, "We took pictures with a camera that had no film in it."

All the blood drained down to the bottom of my feet right there in the cow barn. "No pictures! That means the sheriff is gonna be a free man." I dropped to a sack of grain and let my head rest in my hands. "Ain't fair after all he's done to me. And the Lord only knows how many more young girls."

"I know just how you feel, and I'm so sorry. I could-a swore the camera had film in it. I put the roll in right before Grady's funeral cause I wanted some pictures of you and Granny."

"And you didn't put more in after Preacher Rainey took it out?"

"When did he take it out?"

"Right after we finished the funeral dinner when me and you was talking and making our plans, but as Granddaddy used to say, 'Don't guess there's no use crying over spilled milk, can't put it back in the pail."

I studied a few more minutes and then it hit me just like the idea of moving to Atlanta had earlier. Must be the Lord trying to get my attention. "But the sheriff don't know there was no film in the camera, does he, Sadie? All we got-a do is make him believe there's pictures. We don't have to show them to him."

"Ollie, I've been telling you all along how smart you are. We'll take the funeral pictures and hold up the envelope they're in and he will think we have the real thing. Come on, let's go eat and this Friday we'll take a little trip into town and fix Sheriff Carlson for good."

"Why can't we do it tomorrow?"

"He'd know we couldn't a-got the pictures back that quick. We'll be safe if we wait till Friday."

I followed her toward the house. Granny's fried chicken was gonna taste extra special tonight but not quite as good as the taste of sweet victory on Friday.

* * *

The sheriff was waiting for us when we reached his office on Friday. I'd never seen a more smug look on any body's face, sump'n like the cat that had swallowed the mouse.

Sadie Jo held up the envelope. "Here's the proof of what you tried to do to Ollie."

"You think I'm gonna run scared from some old envelope. Show me the pictures."

My heart sunk. I hadn't expected him to ask to see them. What was we gonna do now. There was no pictures to show and maybe somehow he knowed. I watched to see if Sadie's eyes or hand showed the truth, but her hand never moved. Her gaze held and she said,

Eva McCall

"Do you think we're stupid enough to show you our winning hand? You'll see them in the paper along with half the county."

The sheriff's face grew red, and he grabbed at the envelope. She passed the pictures to Preacher Rainey, and he slipped them in his coat pocket.

"What do you want, Rainey? Money! Ain't you making enough at that preaching job?"

Preacher Rainey grabbed him by the front of his shirt. "Why you little weasel. Money ain't got nothing to do with it. It's called justice and that's what we want. Now take off that badge and lay it there on the desk. I would take your uniform and send you down the street in your drawers, but I won't do that cause there's women present."

When the preacher loosened his grip, Sheriff Carlson unpinned the badge and laid in on the desk.

Preacher Rainey shoved him toward the door. "Get on home and change out-a that uniform and bring it back and put it by that badge. I'd advise you to tell people you've found a better job over in Knoxville, Tennessee. If that don't happen these pictures will find their way to the paper."

I watched the sheriff go and took a deep breath. The sheriff is gone — what a relief — no more creepy looks or sickening touches from him — no more fear! But there was still a rocking granny to fix and no granddaddy to help me. What was I gonna do?

* * *

Birdie saw the preacher's truck head down the road with Ollie in it. She'd get on over to Eula's and see if she could straighten Eula out on telling Ollie the truth. Ollie had been told all her life that when she growed up she'd be told the truth about her mother and it looked like she was just about grown up. If she knew Eula Sanders, she'd never get around to talking to her. And if she didn't, there wouldn't be anything else left but for her to talk to Ollie.

When she reached the house, Eula was in her rocker going at full speed. She walked around in front of her and took hold of the chair, bringing it to a stop.

"You're gonna listen to me, old woman. You've had your way much too long."

Granny jumped up from the chair and went into the kitchen and started washing dishes. Birdie followed and sat down at the table.

"You're gonna tell Ollie the truth. She's a big girl now, and she needs to know where she come from. Grady is gone, and if you don't tell her the truth, I will."

Granny whirled. "The way I see it is that I growed up with out a mother and done all right and Ollie is doing the same thing. I think you'd better get on up the mountain and tend to your own knitting and leave Ollie and her up-bringing to me."

She went back to her rocking chair and Birdie followed. "You're punishing a child for what you didn't have. How sad and sick! I'm going. But if you don't tell Ollie soon, I'll be back and fully armed with every thing that young'un needs to know to live a good life."

"It seems to me like you've done enough damage to this family. Now get and don't waste your time coming back. I'll tend to Ollie!"

Birdie left the old woman rocking with her lips set in a hard straight line. She was all too familiar with that look. She'd love to be able to erase that look, but she knew that Eula's cure wasn't hers to fix.

* * *

When me and Sadie returned from our sheriff mission, Granny

was rocking at full speed. We tried to slow her down but nothing we said helped, she just rocked on and on.

By the time Sadie and Preacher Rainey were ready to go home to Atlanta, she'd not eat for two days and the chair had been on the move day and night.

When Sadie come by to tell me that I didn't have to worry 'bout Sheriff Carlson anymore cause he'd left on the bus the day after we'd threatened him with the pictures, I started bawling. She figured it was because I was so relieved that the sheriff was gone. That was part of it, but I sure didn't want-a be left here with a rocking granny. When I confessed that to her, she set 'bout to try and figure out some way to fix things.

We both sat there at the kitchen table for a long time trying to think of sump'n but my mind was as blank as the boards Granny was rocking on.

Finally, Sadie said, "I guess I could stay here with you."

That was the best idea I'd heared since Granddaddy had died but I knowed from the look on her face it wasn't sump'n she wanted to do. Then I remembered me and Granny's talk and how she'd laughed at being in Atlanta. "Sadie, me and Granny was talking last week, and I said sump'n 'bout us going to Atlanta."

"What did she say?"

She said she'd be like a bull in a china shop. Guess she was right, but the way she is now she'd never know, would she?"

You're right, Ollie. I swear you're the smartest young'un I've ever seen. Come on, let's get the packing done. You and Granny are going to Atlanta, and we're gonna find some way to fix her for good."

Sadie set 'bout getting together stuff we'd need in the big city, and I set down to write a note to leave in Aunt Birdie's mailbox.

After all, me and Granny couldn't just disappear off the mountain without a word, but there was no way I wanted to spend the winter all alone with a rocking granny. If I went up to talk to Aunt Birdie, she'd start that bawling again, and I had enough to deal with right now. Tomorrow, we'd tie Granny's rocker on the back of the truck and head south. South, where I hoped we'd find a fix for Granny that would last forever.

25

The truck was loaded. Sadie helped Ollie get Granny out to the truck, then returned to the house to make sure every thing was closed up.

She stood looking out the kitchen window toward the Sanders cemetery. She wished she had the time to go and tell Charlie she was taking Ollie and Granny to Atlanta with her, to tell him she'd see that they were taken care of, since his father was now resting on the same hill but there wasn't time, and maybe it was for the best. She'd said her final goodby to him before she'd married her preacher husband. Life was good now, and she planned on keeping it that way.

Ollie came to the door. "Come on, Sadie. Preacher Rainey says we're ready."

"I'll be right there just let me dump some water on these ashes in the stove." She let a dipper of water dribble over the coals then followed Ollie out to the truck.

"I can ride in the back so it won't be so crowded up front." Ollie walked toward the back of the truck.

Sadie called for Ollie to wait up. "We'll all crowd in the cab for a little ways. If it gets to uncomfortable then me and you will ride back there. It won't be as breezy when we're out-a the mountains. That's why I wanted to leave in the middle of the day."

Sadie put Granny in next to the door, then she went around to the driver's side and scooted in, then motioning for Ollie to come sit on her lap.

"How long will it take to get there, Sadie?"

"I guess about three hours. That's how long it took us to come up." Sadie looked over at her husband. "Will you stop at Ray Sanders' mail box? Ollie has a letter to leave for them."

He nodded, and they were off for Atlanta. Then Sadie remembered how Birdie had always stood between her and Charlie. How would she feel about her taking Ollie and Granny away from the mountains? "Ollie, what did you tell your aunt in the note?"

"Granddaddy used to say everybody needs to dump their bucket ever once in a while so that's what I done. I told her how bad Granny's rocking had got since Granddaddy died and that I didn't want-a be left alone with her. I said since her and Granny didn't get along so well, it was best that I go home with you and try and get some help for her. I promised to write and let her know how we were doing and I also said that when I returned I'd be all growed up."

"You don't think she'll be to upset, do you?"

"No, her and Uncle Ray have their own problems and they don't need to be bothered with us."

The truck ground to a stop at the mailbox, and Sadie reached over Granny's rocking body and slid it into the mail box. From what she'd seen and heard, Birdie wouldn't be too sad at Eula leaving, but Ollie, well, only time would tell.

* * *

In a million years, I'd never dreamed the big city would be like this. I thought for a place to be this big there would have to be some sort of system. Order, as Granddaddy used to say, was what made the world turn. Well if he could see this, he'd have to re-think his saying.

The edge of dark had started to settle in as we drove down Peachtree St. In all directions, ghost-like shadows crept from behind giant building. People wandered up and down the streets looking like they didn't have any place to go. The drivers of cabs zigzagged in and out of traffic as though they owned the streets.

I glanced up at Sadie, who looked as comfortable in this madhouse as if she'd always lived here. She smiled at me and patted my arm.

"Don't worry, Ollie. You'll soon get use to all this hustle and bustle, and the quietness of the country will be as though it's something you dreamed."

Right then and there I decided I never wanted to forget the life I'd left behind. Yes, it was quiet and peaceful, but what's wrong with that? It was a place where a body could get in touch with who they were. "Franklin will always be home, Sadie. This is just a place to visit."

"Don't be too quick to judge. We'll see if you feel the same way in a few weeks."

We parked in the back of a huge apartment building and me and Sadie pushed and drug Granny up two flights of stairs. Inside their apartment, I tended to getting Granny settled while Sadie went back down to help Preacher Rainey bring up our belongings. This sure was a far cry from our home on Haint Branch. Our house wasn't a castle, but it had one thing this place didn't and that was privacy. All I had to do was sit at the kitchen table, and I could hear the people next door as plain as if they was in the kitchen. I was trading the sound of birds singing and crickets calling for this. I must have been out-a my mind to want to come here. Hopefully, we could get Granny fixed in a hurry, and we could be home for Christmas.

"I know you'll just love this place, Ollie."

I turned to face Sadie. "It's all right I guess, but it ain't like home."

She come over and took my hands in hers. "I expect you to feel a little homesick at first, but I promise It'll change. It did for me. At first I thought I'd die away down here by myself, but it didn't take long till I wondered what I done with all my time up in the mountains."

"Don't you get tired of listening to everything your neighbors say?"

"For the most part, I don't hear them. Oh, sometimes if someone raises their voice I'll find myself listening but not often."

"When can we see 'bout fixing Granny?"

"Ernie said he'd talk to his doctor friend tomorrow, and hopefully before next week is over, we'll have her on the road to getting well. In the meantime, we'll need to see about getting you in school."

"No, I don't want to go to school. All I want is to fix Granny and get on back home. I'll go back to school then. I'm good at my school work, so I can catch up by the end of the year."

"We'll see, now come and let's get your granny settled then we'll get a good night's sleep and see what tomorrow brings."

I followed her into the other room. I'd make the best of being here, but I knowed this would never be home. How could a person live where they never seen a sunrise or sunset or couldn't hear the birds sing for all the traffic. Why Granddaddy would be plain aggravated with me if he knowed I'd decided to live here. The minute the city had come into view I'd wanted to go back to Haint Branch and my home.

* * *

I clutched Granny's hand and looked around the room where we were setting waiting on Preacher Rainey's doctor friend to come tell me if he could help my granny get rid of her rocking problem. This room was a lot nicer than Sadie's apartment and it smelled like medicine of some kind. Hopefully there'd be some sort of pill he could give her that would slow her down.

The door opened and a little man in a white jacket entered and sat down behind a desk that made him look even smaller. He didn't say a word but just watched Granny as she moved back and forth in her chair. Finally he said, "And she does this all the time?"

"It all depends, sir. Sometimes she'll be as normal as me or you, then all of a sudden, she'll take to her rocker and rock for days at a time. The whole time she rocks she looks like she's mad at the world."

The doctor moved around in front of his desk and pushed his skinny little glasses up on his nose then brushed a few strands of gray hair from his forehead. "Maybe she is mad about something. This could just be her way of pouting."

"That's 'bout what me and Granddaddy decided so we got to where we'd just ignore her and go on 'bout our living and in a little while she'd be up at her work again."

"How long has she been rocking?"

"Ever since Uncle Charlie got shot, a couple of years back."

The little doctor pulled at the bunch of hair that growed from his chin and studied Granny some more. Finally, he reached out and touched her on the shoulder but the moving didn't stop.

"Mrs. Sanders, my name's Doctor Wallace. I'd like to help you find a different way to handle your problems."

Granny didn't even push his hand away or act like she heared anything he said. I got down on my knees in front of her. "Granny, don't you want to talk to the good doctor. He might be able to fix you so we can go back to the mountains."

Nothing. If she was in there, she wasn't gonna let us know

it, and it seemed to me that she didn't care if she was here or the mountains. But I sure did. I couldn't wait to get back to where I could hear myself think.

The doctor motioned for me to come with him. We went into another room with another big desk and several chairs. He sat down and patted a overstuffed one. I sat down. "Can you fix my granny? I'm getting awful homesick, and I don't know how much longer I'll be able to keep her here."

"I really can't say, but I'd like to give it a try. Your Granny is a very sick woman."

"Granddaddy used to say that she'd just gone to a place beyond words."

The doctor drummed his fingers on the desk top for a few minutes. "Guess in a way that's what's happening to her."

"What kind-a place was Granddaddy talking 'bout, doctor?"

"It's a part of the mind that people retreat to when life overwhelms them so much that they don't know how to deal anymore."

"Is it a good place?"

"I'd say it is, but it's not good to stay there too long."

"Why?'

"The mind's like soil. If it's not tended and kept active it begins to go bad."

"You mean if we leave Granny in her rocking world she'll spoil."

"Not like rotten tomatoes, but she'll draw so far into herself that she might not ever return to the land of the living. I'll have your granny looked at by some very good doctors and if they say her body's in good shape, her problem is a head problem."

"Doctor, I can tell you right now my granny's problem is a heart problem. Her heart's broke cause she lost her baby girls a long time ago. Then she went and lost Uncle Charlie, and a few weeks ago she lost my granddaddy. Just loosing Granddaddy is enough to break a healthy heart let alone one that's already tore up. I know cause mine's tore in two. That's why I gotta get back, so I'll be closer to him."

I felt tears start to spill down my cheeks. I didn't want-a cry right here in front of this well-educated doctor, but once my tears started to run there was no stopping them. I'd been that way since I was a little young'un. Granny said I'd cried day and night the first three years of my life. You'd a thought a young'un would a-been all cried out after all that crying but here I was, bawling again. Well, a person can't help who they are so the doctor could just think what he wanted. Maybe my tears would do what my words couldn't.

* * *

Them tears must-a worked wonders cause the doctor got busy fixing Granny right away. First thing he done was get her a room in that fancy hospital of his. It was a room that was all locked up so she wouldn't be trying to slip off and go back home. That made me feel real good cause I'd a-hated to have her out there in all that traffic trying to find her way. She might-a got hit by one of them big old trucks and by the time all the wheels run over her, nobody would-a knowed it was my granny.

As the weeks passed, Granny rocked less but she still wasn't saying nothing. I was beginning to be afraid that she'd stay in that place beyond words. It was this kind-a fear that caused me to decide to go to church with Sadie and Preacher Rainey. As you know by now, I take after my granddaddy 'bout church. With him, God wasn't in a building but out'n the woods. I reckoned since there weren't no woods around here, maybe He'd decided to hide in the church to get away from all the noise men was making.

When we got to the church, I was glad to find it wasn't like the ones I'd been to in the mountains. Them up there was just a bunch of people gathered up doing whatever they thought God wanted them to, no order what-so-ever. Why there's many a time the preacher never got a chance to say much cause the altar would be full of people all praying out loud. Sometimes I wondered if they were having some sort of contest to see who could pray the loudest. Guess that's why Granddaddy never liked them much cause like I said, he was a man who liked order.

Right behind the preacher's stand was this tank of water for baptizing, and on both sides was chairs. As soon as the service started, all them chairs filled with people dressed in pretty, long, red robes. A woman sat down at the piano and begins to play "When the Saints Go Marching In." Then the people in the robes sung to the top of their lungs. I sat there spellbound. In all my life, I'd never heard such nice singing.

After the music stopped, Preacher Rainey stood and begin to speak. It wasn't nothing like the way he preached at the tent meetings. His voice was soft as velvet, and he talked 'bout how much God loved us all and wanted us to serve Him. I could see right away that God and Granddaddy had give him a good dose of religion. Thinking bout Granddaddy caused me to want to see him so bad that I almost started to cry. I bit on my lower lip and prayed that Granny wasn't gonna stay in that place beyond words and that we could soon go home so I'd be able to visit Granddaddy's grave and tell him what a good job him and God had done on Preacher

Rainey. When I looked back at the preacher, I seen Granddaddy standing right up there where Preacher Rainey had been standing, and he was smiling right at me and holding out his arms. For the life of me, I couldn't figure out what was happening. I felt like I'd been wrapped in a nice warm blanket. I was gently lifted from my seat, and I floated down the aisle toward Granddaddy.

When I opened my eyes, I was kneeling at the altar and people had gathered around and was laying hands on my head and praying for me. Preacher Rainey had took Granddaddy's place. Here I was, trapped at the altar of Grace Baptist Church in Atlanta, and Granny was locked up in that hospital. And the only place either of us wanted to be, was home, in the mountains.

Sadie hugged me and said, "Ollie, I'm so glad you're giving your heart to the Lord. You won't be sorry. He will make so much difference in your life."

"But I only meant to…" then the light come on in my head like the sun peaking over our mountains on a spring morning, and I understood that the only way me or Granny was gonna be free to go home, was to act like we were both being fixed. Me being saved would cause Sadie to think I'd be able to manage Granny. Now all I had to do was get Granny out-a that strange world that the doctor said she was in, and we'd head on back home where we both belonged.

* * *

I'd begin to see that me and Granddaddy knowed all along how to fix Granny. Not that the doctor didn't try, but none of them pills or all that talking didn't look like it was doing much good.

First thing I'd do was get myself baptized and then I'd work on getting Sadie and Preacher Rainey convinced that taking Granny back to the mountains was the right thing. Maybe I could even get them to move back too. The little church up on Scaly Mountain needed a new minister, and he'd be just the one to lead them.

Sunday morning, Sadie helped me into one of them nice white robes that people wore to get dipped in, and I sat on the front row and waited for the place in the service that Preacher Rainey invited new converts down to be baptized.

This time I walked down front knowing full well what I was doing. What I didn't know was that when I was dipped in that water, I'd come out feeling like a new person. As soon as Preacher Rainey lifted me out-a the water and I opened my eyes, Granddaddy's spirit hovered over me like he was really there, and I knowed he was as pleased as Jesus was for the decision I'd made. Oh, it might-a started out just pretending, but I was surrounded with so much love my heart had melted. Now I was a child of God.

The next few weeks passed without much happening except my praying for a answer to getting me and Granny back to the mountains. Then out-a the blue, Preacher Rainey came home in the middle of the day. Me and Sadie were setting at the kitchen table polishing our nails when he walked in. Sadie looked up. "You home so early. Anything wrong?"

He pulled out a chair, and instead of setting he dropped into it. "I don't have a job anymore, Sadie."

She knocked over the polish, and I grabbed a rag to wipe it up before it got all over the table.

"What happened, Ernie? People liked you … I guess I thought we'd be here forever."

"Nothing is forever, honey, nothing but us. They do like me but that preacher school sent a new educated man out. And he convinced them he was the one to make their church grow."

"What are we gonna do, Ernie. I could get a job and help out until…"

I tightened the lid on the polish. "Remember that little church up on Scaly Mountain, Sadie. They need a preacher. We can all go back to the mountains and you'ns can live with me and Granny till you get settled."

Preacher Rainey took Sadie's hand in his. "What do you think, honey? You think you can become a mountain girl again?"

"When I married you, I promised to be by your side no matter what. If it takes going back to keep doing the Lord's work, I'll get to packing right away."

Preacher Rainey looked over at me. "You know if we go back to the mountains, we'll have to take your granny out of treatment. How do you feel about that?"

"Preacher, I done decided that me and Granddaddy knowed all along how to fix Granny. You get her out-a that hospital and when we get back home, you'll see how much better she'll be."

26

Once we were back in the mountains. It didn't take us long to settle into our old routine. I went back to school and in a few weeks I was all caught up with my school work. Sadie Jo and Preacher Rainey took the church up on Scaly Mountain and were really busy. Sadie had decided to start one of them women's missionary groups so she spent most of her time visiting the ladies and trying to get them interested in coming to her meetings. Granny still rocked some but not like she had right after Granddaddy died. The doctor had sent her home with some little white pills that helped or at least I thought they did until I found that she'd not been taking them but hiding them under the edge of the oilcloth on the table. That's when I decided to slip it in her coffee. After that her rocking slowed, and she begin to do more around the house.

Me and Aunt Birdie spent most of our Saturdays together. She still was sad 'bout Ruth Ann but she said her and Uncle Ray were more in love than they'd ever been. I was glad. It was time she had some happiness.

By the time school was out Eddie Hodgins was hanging around our house like he belonged there. Granny would frown and ask if that boy didn't have a home. One day she said, "Ollie, you know he's hoping to get between your legs, and I'm here to tell you if you turn out like your mama, I'm not raising another young'un."

I was so dumbfounded I didn't know what to say. That was the closest she'd ever come to having a woman to woman talk with me. I didn't know whether to push her into saying anymore or not

Eva McCall

because I already knowed 'bout the birds and bees. What Sadie and Aunt Birdie hadn't told me I'd learned from my friends at school or my health book. I sat myself right down there at the table and looked Granny straight in the eye. "If you don't want me to be like my mama, why don't you tell me 'bout her so I'll know what to watch out for."

"Don't you use that sassy tone on me, little miss smarty pants! You ain't too big for me to spank. And as for your mama, all I know is that she got herself in 'the family way' without having a husband."

"And just how do you know that?"

"Cause if she'd a-had one you wouldn't a-been left on my doorstep."

"Maybe my father didn't want a baby, and she had to choose between us."

"That's even worse. Ain't no woman no good that would pick a man over her child. I loved your granddaddy, but I'd a-never give away one of my babies for him."

I studied the little woman, who I'd always thought was hard-boiled, like I'd never seen her before. She might seem all business but underneath there was a heart as tender as the spring cresses that was popping up down by the branch. I'd do my best not to go wrong and cause her anymore heartache.

"Ollie, would you like to go for a walk down by the swimming hole?"

I turned to find Eddie standing on the back porch. Gosh, he was good looking. Must be the way the sun was hitting all that black hair that lay in deep waves over his head. Why hadn't I noticed before? "I'll be back soon, Granny. Leave the dishes and I'll wash them."

"Remember what I said, Ollie. A apple never falls far from the tree and in your case . . ."

I don't know if she had intended to lecture me more or not for I was out the door and gone like a flash of lightening.

"Your granny don't like me, does she?"

I threw a stone across the pond and watched it skip to the middle then sink. "It's not you that she don't like, Eddie. It'd be any boy. She's got it in her head that I'm bound for trouble, but I don't want-a talk 'bout that." I felt the hand he had around my shoulders slip under my blouse and move toward my back. Tiny goose bumps rippled up my arms.

Eddie pulled off his jacket and laid it on the grass and we sat down. I threw another stone as Eddie's hands roamed over me. He did it sort of sneaky, like he wasn't paying any attention to where they went. Finally he said, "Is this the place where your aunt drowned her baby?"

"Aunt Birdie didn't drown her baby. Ruth Ann died of natural causes, the doctor said so. Besides, it wasn't here where Aunt Birdie fell in. It was further up at the old swimming hole. Me and Granddaddy built this one so she wouldn't have to go back to where it happened then we tore the old one out."

"Your granddaddy was a good man. My grandfather said there'd never been a better person in these parts."

I turned to face him. His brown eyes had that serious look like he was paying his last respects to someone at their funeral. Kind-a made me want to hug him and tell him it was all right. No body had to tell me how good my granddaddy was. I knowed that first hand.

"Sorry, I shouldn't a brought up family matters." He blinked and the twinkle returned to him eyes. "I asked you to come down here because there's something I want to ask you?"

His touch was becoming more intent and his hands were moving more purposely. He cupped my face with one hand and kissed me right smack-dab on the lips. My heart gave a skip and speeded up. For a moment, I thought I'd melt right there on that very spot. When I caught my breath, I said, "I thought you wanted to ask me something."

"Will you be my girl, Ollie?"

I wanted to scream, yes — yes — yes but on the other hand I didn't want to seem too eager. Sadie said you had to keep a man wondering. And the way I seen it, I had time to keep them wondering. After all, I was only fourteen-and-a-half.

When I didn't answer, he put his arms around me and lowered me to the ground and gave me another kiss. This time I kissed him back. I felt myself wanting him to touch me, hold me and kiss me forever. Suddenly, I realized his leg had slid over mine, and I could feel his weight. Granny's words echoed all the way from the kitchen to the pond, 'All that boy wants is to get between your legs'. My little serious granny actual knowed what she was talking 'bout. My senses returned and I pushed Eddie away. He looked confused. "I thought you wanted …"

I felt tears gather in my eyes and spill down my face. "I don't want-a be like my mama was."

"And how was your mama?"

"My Granny says she was a good girl gone bad. I don't know cause I never knowed her."

"You're a pretty girl, Ollie. I like you a lot but if you don't give me what I need there's girls who will."

I got so mad I jumped up and clenched my fist. "I thought you wanted me to be your girl because you loved me. Because — because — because." I turned and fled toward the house then stopped and faced Eddie again. "Just go on and have your way with that Trixie Collins. I hear she'll do it with any boy who'll have her. Just remember if you leave your seed in her somebody is gonna have to raise the baby."

I didn't wait for him to say anything but headed on toward the house. Right there on the path leading up to the house lay a-apple and way up at the top of the hill stood a June apple tree. I picked it up. I'd show my granny that even if a apple didn't fall far from the tree it could roll a long ways from the place it landed.

* * *

The days following my telling Eddie he could go have his way with Trixie, I mopped 'bout the house so bad that even Granny started worrying bout me. She even asked why Eddie wasn't hanging around. I told her that I'd told him not to come back since it was such a worry to her. She patted me on the arm and said, "Ollie, young'un, there'll be plenty of time to find a husband when you grow up."

I wanted to scream. When did she think a young'un growed up? Why if the truth be knowed, I bet she was married when she was my age but if I said anything she'd just say, "It was different in my time." So I just agreed with her and went off out to the barn to practice shooting Granddaddy's little pistol. Granddaddy loved his shooting 'bout as much as he liked his whiskey. I guess thinking 'bout him was what give me the idea to go on up to the cemetery where I could be closer to him.

When I got there, I went straight to his grave and with the tail of my dress wiped off his headstone and read the inscription, "Rest in Peace." I smiled. There wasn't any words that could describe the man who was buried here. Oh Lord, how I missed him. How I wished I could feel his arms around me. I knelt and let my tears soak into the ground. Maybe he could feel the warmth of them. As my tears bathed the soil, thoughts of Uncle Charlie, lying right over there, replaced Granddaddy's memory. The law said he was dead from blowing a hole in his chest. Was that possible? I found me a stick about the length of a shotgun then I sat down and leaned back against Charlie's tombstone. Of course, Uncle Charlie was taller than me. As I placed the stick against my chest, I realized that, even if he could have somehow pulled the trigger with his toe, he couldn't have placed the gun back on the bed by his side. The law was wrong. Somebody killed my uncle in cold blood.

A sudden chirping brought me to my feet. Right above Granddaddy's headstone coils of a diamond patterned snake filled the tiny space under a wild Rose bush. The snake's skin was so tight that it looked like it might burst with the hardening muscles. The only movement was the rapid in and out of a forked tongue; the only sound come from the constant chirping of a redbird. The snake's eyes held the bird as surely as if iron fist grasp it.

I slowly removed the little thirty-eight special from my pocket and aimed. Beads of sweat trickled down my neck and puddled between my breasts. My sweaty palm squeaked against the pearl handle as my finger tightened on the trigger. My tongue wiped at the moisture on my upper lip. God, all I've got to do is pull this hammer and the bird'll be free. "Pull you coward, pull!" I told myself. My index finger remained frozen as my legs started to shake. Finally, a limp hand dropped to my side. Dropping the gun in my pocket, I walked away. Glancing back at the rose bush, I saw the bird break free and fly higher. My fingers touched the cold steal in my pocket. No, Uncle Charlie hadn't taken his own life, and I was all growed up now and it was time that I got the answers I deserved.

* * *

Birdie saw Ollie coming up the mountain. She could tell by the way she walked that she was a girl on a mission. Deep in her heart she had known this day would come, a day of reckoning. Was she ready? No, but that didn't matter. What mattered was that Ollie left here knowing the truth.

Birdie busied herself in the kitchen and pretended she hadn't seen what she'd noticed as Ollie hurried into the kitchen. She looked up and said, "What brings you up here in the middle of the week?"

Ollie dropped in a chair at the table. "Aunt Birdie, since school was out and I'm home all day with Granny, it's been hard."

"Your granny back to lots of rocking?"

"No, the medicine the doctor give her is helping. She rocks some but not like before. It's her attitude toward me. She still treats me like a little young'un. She keeps telling me that when I grow up I'll understand."

"Does your friend Eddie still come around?"

"No, Granny said all he wanted was to get between my legs."

Birdie got up and started making hot chocolate. "That woman doesn't see any good in anything."

"She was right this time."

Birdie dropped the spoon she was stirring the chocolate with and turned to face Ollie. "Please tell me you're not . . ."

"No, Aunt Birdie, he's not had his way with me. I told him to go see that Trixie Collins that she'd give him what he wanted. I guess he did cause he ain't been around all summer."

Birdie took a deep breath. Thank God, Ollie hadn't gone astray. She'd do what ever had to be done to save this young'un from setting foot on the wrong path like she'd done when she was her age. She set the cup of hot chocolate in front of Ollie. "Honey, I know there's lots you don't understand and if there's anything I can say or do to help you, I will." She watched as tears filled Ollie's eyes and ran down her cheeks. Her breath stuck in her throat as Ollie pulled the little pistol from her pocket.

"See this gun? I was practicing this morning, and I got to thinking 'bout how much Granddaddy loved shooting so I went up to the cemetery. I done me some powerfull thinking up there. I figure it was nigh on to impossible for Uncle Charlie to shoot hisself. "

Birdie felt little beads of sweat form on her forehead.. It was time Ollie knew the truth and she was the one that was going to have to tell her. "What made you realize that Charlie hadn't took his own life?"

"There was a big rattlesnake that had a bird charmed in the brush. I tried to shoot it but couldn't. That's when I knowed if I couldn't shoot a snake to save that bird, then Uncle Charlie couldn't take his own life. Killing just ain't in the Sanders blood so that leaves out Granddaddy and Uncle Ray. Do you think he killed hisself?"

"No, I don't, but I don't know who done it?"

"Me either. I know that lots of people right here on the branch had reason to want him dead, and I think one of them put a hole through his heart. From the day he died, I started out to find who killed him but when I realized it might be someone I loved, I quit."

Birdie remembered the day she'd had her talk with Eula. She wanted to ask Ollie if she'd overheard them, but she didn't have the nerve. "It's a good thing you did. Could have got yourself in lots of trouble and it wouldn't-a brought Charlie back."

She sat down across from Ollie and studied the young lady in front of her. It was time she was told the truth, but who was gonna do it? Then it struck her that no one had to. "Ollie, come in the other room with me, will you?"

As Birdie moved toward the front room, she wondered if she'd make as big a mess of the future as she had of the past. So much depended on Ollie's reaction to what she was about to see. She stopped and looked into the mirror then motioned for Ollie to look. "What do you see, Ollie?"

"You and me and the reflection from the window over there. What am I suppose to see?"

Birdie felt a jab of disappointment. Maybe she'd have to put into words what she'd wanted Ollie to see in the mirror. She placed her hand on her arm and started to speak but as she turned she saw the look in Ollie's eyes. Maybe she wouldn't have to say the truth. She watched as the light of knowing brightened in Ollie's eyes. They just stood there looking at each other's reflection in the mirror as tears gathered in both their eyes and streamed down their faces.

Finally, Ollie turned and slid her arms around her neck. "You're my mother, aren't you?"

Birdie raised Ollie's face so she could look her in the eyes. "Yes, I'm your mother, but that's all I can say."

"Why?"

"You'll have to get your granny to tell you the story and you can't tell her that I told you. Just tell her that you guessed the truth."

"And that is the truth? I don't see why I didn't see it a long time ago. Is your being my mother why you and Granny have never got along?"

"Partly."

"And if she won't tell me the truth, will you?"

"If I have to, I will, but I think she'll tell you everything now." She wiped the tears from Ollie's cheeks with her forefinger. "Remember, I have always loved you and that's why I did what I did."

"I will . . . mom."

Birdie felt a new bunch of tears gathering in her eyes. "You don't know how long I've wanted to hear you say that word."

"And you'll never know how many times I've wanted someone to call mom. Now, I've got to go and talk to Granny, but I'll be back."

Birdie watched her daughter hurry back down the mountain. She could tell by the way Ollie walked that her load was lighter than when she'd come up the same path.

* * *

I didn't know that finding my mother would fill that great big hole that had been down deep in my gut since I was a little young'un, but on my way down the mountain I felt as good as I did at my baptizing. Would God be mad at me for feeling that way? Right there on the trail I started praying. I thanked Him for giving me Birdie for a mother and for keeping us close all these years. I also ask him to open Granny's mouth and let her speak the truth that had been buried deep inside her. If I'd a knowed how loose her tongue was gonna be, I'd ask Him to keep one end tied down long enough to give me time to digest what she was saying. The things she was fixing to tell me answered every question I'd ever had.

When I got to the house, she was sitting in the porch swing, swinging and a-humming. I hadn't seen her so content in years, and I almost hated to bring up the mother subject. After all, I knowed who she was now and I no longer felt empty.

I eased down by her and let my hand rest on hern and give it a gentle squeezed. She looked over at me and said, "I guess it's time we had our little talk, don't you?"

"Yeah, I'm as growed-up as I'm gonna get. You want me to get the crosscut saw so we can cut down the family tree?"

Granny smiled and patted my leg. "You sure got your granddaddy's sense of humor. I wish he was here to help me unburden my soul. He always said I'd be sorry for what I done. Lord, if he'd only knowed . . ."

I could hear the tears in her voice, and I knowed she'd suffered. But I also felt that it wouldn't stop until she'd told me the truth, and I wanted to help her. "Granny, I know that Aunt Birdie is my mama."

"I figured as much. Did she tell you?"

"No, I stumbled on the truth."

"How'd that happen?"

"I'd say it's as plain as the noses on our faces, wouldn't you?"

Granny nodded. "I was always afraid you'd see it. That's why I didn't want her around."

"So you don't hate her?"

Granny's famous scold appeared. "I don't know what I feel anymore. But hate ain't the word for any of the stuff that's happened in this family. Your aunt, or mother, was about your age when she started messing with my boys. I tried to warn them just like I've warned you, but they didn't listen. The day your mama come over here and told me she was having a baby was just the beginning of all our troubles. No, that ain't right. I guess it all started when my little girls died. You've seen the things I keep in the trunk."

I'd seen her looking at the stuff that she kept in that old trunk in the far corner of the living room. "Do you want to tell me what happened to them, Granny?"

"I guess that's as good as any place to start. The first one, didn't live long after she was born. I found her dead in her crib one evening. The doctor couldn't give us a reason, just said it happened sometimes. That's when we started the cemetery up on the hill. Your Granddaddy said he wanted his baby buried on our land. That was like him, wanting to care for his own even in death."

I remembered how he'd set a headstone for Uncle Charlie and I knowed she was right. He'd take care of us from the grave if it was possible and in a way he was cause I felt his presence right here helping Granny tell me the truth. "And your other little girls, did they die the same way?"

"No, the other one was born the next year but she was born dead. When I was forty Sarah was born and lived till she was eight. There was a-outbreak of typhoid fever and folks were dying left and right in the community. I tried my best to keep her home but she sneaked off one day and went down the road to the Roper house. I'm sure that's where she got it because the little Roper girl come down with it the next day.

"I never knowed Mrs. Roper was a mama."

"She was, but it was Mr. Roper who died of a broken heart. He thought the world turned around his little Mattie."

It was hard for me to picture old Mrs. Roper with a child and a husband, but maybe I still had some growing up to do.

"Some day I'll show you the things in the trunk, but right now let's talk about how you come to be. After Sarah died, my boys were all I lived for. In a way I guess I become over protective. That's why it hurt me so bad when your mama got in 'the family way.'"

"What's that got to do with your boys?"

"Every baby has to have a father."

It took a few minutes for what Granny had said to sink in. I'd always wondered 'bout who my mama was, but I'd never given too much thought to who my father was. It fact, the only time a father had been mentioned was early this summer when Granny had been lecturing me on being a good girl. Now, things started to make sense. One of Granny's boys was my father. Why else would Aunt Birdie come to see her? "Which one was it, Ray or Charlie?"

"Charlie. Your mama said she'd give in to him just once but that had been one time too many."

"What did you say to her?"

"I told her she wasn't about to wreck either one of my sons young lives by saddling them with a child. She said she could go live with her aunt and have the baby but her aunt wasn't able to raise another child."

"Did she want me?"

"I guess she did but you have to remember she wasn't much older than you are right now. How would you feel about having a baby?"

The thoughts of being in 'the family way' caused me to shudder, and worse yet, what if the baby turned out like little Ruth Ann. "I'm not sure I ever want young'uns."

"That'll change when the right boy comes along."

"I guess you're right but how'd Uncle Charlie feel 'bout being a father?"

"He was never told. Your mama went to Canton and stayed until you were born. Her daddy brought the suitcase with you in it and left it on our porch. Me and your granddaddy was the only ones that ever knowed the truth about your birth. He was against the plan all along. Said it wasn't right, but he also knowed how much I wanted a little girl so eventually he went along with our plan."

"But my granddaddy loved me."

"Of course, he did."

We sat there in the silence of the dying day not saying anything. I knowed now that I really did have a true family tree, but I wouldn't rewrite it for my teacher. This was my story, not one to be shared.

"Why did Uncle Ray marry my mother?"

"I think he loved her all his life. He was always her defender. Anytime Charlie did her wrong, he was there to pick up the pieces. It about broke my heart to see what was happening. Charlie was what people call 'a lady's man'. He also loved to drink and play cards. He was the wild one. Anyway, he started fooling with other women and Ray and your mamma started dating. First thing I knowed they were married."

"What did Uncle Charlie say?"

"He just fluffed it off. I knowed it wasn't over between them. I could see it in his eyes. That's when I warned your mama about carrying on with him."

"But she was married."

"Yes, I know and so did she, but Charlie could be mighty charming and persuasive." Granny stood up. "You sit here and digest what you've learned, and I'll go fetch us some hot chocolate."

As I listened to her rattling pots in the kitchen, I tried to sort out all that I'd learned. Did any of this have anything to do with Uncle Charlie getting shot? Did Uncle Ray find my parents together and killed Charlie? Or maybe my mother tried to break it off with him and he threatened to tell Uncle Ray and she shot him? Even though there was a warm summer breeze, I felt chilled. If that was so and the law found it out, she'd go to jail. Surely I hadn't found my mother just to lose her again. Granny come out with a lamp and two cups of hot chocolate on a tray. We set there sipping it and listening to the quiet as the edge of dark crept closer. There was so much I wanted to say to Granny but I guessed there'd be lots of time for talking. I'd let her decide the time.

Finally, she said, "Ollie, do you remember the Cain and Abel story in the Bible."

"Are you talking 'bout Adam and Eve's sons?

"Yes, Cain killed Abel because he was jealous of him."

"Are you trying to tell me that Uncle Ray killed my father because he was jealous?"

Granny pushed her foot against the floor and set the swing in motion. "No, but that could have happened if …"

The swing moved a little faster. "If what, Granny?"

"Never mind, child."

"Granny, do you think it could-a been my mother who killed Charlie?" I prayed as I waited for her to answer. Off in the distance what sounded like a dog howling echoed through the night air and then on the other ridge another answered. I hadn't lived here all my life to not know this was the moonshiners at work? If Uncle Charlie had lived, he probably would be the one giving the signal. Maybe it was just as well that he was dead. Then between the howls come the whisper of an old woman who needed to bare her soul. "No, it wasn't your mother, it was me."

I wanted to pretend that I hadn't heared her, but I knowed it wouldn't do any good. I'd wanted to know, and now that I did, I'd have to face the music as Granddaddy used to tell me when I got in trouble. "Granny, you can't blame yourself. He was a grown man who got hisself in trouble."

"But I'm the one who pulled the trigger."

"Granny, don't talk like that. You're scaring me."

"I killed him, Ollie. I've been thinking about Eve, in the Bible, and if she'd a seen the same thing between her sons, she'd a done what I done. She'd already sinned and got them thrown out-a the garden and if she'd a just killed the bad son then she'd had a good son left. That's what I done so I'd have my good son."

"Granny, that doctor medicine must-a went to your head!"

"No, Ollie. Listen to me. You wanted to know the truth so you have to hear it all. I found them, your parents, making love right there in Ray's house, his bed. They didn't even have the decency to use the hay loft. I should-a stopped it then but I didn't. I just went on about living like I'd never seen anything. Then the morning Charlie took his squirrel gun and headed up the mountain toward Ray's I knowed I'd have to stop him someway, somehow."

I stood up and faced her. "Granny, please stop. You're like me. You couldn't kill a fly and you know it."

She grabbed my arm and pulled me back down in the swing. "Listen to me, Ollie! I've got to tell somebody. Please, honey, help your old Granny."

I sank down beside her, knowing that whatever come out-a her mouth would be the truth, and I'd have to be the one who decided what to do with it.

"I put off going up there as long as I could stand it. I was hoping if I waited long enough, they'd be through their frolicking, and I could talk some sense into them both." She took a deep breath as she squeezed my hand real hard.

"Were they through frolicking when you got there?"

"I only found Charlie. He was lying on the bed when I got there. He wanted to know what I was doing coming up here. I told him I knew he was carrying on with his brother's wife and I wanted him to stop."

"What did he say?"

"He laughed, Ollie. Plain out and out made fun of his mama. Can you believe it? He said they were both growed up and they could make their own decisions without any help from me. Right then I knowed he was a bad seed just like Cain was in the Bible and I wanted him gone … dead. That's why I know Eve would-a wanted the same thing if she'd been given the chance. Anyway, something happened to me. His gun was standing by the door, and I picked it up and fired. I can still see that look of disbelief on his face."

"Granny, you didn't mean to. Please, tell me you didn't mean it!"

"I did mean it, young'un. You see I done it so my good son would be saved."

"What-a you do then?"

"I laid the gun by his side and walked out-a there. I knowed your mama would be the one to find him, but that was all right. She needed to pay for her sin, also, and finding her lover, dead, served her right."

"But Granny, you blamed the sheriff."

"That no-good scum, course I did. Somebody had to take the blame."

I could see her way of thinking. Who better to accuse than someone you thought deserved it.

"Now, you can call the law and have your granny locked up. Then you can go live with your mama."

I slipped my arms around Granny's frail little body. "No, I think there's been enough paying. We're gonna do us some living while there's still time." I heared the sniffles but I knowed they weren't tears of regret but tears of relief and gratefulness.

Granny stood, picked up the lamp, and turned toward the door. I heared her mumble something that sounded like "but he really killed hisself" then the door slammed. The swing slowed, and I sat in the twilight trying to adjust to what Granny had told me.

A dog howled and another answered from the other side of the mountain. Moonshiners on the move, the one thing that hadn't changed was moonshining. Men had to feed their families, law or no law.

Inside the house, the rocking started again and as each squeak grew louder it sang out brok-en, brok-en, brok-en. Yes, Granny was broken, and I'd have to do like the moonshiners, law or no law. Granny needed me now more than ever.

Discussion Questions

- Can Ollie's situation relate to today's youth?
- McCall included several controversial issues from the forties that are still relevant today. Which issue was your hardest one to read?
- It is clear that there were a lot of people who could have killed Charlie throughout the book. When did you figure out who actually killed him?
- Ollie made it clear her Granny needed her. How do you picture the future for Ollie now that she knows the truth about her family?
- How would you feel if you were in Ollie's position and find out that both her aunt and uncle were actually her parents?